THE WOLF WHO CRIED GIRL

Geonn Cannon

Supposed Crimes LLC • Matthews, North Carolina

The Wolf Who Cried Girl

PROLOGUE

Kloesterle Castle
The edge of the Black Forest
Six Months Ago

MILO DUNCAN walked to the chest-high stone wall, put her hands on top, and leaned over to look down at the unpaved road below. The ground fell sharply away on the opposite side of the road and, in the distance, she could see the cluster of white buildings inside a grid of curving lines that she assumed were roads. Even with these signs of modern civilization, the endless green hills veiled by thick fog made her feel like she'd been transported back in time.

She ruined the illusion by taking out her phone to take a photo, framing the town at the bottom of the screen.

"Milo?"

"Up here on the..." She turned and examined the walkway on which she'd found herself. "I don't know what this is. A parapet?"

She heard footsteps from the stairwell. The castle must have been built when humans were much smaller, because Milo considered herself fairly slight and still had to stand at an angle to prevent scraping her shoulders on the stone walls as she'd ascended. Gwen Willow appeared in the doorway with her body similarly twisted before she stepped out into the open air.

The wind caught Gwen's hair and tossed it across her face, and she tucked it behind her ear as she looked out over the hills. "Wow, this is absolutely gorgeous."

Milo smiled, now seeing nothing but her lover's profile. "Yeah, it's pretty swell."

Gwen caught the tenderness in Milo's voice, looked at her, and smiled. She walked forward and rested her elbows on the wall. Milo joined her. For the past month, they'd been slowly making their way south from Potsdam trying to find a safe place for the Magnusson book of essays. They still didn't know how Isaac Hayden found its previous stronghold, but they weren't taking any chances. The book had almost turned Dale Frye into a hunter. Anything that powerful should never be allowed to fall into the wrong hands. Milo thought they should destroy it, but Henrik Bayer, their host, was adamant that it had to be preserved.

"That's like keeping a bottle of poison on the shelf and hoping it never falls into your food. What good is it doing by existing?" Milo had asked at one point while they were driving south, following a lead about a potential safe place to leave the essays.

Gwen shrugged without taking her eyes off the road. "Why is *Mein Kampf* still being published?"

"Why *is* that book still being published?" Milo had asked.

"The ideas in *Mein Kampf* weren't invented by that book, and the monster who wrote it wasn't the first man to have them. The writing gives us insight into an evil mind, so we can recognize one when it rears its ugly head again. The same goes for Magnusson's essays. We learn from the monsters we've vanquished so we can defeat the ones who follow in their footsteps."

Milo still didn't buy it. "I think it's a lot less likely to have people following in his footsteps if we just erased him from history. Maybe the Nazi book has been spread around too much to get rid of it forever, but there are only a handful of copies of these essays. We can wipe it off the face of the planet and just be done with it."

Gwen said, "It's tempting. But it's not up to us."

Milo had let the subject drop, but every night since then, she'd imagined climbing out of bed and taking the essays outside with a bucket and a lighter. Even now she was tempted to suggest the safest place to hide the book was at the bottom of an ash pile. They could do it up here in the tower of an ancient castle. It would be poetic and ensure no one would ever lay eyes on it again.

"We can't burn it," Gwen said.

"Gah, stop peeking in my brain."

Gwen smiled and reached over to put her hand on top of Milo's. "Ignoring the hunters won't make them go away. Hayden is proof of that. He was a bad man long before he laid eyes on the book."

"And he killed a lot of wolves to get his hands on it." She grunted. "Look, I get what you're saying. Learn from the past, understand the baddies, learn how their brains work so you can fight them. But this book is actively harmful. I don't see how the benefits of having it outweigh the dangers. We came all this way because some monks allegedly lived here and fought ghosts a thousand years ago."

"It was eight hundred years ago," Gwen corrected, "and the last known sighting of them was in 1860. There's a reason the Black Forest is the setting for so many fairy tales and legends. The monks fought ghosts, witches, and werewolves. Only the bad kind, obviously."

"Obviously."

"It seemed like our best shot." She sighed and looked over her shoulder at the ruined castle behind them. "I guess there's a reason they haven't been mentioned in a few decades."

Milo blew air out past pursed lips. "Okay. So how long are we going to keep up like this? If we're out here chasing down mythical monks, it seems pretty clear that we're running out of options."

"We have to find a safe place for the book." She looked at Milo. "It means a lot to me that you've stuck with me all this time. I know if you had your way, the book would've been ashes a long time ago and we'd be back in Seattle."

"We're in this together," Milo said. "And hell, a couple years ago, I was working eight to four delivering packages around Canary Wharf. Now I'm standing in a fairy tale castle trying to hide a cursed book with the woman I love. The last part of that sentence is the most important. I don't care what the first half is as long as the second half stays the same."

Gwen turned to face Milo. "We'll give it another week. We've traveled around most of Germany looking for a place to leave this damn thing. If we can't find it in a week, we'll head back to Potsdam to brainstorm with Henrik and his pack." She brushed her thumb over Milo's cheek. "I love you."

"I love you," Milo said.

It was close enough to nightfall that they decided to camp out in the castle. There was a room on the lower level where they would be protected from the winds and any wild animals that might wander through the area overnight. They made love, considered going for a run, but eventually decided they were both too exhausted and fell asleep in each other's arms.

Milo didn't know how long she'd been asleep when she heard movement elsewhere in the castle. She pushed herself up on her elbow and listened carefully, scenting the air. It could have been any number of creatures: deer, elk, a badger... She didn't smell anything, though.

She pulled on her T-shirt and shorts, slipped out from under Gwen's arm, and went to investigate. Her bare feet didn't make any sound on the stone floor, and she stayed close to the wall so the shadows would conceal her. The entrance to the foyer was an archway and she paused at the threshold to listen for more movement.

"You might as well keep coming, dog." The man's voice was shockingly loud in the silence. She heard it echo off the stone corridors. She tightened her jaw and looked back the way she'd come. "We had someone waiting outside the room. They already have your woman." He let out a painfully shrill whistle, and Milo heard sudden movement from the way she'd just come.

Milo tensed. "I would have smelled anyone lurking."

"You rely too much on your dog senses," the man said. "Leaves you vulnerable."

A light came on down the hall, its beam appearing from around the corner. It bounced, which meant either someone was carrying it or it was mounted on their body. Milo braced as the man stepped into sight. He was with another man, both of them dressed in full tactical gear that covered their faces. The man with the light had a vice grip on Gwen's upper arm, forcing her to walk alongside him. The second man, who was mostly in the dark, walked behind them. Milo could see the gun he was holding on Gwen's back. Gwen caught Milo's eye and gave her a look that screamed *run*.

"Why don't you come on out here?" the man said from the foyer. "This will all be a lot easier if we're all in the same room."

Milo considered Gwen's plea, tried to imagine herself running away from this decrepit castle and leaving her behind.

She stepped away from the wall and put her hands up. Gwen closed her eyes and let her head drop. The second hunter came forward and grabbed Milo's shoulder, shoved her through the archway into the foyer.

The speaking man was standing near the large double doors to the castle. He was dressed in gear like the other men, but his face was exposed. His hair was silver in the moonlight, and his eyes were shaded by his brows, giving him the appearance of a bleached skull. The hunters forced Milo and Gwen to their knees, pulling their arms back to restrain their wrists.

"The book is hidden," Gwen said. "We don't have it with us. You kill us, you'll never find it."

It was a lie. The book was in their car, wrapped in a blanket in a compartment under the backseat. They hadn't thought they would need to take more precautions than that given how isolated the castle was. As it turned out, their bluff apparently didn't matter.

"We don't need the book," the leader said, stepping forward. "And we have no intention of killing you. At least not yet."

Milo sniffed the air. "Gwen, do you smell anyone in this room?"

"Just you, love," Gwen said.

The leader smiled. "We have a lot of things to discuss, and a long time to have those discussions. But right now we should get a move on. We've got a very long trip ahead of us." To one of the guards, he said, "Go gather their things. Load it all into the truck. I want to be out of here in fifteen minutes."

"Where do you think you're taking us?" Milo asked.

"Home, Miss Duncan," the man said as he walked to the door. "I'm taking you back to Seattle."

Milo looked at Gwen, so her face was the last thing she saw before the remaining guard slipped a black bag over her head.

CHAPTER ONE

Seattle, Washington
Now

ARIADNE WILLOW didn't know, or care, how many traffic laws she broke on the way to Dr. Frost's house. Milo crouched in the passenger seat, knees up and hands on the dashboard, head on a swivel to keep an eye out for anyone who might be coming after them. She was still wearing the hospital johnny, thankfully the kind that came with pants, and she looked like she had just been dragged out of the woods.

"Where the hell you been, Milo?" Ari muttered as she blew through a red light.

Milo swung her head around at the question. Her hair hung over her eyes, but Ari could see there was only a wolf's intelligence behind them. Milo's brain thought she was in wolf form, thought she was incapable of speech or sitting properly. It was hard for Ari to look at, as if just seeing it was enough to make it contagious. It was probably better to keep her eyes on the road given the way she was driving.

"We're going to figure this out. Don't worry."

Milo spun in the seat, gripped the headrest, and watched out the back window for the rest of the journey.

Ari realized she should have called ahead, but the front door opened as she was getting Milo out of the car. Dr. Frost was *canidae*, retired, and the man who saved her life on too many occasions for her to count. She owed him far more than she could ever repay, and now she gave him an apologetic look as she walked Milo up the driveway. Milo was on all-fours again, palms flat on the pavement with her knees tucked against her flanks in a way that a human skeleton really shouldn't have allowed.

"What seems to be happening here?" Frost asked, tilting his head to regard Milo.

"Her brain thinks she's in wolf form."

Frost's eyebrows arched. "Well, Miss Willow, you certainly do bring me the most interesting patients. Bring her inside."

Frost took them into the house and guided Milo into the office he kept near the kitchen. Ari stayed behind in the living room and took out her phone. She planned to call Dale, but she had no idea what she would say in the call. There was just too much to sum it all up in a quick message when all she really wanted to say was "Milo and Mom are both alive, Mom's still missing. I'm at Dr Frost's. Please come be with me." So she just sent that.

Dale replied within a minute. "On my way."

Ari sat on the couch and slid down until she could rest her head against the back. She closed her eyes and gave herself a second to absorb everything that had happened in the past half hour.

Her mother was alive, but still missing. Milo was alive but afflicted with something horrifying, bizarre, and possibly permanent. Isaac Hayden was back. And the last time she'd seen Diana, she was surrounded by a bunch of people who were probably hunters.

She'd been foolish enough to think she'd eliminated the hunters as a threat years earlier when her father tried to get wolf manoth going again. Jacob Keighley had gotten some of his rich and powerful friends to fund a drug called wolfsbane that caused *canidae* to go feral. It had caused a few deaths before Ari and Dale tracked down the members of his little Venatorial Club and convinced them to back off. They folded without much pressure once confronted by the reality of what they were doing, and Keighley had gone to prison. Since then, hunters hadn't been much of a concern.

Now, with Hayden and that damned book of essays, they appeared to be making a comeback. She didn't even know what an actual war between hunters and wolves would look like. She'd always hoped she would never find out. And given the state Milo was in, she dreaded what new tactics they might have picked up since their last dust-up.

She was aware of drifting off, but she only knew she'd fallen asleep when she heard the front door open. Dale came into the living room and went directly to Ari, embracing her.

"Milo's safe?" Dale said.

"She's... yeah. Something isn't right with her, though. She's in human form, but the wolf is in charge."

"How does that happen?"

Dr. Frost came out of his office.

"I'm hoping he's about to tell us," Ari said.

Frost sighed and gave Dale a tired nod of greeting. "I've never seen anything like this. I've never even heard of anything like this. It shouldn't be possible. But I think it's similar to automaticity. Driving home from work, day after day, the same route, your brain focuses on other things while you go through the motions of safe driving."

"Like muscle memory?" Dale said.

"More like hypnosis," Frost said. "Miss Duncan's conscious mind is, um, asleep. Shut down. Whether that's due to trauma or something else, I can't say. But rather than leaving her catatonic, the wolf simply took control."

"Milo's catatonic?" Ari said.

Frost nodded. "It seems so. I'll need to examine her further, but at the moment it seems to be the only conclusion that makes sense. I don't know what effects this will have on her in the long-term, but her hands don't show evidence that she's been walking on all fours. It may be short-lived. It may fix itself when she transforms into the wolf and then back into her human form. We simply have to wait and see."

"Where is she now?"

"She's sedated, resting. There's a chance that's all she needs and she'll wake up being her old self again."

Ari said, "When will she wake up?"

"A few hours."

"Okay. Diana said the uniformed cops found her on Alaskan Way by the stadium. I'm going down there to see if I can pick up her scent, backtrack to wherever she came from."

"Are you sure that's safe?" Dale said.

Ari shrugged. "I don't know. I'll be as safe as I can be, but we need to know where she's been this whole time. If we're not going to get answers from her..."

"Right. Do you want me to go with you?"

"I'd rather have you here in case Milo wakes up."

Dale nodded and squeezed Ari's hand. "I'll call you if anything happens."

Ari kissed her, thanked Dr. Frost, and headed out. She didn't like that she still had Diana's car, but she didn't know if it was safe to return to the medical center yet. She sent Diana a text, asking for an update, then drove south through the city. Just before she reached CenturyLink Field, traffic narrowed to a single lane thanks to the crews finishing up the demolition of the viaduct. Cranes, excavators, and water trucks spraying down the skeletal remains had been cluttering up the waterfront for months, and she was glad the project was finally nearing an end.

She pulled into the ferry waiting zone and parked as far from the main road as she could. She checked to make sure she was alone, then quickly undressed and opened the door a crack. She transformed while she was still sitting in the car, rolling to her left and falling onto the pavement with the elegance only a wolf could achieve. She shook out her fur, stretched, and bumped the car door shut with her shoulder.

She didn't know exactly where Milo had been picked up by the cops, but she knew her friend's scent well enough to pick it up from a fair distance away if she put her mind to it. She smelled the air and isolated out the grease, gas, and oil of the cars from the saltwater of Elliott Bay, and set out at a fast trot. There were so many things to smell, to look at, but she forced herself to stay on task. There were people out walking but she ignored them as she weaved around their legs, looking for any hint of Milo or her mother.

There was something. Faint, but undeniable. The wolf part of her brain locked onto it and Ari let her body follow. Dale had once asked her what it was like to track, and she couldn't think of a comparison that effectively explain it. The closest she got was telling her it was like heat that makes a sound. "Imagine a room with lots of different temperatures. Hot in one corner, cool in the other, warm in the center, with spots that spike one way or the other. Now imagine each one makes a noise so you can cross the room without ever breaking a sweat. That's pretty much what it's like. Only without heat. Or sound. Just smell." Dale hadn't quite understood, but she declared the explanation was good enough to satisfy her curiosity.

Ari crossed the street and squeezed through the chain-link fence separating the flow of traffic from piles of rubble and continued running along the last remaining segments of the viaduct. Construction workers saw her, and one man operating a spray truck swept the stream around near her. She chose to believe he was doing it to keep her away from the dangerous equipment rather than just being a dick.

The scent took her south, to Dearborn, in front of the large glass building that housed the ventilation system for the SR 99 tunnel with its bright yellow smokestacks. She paused on the sidewalk and sniffed the air again to re-center her focus, which is why she was doubly alarmed when something heavy dropped onto her back, knocking her hind legs down and pinning her to the pavement.

She twisted and managed to wriggle free from what turned out to be a weighted nylon net. It had been thrown by one of two men currently running toward her, one of them fumbling with what looked like a garage door opener. She realized what it really was when he extended his arm, pressed a button, and the air filled with a piercing whistle so loud that she couldn't focus on anything else.

Ari flattened her ears to her skull and let the wolf's survival instincts take over. Her claws skittered on the ground as she ran. The whistle fell silent and, when its echo faded, she could hear the men shouting to each other as they pursued.

"~not her!"

"But look at the size of the thing! It's gotta be one of 'em."

They were looking for Milo. They were the people, the hunters, who had been holding her hostage. That meant they were probably the ones who had her mother.

But she couldn't let them catch her, so she ran. She scrambled through a chain-link fence and back into the demolition zone. Buildings that ran alongside the viaduct were boarded-up and sheathed in sheets of plastic that waved in the wind. She heard the rattle of the fence as her pursuers tried to get over it and continue the chase. She jumped large chunks of concrete, not bothering to look back as she ran.

Workmen shouted at her pursuers. "Yo, you guys can't be here. Turn around."

"That wuh- the dog, we have to-"

"The dog is gone, pal, we can't have you back here. Go. Now."

Ari didn't wait to see if they complied. She kept running until she was out of the demolition zone. She didn't plan to go back for Diana's car. If the hunters were lurking around the area, it was far too dangerous to risk transforming anywhere nearby. The wolf could get her back to Dr. Frost's house, and then she and Dale would go back for the car later on.

Second car I've abandoned today, she thought. *I'm on a roll.*

The realization was almost enough to amuse her. At the moment, though, she was too focused on escaping before the hunters pulled out any more tricks like the whistle.

***

Dr. Frost loaned Ari a pair of his slacks and a dress shirt, both of which almost fit her. Still, it was better than staying in wolf form or hanging out in the nude until she had a chance to get back to her apartment. Dale went into the bedroom with Ari so they could talk while she dressed.

"I've been trying to call Diana," Dale said. "No reply. Hopefully she's just busy and not something worse."

Ari nodded and tucked the shirt into her borrowed pants. It was still too baggy, but it would suffice. "I, uh, I didn't find anything on my end, either."

Dale narrowed her eyes. "Puppy..."

"Some hunters were apparently looking for her, too." She focused on rolling her sleeves up so she wouldn't have to look at Dale. "I managed to get away, but it was a close call. But really, I swear, it was nothing."

"Nothing? These are people who not only managed to capture your mother and Milo, they managed to keep them both prisoner for months. They did god-knows-what to Milo. So forgive me if I look at the glass as half-empty here. You got lucky escaping them this time."

Ari said, "I did. I admit that. But they got lucky, too." She furrowed her brow and shook her head, leaning against the dresser. "I should have smelled them. They were really damn close, and I was in full-on bloodhound mode. There's no way they should have gotten anywhere near close enough to throw that net. And even after I knew they were there, I never picked up a scent from them."

Dale crossed her arms over her chest. "What does that mean?"

"I have no idea." She sighed and ran her hands through her

hair. "And trust me, it's just as annoying to say that as it is for you to hear it. I don't like not knowing this much, and I don't like the idea of hunters being able to sneak up on us."

"Me neither." Dale thought for a second and then tilted her head to the side. "Why are they out looking for her?"

Ari said, "She escaped."

"But Hayden was at the hospital. They know where she is. They wouldn't have to look for her in the same place where she escaped."

Ari started to answer, but it was a very good question. Hayden and his goons knew that Milo was nowhere near the demolition site. So what had those two hunters been doing?

"The simplest theory is that there are two groups of hunters at play. But I'm having a hard enough time worrying about one, so let's wait until we get to that bridge before we worry about it."

"Fair enough," Dale said.

They returned to the living room and found Dr. Frost had just come out of his office. "Ah, there you are. Milo is awake."

"She's..."

Frost smiled, relief clear in his expression. "She's herself again. Come on. I still want her to rest, but I think we all have questions for her."

Ari breathed a sigh of relief and gripped Dale's hand, then followed Frost into the office. The front half looked like a typical older man's study: massive desk, bookshelves neatly filled with leather-bound books and a variety of small doodads. The far side of the room, on the other hand, looked like a hospital room. Milo was in a bed with her head and shoulders elevated, a blanket tucked around her legs, hands folded in her lap. She'd been cleaned up since the last time Ari saw her. Her hair was wet and slicked back from her face, and she was wearing an old Mariner's T-shirt. Most likely it was another loan from Dr. Frost's closet.

She had been staring out the window but sat up straighter when they came in. "Ari. Dale. Apparently I really am in Seattle."

"Apparently so," Ari said.

Milo looked between them. "Where's Gwen?"

Ari's shoulders slumped. "Ah, pup, we were hoping you'd be able to answer that one." She sat on the edge of the bed as Dale went around to the other side. "How are you doing?"

"Confused, obviously." Milo reached out for Dale's hand. "I don't know how I got here."

"Cops found you by the arena," Ari said. "You were out of it. Your wolf brain was in charge even though you were in human form. You don't have any idea how you got there?"

Milo searched her memory, but she was slowly shaking her head. "I'm having a hard time remembering anything."

Frost cleared his throat. "It's not surprising. Considering the trauma your mind has gone through, it's highly unlikely your memory escaped unscathed. What's the last thing you remember clearly?"

Milo closed her eyes. "Germany. With Gwen. We were on the road, going... somewhere. We had to find a safe place to leave the book. I don't... I..." She squeezed her eyes shut tighter, like she was trying to force her brain to work. "I don't remember if we found a place. I don't know how I got from there to here. I remember... a plane. I was laying down on a plane. Then dark rooms... It's like trying to remember a dream. The harder I push, the more I lose."

"Then maybe just let it rest for now," Dale said.

Ari shot her a look. Dale responded with a look that said they weren't going to gain anything by damaging Milo's already injured brain.

"Dale's right," Ari conceded. "For now you just have to rest. We'll keep an eye on you." She brushed Milo's arm and squeezed her hand. "Is there anything you need?"

"Water. I'm dying of thirst."

Frost was already halfway out of the room by the time she finished speaking. Ari waited until he was out of earshot and lowered her voice.

"There might be something you can answer from before the blackout."

"Anything that might be helpful."

"When Dale talked to Henrik Bayer, he referred to you and Mom as 'the Willows.' He seemed to be under the impression you were married."

Milo smiled weakly. "Oh, that. We met with a lot of *canidae* when we were over there. Every time we had to introduce ourselves, Gwen stumbled over herself because she doesn't like the word 'girlfriend' and 'partner' is too vague. By the time we met Henrick she decided to just introduce me as Milo Willow and let people draw their own conclusions." She shrugged. "I didn't mind it. I mean, I still think it sounds silly. But... yeah, I didn't mind it."

Ari smiled. "I don't mind it, either, if you want to know the truth. But I'm not calling you Mom."

"Fair enough."

Frost came back with the water. "Okay, ladies, let's go. Give her memory some time to recharge and heal, hm?"

Milo said, "Here's hoping."

Frost left the glass on the nightstand, then held out his arms to herd Ari and Dale from the room.

Milo stopped them. "Ari, can you stay for a second?"

Ari went back to the bed. Dale closed the door behind her, leaving them alone. Milo held her gaze on the door, then switched her focus to Ari.

"How is she?"

"Who, Dale? She's fine. Perfect."

Milo said, "She read the book, Ariadne. Gwen and I got a crash course on that thing the past few months. It's fucking insidious. It can change anyone into a wolf-hating maniac. A member of Henrick's pack knew someone who read the books and then poisoned sixteen *canidae* before they finally put him down. If it can change a wolf..."

"I trust Dale."

"It's not about trust, Ari. It's not even really about Dale, or how we feel about her. I need to make sure you know how powerful that book is."

"I understand," Ari assured her, "and I know Dale is stronger. It's been months since she read it. She's had countless opportunities to hurt me. She's the same person we've always known. If you can't trust her, then trust me."

Milo pressed her lips together. "I do. You know I do. But mainly because you're the one she'll go after first if she does snap. If anything happens to you, I won't hesitate to go after her."

Ari bristled at that, but she tried to understand where Milo was coming from. Instead of arguing, she nodded. "Okay, Milo. If that's what it takes to get you on board with her, then I accept it. But you don't have to worry."

"I hope you're right, pup. I love Dale, I do, but I'm not going to stand by and let her turn into something she'd hate."

Ari squeezed Milo's hand. "I'm glad to have you back."

"Glad to be back," Milo said. "I just wish I could fill in some more blanks for you."

"All in good time." Ari bent down and kissed Milo's forehead. "We can talk again when you've gotten some of your strength back."

She got up off the bed and left the office. She knew Milo's concern wasn't baseless, but she also knew the idea of Dale still being under the control of that book was preposterous. She could only hope Milo's current paranoia would fade when she was feeling more like herself.

CHAPTER TWO

GWEN WAS getting pretty good at counting time. Her window was fogged glass, barred on the outside, and covered with a thick sheet of plastic, but sunlight still passed through. She could tell the difference between morning, afternoon, and evening, and could make a good guess about how far into each part of the day she was. They didn't take her out of her cell according to any schedule she could recognize, but it helped break things up a little. Guessing was harder on the days when they drugged her but, for the most part, she felt her accuracy was good.

She was almost positive it was just before noon when the door to her room was unlocked. She was sitting in the middle of her bed, feet up on the mattress so she could rest her arms across her knees, staring straight ahead as Valerie Byrne came in. She had a tray of food, a combination of breakfast and lunch, which she placed on the desk under the window. Gwen was wearing her usual outfit of sweatpants and a T-shirt. Her hair hadn't been cut in months and sat heavily on her shoulders in a rats-nest tangle.

Val looked equally disheveled. It was clear she hadn't had a quality shower in a while, but at least her scrubs were clean. Her hair was long and ratty, but she had it tied back in a ponytail to keep it out of her way. She rested her hands on the back of the chair before she turned to face Gwen.

"She's gone."

Gwen perked up as if a power button had been thrown. Her eyes, once flat, filled with life as she focused on Val. "What do you mean 'gone'?"

"Her room is empty." She kept her voice low and one eye on the door. "A bunch of the guards are also gone, presumably out looking for her, but judging from how pissed off everybody is, I don't think they're having much luck."

Gwen put her feet on the floor and stood up. "If Milo got out–"

"We don't know for sure that she did," Val said. "They would be equally pissed off if she got killed trying to escape. The guards may be gone to dispose of her body."

Gwen refused to hear that theory, shaking her head until the visuals were gone. "She said she had a theory. A way out. If she found a way..."

Val stepped closer so she could lower her voice even further. "This isn't necessarily a good thing, Gwen. If Milo really did get away, who do you think they're going to take it out on? The only other *canidae* they have prisoner? No. It'll be me."

Gwen flinched and looked away. "I'm sorry. Milo and I promised we'd get you out of here, and I still intend to do that. I won't leave you behind. Milo won't, either. If she did get out, she's probably getting help as we speak."

Val still looked concerned, so Gwen took her hand. "Look at me, Valerie. We're getting out of here. It's just a matter of time."

"I hope you're right." She squeezed Gwen's fingers before letting go. "I should get back. We don't want them to come looking for me. I'll let you know if I hear anything else."

Gwen nodded. "Thank you. Is there anything planned for today?"

Val hesitated. "Not that I know of. I don't know what Milo's disappearance will do for their mood, so we should be prepared for anything."

"Okay. Thank you, Val."

"Yeah," Val said softly. She let her hand fall from Gwen's and left the room.

Gwen went to her desk and looked down at the food. Another frozen dinner. Definitely not the worst food in the world, but it was the only thing she'd eaten in months. It was better than starving, barely, so she sat down and started to eat. She focused on the bare wall in front of her and, for the millionth time, went over how few options she had.

Her jailors didn't seem to have any issue with letting her see where they were holding her. It was an abandoned building, all the windows on the western side boarded and covered with plastic. All the ground floor windows were barred, and most of the rooms had been completely gutted. The room she was in had a reinforced door, naturally. She assumed Milo and Val's cells were equally secure. There were always at least two hunters on duty, and Val said they had more outside. The only other exit she'd seen besides the main door was a loading bay which had been bricked over.

It clearly wasn't impossible to get out. Milo had somehow managed it. The thought made Gwen smile, despite everything. She might not know the details, but Milo had definitely thrown a monkey wrench in Silver Skull's plans. That alone was worth celebrating. And while she knew it was certainly possible that she'd been hurt or even died in the attempt, she couldn't make herself think about that version of events. She had to imagine her free, safe, and looking for help, because the alternative would make her shut down. She needed to keep her wits about her.

Her right foot bounced. She stared at the window in front of her, imagining if she stared hard enough she could see through the blurry glass and the plastic. There was a world out there. She could hear traffic and the sounds of demolition, heavy trucks moving around and beeping when they moved in reverse. Men and women were working less than a hundred yards from where she'd spent the last few months. But their voices might as well have been a radio broadcast from Mars for all the good they did her.

When she first woke up in this place, brain still foggy from whatever drug they'd given her for the flight from Germany to Seattle, she'd assumed Val was one of them. When she came in to do the initial examination, Gwen had attacked her. Val endured the punching and kicking, letting Gwen tire herself out before she wrestled her onto the bed and got the restraints around her wrists.

"We've met. Remember? I helped Ariadne. I'm a friend."

Gwen's brain was scrambled, but she did seem familiar. She couldn't remember where exactly they'd met, but she did have a memory of this woman. It was enough to make her stop fighting and pay attention to what Val was saying.

"I'm a prisoner just like you," Val had said. "I'm going to make this as painless as possible but you've got to fucking cooperate. Understand?"

Gwen truly hadn't known whether or not she could trust Val, but all the fight had gone out of her. She surrendered, let Val administer the sedative, and felt the fog close over her mind again.

Since then, she'd been subjected to a series of tests and experiments that verged on sadistic. The hunters in charge never told her their names, so she was reduced to identifying them by physical characteristics. The man who'd captured them in Germany was the Silver Skull, due to his hair and sharp cheekbones. His partner was Walrus, from his bushy mustache. The ones who took her out of her room and "escorted" her to the lab were Goon One and Goon Two, since she didn't think they deserved proper names. The only other one she saw with any regularity was the Geek. He had black-rimmed glasses and a generally nerdy demeanor; shirts buttoned to the collar, pencil-neck, hunched posture. He observed the tests, rarely speaking to her.

Gwen flexed her hand. The hunters holding them hostage were trying to understand *canidae* physiology. They wanted to know exactly what happened before, during, and after a transformation. She didn't know what they intended to do with this information once they had it, but she fought with every fiber of her being to keep them from achieving their goals. She'd transformed ten times since being taken prisoner. She tried to time them for odd hours, to quietly transform in her room behind a locked door, and so far she hadn't been caught. It was only a matter of time, she knew, before they succeeded.

In the meantime, they ran their evil little experiments. They took her blood. They administered electric shock. They experimented with extreme heat, extreme cold, and had once submerged her head in a basin of water so long that she thought they were trying to drown her. They stopped just before she blacked out. They gave her a fitness tracker which was never unstrapped from her wrist. She didn't have to take it off to bathe because they only gave her a bucket of water and towels for that. She hated that, but if the alternative was showering with one of the hunters standing watch, she would take the bucket every time.

Val had proven herself to be a true ally many times over the course of their mutual incarceration. Insisting the experiments had to stop, making sure Gwen was safely returned to her room when the sadists were finally done, sneaking her extra food when she could. Most importantly, she was a conduit of information and provided communication between Gwen and Milo. They hadn't seen each other since Germany, but Gwen could sometimes hear her shouting at their captors through the walls.

Now she was out. Whatever that meant, and she could only hope it was the turning point of this whole damn ordeal.

Back in Dr. Frost's living room, Ari stood in front of the couch, uncertain of what her next step would be. She looked at Dale for help, but her expression revealed she was equally clueless.

"So what the hell do we do now?" Ari asked Dr. Frost, the default grown-up in the room due to his advanced age. "Do we just go to the office and pretend like it's a normal day?"

"Well, I can tell you that Miss Duncan isn't going to be much help to you any time soon. She needs a lot of rest. She needs to recuperate. And she can't do that with all of us looming over her asking questions she can't answer. Her body and mind both need time to mend." He pressed his lips together and glanced over his shoulder as if making sure he'd closed the door to his office before he continued. "There's evidence she's been electrocuted."

"What?" Ari and Dale said at the same time.

"Contact burns on her arms." Frost tapped his own arms just above the elbow to show where the marks had been. "Some were old, some were fresher."

Ari clenched her jaw and began to pace. "Why would they kidnap Mom and Milo just to torture them for six months?"

"I don't know," Frost said. "But torture might explain Milo's mental state when she was found. We won't know more until her memory starts coming back. If it ever does."

"If?" Dale said. "It's six months of her life. Are you saying it could just be gone?"

Frost nodded. "If the damage is bad enough. And honestly..." He sighed and shook his head. "I don't want to make assumptions about what she went through. But if it was bad enough to make her conscious mind retreat so the wolf could take over while she was still in human form, then she might be better off not remembering."

Ari shuddered. "Thank you, Doctor. Not just for this, but for everything you've done for us. We show up and dump huge problems on your lap, and you rise to the occasion every time."

"Always happy to patch up you or your friends, Ariadne. I am looking forward to you dumping your mother's problem on me very soon."

Ari and Dale left the house and went out to the car. Dale got behind the wheel and turned to face Ari, reaching over to touch her thigh. Ari stared straight ahead out the windshield, holding her head very still, refusing to meet Dale's gaze.

"Are you going to drive?" she finally asked.

"I'll drive if that's what you want," Dale said softly. "But I'm willing to wait here if you want that, too. And once I drive, I can go wherever you want."

Ari kept her voice quiet. "We should go to work. We have that... there's that case..." Her bottom lip trembled and she felt tears in her eyes. She turned to look out the window quickly. Dale moved her hand to Ari's shoulder. "I'm fine," Ari said, though her voice betrayed the lie.

"Hey. Look at me, Ariadne."

It took her a few seconds, but she finally turned around to look at Dale. She didn't bother hiding the fact she was crying. Dale brushed away the tears with her thumb.

"You made peace with losing your mother. Now she's out there, but she's maybe being hurt. You don't know if it's safe to hope yet. But the carpet got pulled out from under you. It would be worrying if you weren't a wreck right now."

"I feel like I got my hope back just to have it taken away again," Ari said.

"I know, puppy. I feel that, too. So just tell me where you want to go and I'll take you there. And I'll sit with you, or talk with you, or do whatever you need for as long as you need."

Ari took Dale's hand, kissed the knuckles. "I love you." She kissed Dale's hand again, then let it go and faced forward again. She wiped her eyes and cleared her throat. "Drive."

"Where to?" Dale asked.

"West."

Dale started the engine and pulled out of the driveway. "I can only go so far west, given where we are now," she pointed out.

"I'll think of something before we hit the water."

"Okay," Dale said, turning the car west. "I trust you."

***

They picked up lunch and took it to the Olympic Sculpture Park. It was really too cold to sit outside and eat, but at least that meant there weren't many other people around. Dale sat close to

Ari and huddled against her, watching the water as Ari mechanically ate her sandwich in silence. When the food was gone, Ari wadded up the paper and slipped it into her pocket, and stared straight ahead like she was an actor waiting for a cue. They'd tried Diana's cell phone twice in the car but it still went directly to voicemail. Dale was starting to wonder when they should call her wife to let her know what was happening.

"She's somewhere in the city," Dale said. "We know that much, at least."

Ari nodded slowly.

"And Milo was in bad shape, but she's doing better now. That means there's a good chance Mom's doing okay, too."

Ari's lips twitched and some life came back into her expression. She moved her hand to Dale's thigh. "I really like that you call her Mom. I know how big of a deal that is for you."

"She means a lot to me." The wind blew her hair into her face and she brushed it away, not taking her eyes off Ari. "We'll find her. We know she's here, we know she needs us, and Milo's going to do everything in her power to remember what happened."

"What about in the meantime?" Ari said. "We just have to sit and wait while Mom is in a hole somewhere, having... who knows what done to her..."

Dale took Ari's hand. "I know it's tough. But it's too dangerous to just start kicking down doors. We have to be careful. We have to do it right. Mom's tough. She's survived this long. We have to have faith that she's strong enough to stick it out a little longer."

"You say that like it'll be easy."

"No, definitely not easy. But we'll figure it out." She put her head down on Ari's shoulder and looked out at the water. "Do you want to go over what we know?"

Ari said, "Yeah, go ahead."

Dale put her thoughts in order before she started speaking. "Someone, presumably a group of hunters, kidnapped Gwen and Milo in Germany. Brought them back here."

"Why?" Ari interrupted. "What's the point of bringing them all the way back to Seattle just to lock them up?"

"That's question number one," Dale said. "So they've been held captive for about six months. Going by Milo's condition, there's... been some torture involved. Question two is what the torture is intended to reveal."

Ari said, "Maybe the location of the essays."

"Maybe. Question three is the biggest one. What happened to Mom and Milo over those six months, and how did Milo escape? That's two questions."

"And another one is why she left Mom behind," Ari said. After a moment she clarified, "I'm not blaming her or holding her responsible. I know she wouldn't have done it if she had a choice in the matter. Maybe question four should be what would make Milo leave without Mom."

"That's a good addition," Dale said, sitting up now. "Five. Why were there hunters looking for Milo at the viaduct when Hayden knew she was already at the hospital?"

Ari nodded. "I'd like to believe it was stupidity or a lack of communication, but I don't think we can count on them being dumb."

"Unfortunately," Dale said.

"And then there are the general questions. How many hunters there are, what they're planning, when it'll happen. We're still a few months away from wolf manoth, if that's their goal, so I don't think it'll be that. I hope it's not that. We cannot have another wolfsbane threat."

Dale shuddered. "Definitely don't want that."

Ari was quiet, then shifted so she could turn on the bench to face Dale. "I haven't forgotten that today is your birthday."

"Oh, hey, no." Dale shook her head. "We never celebrate anyway, and what you did this morning was so sweet."

"Are you sure?"

Dale smiled. "Yes. And I know there weren't any candles, but Milo showing up okay and giving us hope that we might find your Mom feels like a birthday wish coming true. You don't have to worry about me. I'm very, very satisfied with how this day has gone."

"Truly?"

"Best birthday ever." Dale leaned in and kissed the corner of Ari's mouth. Ari turned her head, turning it into a proper kiss.

"Tell me we'll find her," Ari whispered against Dale's cheek. "It's easier for me to believe things when you say them."

"We'll find her," Dale said. "Whatever that means, and whatever it takes, we're going to find Mom and we'll bring her home."

Ari kissed Dale's cheek. "Thank you."

"Any time, puppy. Any time."

Ari put an arm around Dale and drew her close so they could look out over the water for a little while longer.

Chapter Three

Their first mystery was solved when they arrived at the Bitches office. Ari was still in a funk despite Dale's best efforts, but she was determined not to let the unknowns outweigh the good parts of the day. Milo was alive. She'd gone to sleep the night before positive that she'd never see Milo or her mother again, and now her friend was back. There was hope. But with hope came the potential for being knocked back down, and she dreaded that fall.

Dale had convinced her to spend a few hours at the office. They had a few open cases which required very low effort, and she was sure that it was just what Ari needed to distract herself. Dale opened the door to the building and Ari followed her in, stopping immediately upon stepping into the hall. Dale sensed her hesitation and turned to look at her.

"Everything okay?"

Ari sniffed the air again to be sure. Shampoo, chamomile, and hand lotion. Shae butter. She moved without thinking, brushing past Dale and hurrying to their office door. She twisted the knob and pushed the door open. She held her breath until she saw Diana sitting behind Dale's desk, looking exhausted but uninjured. Ari exhaled with relief as Dale caught up to her and saw what had caused the mad dash.

"Diana! You're okay!"

Diana stood and accepted hugs from both of them. "Yeah, I'm fine. I was snooping in your desk to see if I could find either of your cell phone numbers."

"We've been texting and calling you all day," Ari said.

"My phone is in my car. Which, last I saw, you had it."

Ari said, "Oh. Right. I know exactly where it is."

"That's what you like to hear from someone who borrowed your car." She stepped out from behind the desk so Dale could take her seat. "How's Milo?"

"Much better," Ari said. "A sedative and a little rest woke her back up. Unfortunately she's got a big frustrating gap in her memory that keeps her from answering any questions, but the important thing is that she'll recover. What about you? The last I saw, you were on the ground recovering from a taser shot."

Diana shook her head. "Yeah. Remind me to avoid doing that again any time soon. I was hearing static for an hour. Hayden got away, unfortunately, but I arrested both of his goons for assaulting me, two uniformed officers, and Dr. Kalwar. We had some cruisers go around the area looking for Hayden but we never found him."

"He's definitely in town, and I don't think he's going anywhere any time soon. We'll find him."

Diana leaned against the desk. "In the meantime, we have his men in custody. They were wearing suits, like him, so hopefully they're more than just random goons. At the moment they're refusing to speak, but I'm sure it's only a matter of time before they get sick of the silent treatment. Even if we have to talk in front of their lawyers, we're going to hear what they have to say."

"They *were* in suits, weren't they?" Ari thought back to the men who had almost captured her. "The men on the viaduct were dressed all in black. Like commandos."

Diana held up a hand. "Whoa, whoa, what men on the viaduct?"

Ari quickly filled her in on what happened. "That's where I left your car, in the ferry lot. I figured I had a better chance getting away as the wolf."

Dale said, "I can drive you over there to pick it up."

"Thank you." Diana looked at Ari. "What are you going to do?"

Ari shrugged and held out her hands. "There isn't much I can do unless Milo's memory snaps back. We're just going to try to take everything as it comes."

"You can't ignore the fact that Hayden is back in town," Diana said. "He knows he can find you here. You might want to think about precautions."

Dale said, "He's apparently been back in town for a while and he hasn't come by."

"He may have wanted to maintain the element of surprise. But after what happened this morning, I don't think you can count on that. Be careful, Ariadne, okay?"

"We will," Ari promised.

Diana looked at Dale. "Can I take you up on that offer to drive me to my car?"

"Sure," Dale said, rising from her chair. "Want to come with us?"

Ari said, "If those hunters are still around, it might be better if I'm not there. I'll hold down the fort here." She pulled Dale into a hug and whispered, "Be careful," into her hair.

"You too," Dale said, then kissed Ari's neck before stepping back.

When they were gone, Ari went into her office. It felt like a thousand years ago when she'd come into this office as an employee. She worked with Glory Bennett to get her private investigator license, a job she'd never intended or expected to have. She'd been living on the street for a long time, and a steady paycheck would give her the chance to start a real life. An apartment, new clothes, shoes that weren't held together with duct tape.

And if that was a thousand years ago, it felt like five hundred years since the redheaded business school dropout agreed to stick around for "a day or two" so she could straighten out Ari's books. A day or two ended up being a week, and brought with it a realization that the books would just descend into chaos again without someone staying on top of them. Her files were also a hopeless mess, but Dale was able to get those under control as well.

Ari was still thinking about those early days, when Dale was her employee rather than a friend or partner, when she heard the outer office door open. She tensed and smelled the air, but it was immediately apparent her visitor wasn't Hayden. She went back out into the waiting room and saw a girl - college-age, brunette, clearly nervous - standing just inside the doorway. She jumped when Ari appeared, then tried to cover it by tucking her hair behind her ears.

"Hi, um... this is..." She gestured at the glass door behind her.

"This is Bitches Investigations, right? And you're Ariadne Willow?"

"That's right. I'm sorry, but we're not really accepting new clients right now." She hadn't discussed it with Dale, but taking a break felt like the right thing to do until things were a little more settled. "I can recommend some other agencies that could help you..."

The girl's face fell. "Oh. Okay. Um..." She looked past Ari into the office and then scanned the small waiting room as if someone had snuck in when she wasn't looking. When she spoke again, she kept her voice at a whisper. "Are they also *canidae*...?"

Goosebumps rose on Ari's skin. "Are you?"

The girl nodded.

Ari stepped back and gestured into her office. "Come on in. What's your name?"

"Eva Cardoso. But I don't... i-i-if you're not taking clients, I don't want to be a bother..."

"If you're a *canidae*, I want to help. Come on. You can call me Ari."

Eva hesitated another few seconds before she came forward. Ari followed her into the office and closed the door behind them. Eva looked at the big clock on the wall, the couch, the currently-bare bulletin board, and then went to sit in one of the chairs in front of Ari's desk. Ari went around to her own chair and sat down.

"Why do you need a *canidae* private investigator, Eva?"

"It's my sister. Marin. She was out for a run last night and didn't come back this morning. I know it's only been a couple of hours. But if you know Marin, that's enough to be panicking. And I think it's a myth that you have to wait three days before you report a missing person to the cops, but it's not like I can tell them that she was last seen naked and running through the Arboretum on all fours."

Ari smiled a little at that. "Yeah, they tend not to take those reports seriously. Do you have a picture of Marin?"

Eva fumbled in her coat pocket and handed a pair of photos across the desk. One showed a young woman, older than Eva but clearly related to her, smiling next to a river. The other photo was of a tall, broad-shouldered wolf in a wooded area.

"I also brought you a shirt of hers so you can get her scent."

Ari chuckled. "It's really convenient having a *canidae* client. You said the last place you saw her was the Arboretum?"

Eva hesitated. "I actually didn't see here there. That's where she usually runs, so it's a safe bet. I went around this morning to see if I could pick up her scent, and I'm pretty sure she was there."

"You couldn't track her yourself?"

"I've never been much of a tracker. I tend to get distracted when I'm the wolf."

"I've been there," Ari admitted. She looked at the photos again. It sounded like an easy case, but she knew better than to curse herself by saying so out loud. Still, she had more leads in this case than her mother's. It would be nice to bring home somebody's missing loved one. "Let me get a little more information and then we can get started." She pulled the keyboard closer and squinted at her screen. "Sorry, my assistant usually does this part..."

"Um, before we actually start, I wanted to talk about how much you charge. I can pay, I'm sure I can get the money, but if there's some kind of payment plan..."

Ari shook her head. "This one will be on the house."

"You don't have to do that."

"It's a missing person, a family member," Ari said. "You caught me on a really, really good day for that." She winced. "Sorry. I didn't mean to trivialize what you're going through."

Eva offered a weak smile. "It's okay. I appreciate dark humor. Just... just I really hope I'm wasting your time."

"Me too."

Dale parked next to Diana's car. The lot was almost empty as the ferry had just left, still visible out in the bay. The ride over had been silent, but Dale stopped Diana from getting out.

"What really happened this morning?"

"What do you mean? At the hospital? I thought Ari told you."

"She's been known to polish off the rough edges when it comes to danger. I want to hear your version of events."

Diana nodded slowly and settled back against the seat. "I'm guilty of that, too. With Lucy. We only do it so you won't worry about us."

"It doesn't work."

"Yeah," Diana said softly. "Thankfully. We hate making you worry. But at the same time, knowing someone is out there worrying... sometimes it's what gets us through." She sighed. "Okay. Ari and I went to the hospital. She talked to Milo, and then Isaac Hayden showed up with two other men in suits. Ari assumed, rightfully so, that they were coming to grab Milo. There was a scuffle, Ari ran off with Milo and took her to Dr. Frost~"

"The scuffle. You said there was a scuffle, Ari said there was a fight..."

"There were tasers involved. I got zapped, got my bell rung pretty good, but I don't think Ari got hit with anything."

Dale breathed out slowly. "Okay. Thank you."

Diana nodded. "I understand the need. And I'm sure you understand the need for me to say this to *you*, because I think you'll actually listen. Be careful. Hayden is still out there. The man assaulted three police officers this morning and didn't blink an eye. He's out there somewhere and he's pretty pissed off. I don't want you or Ari taking that lightly."

"Oh, I'm taking it seriously enough for both of us. That man almost turned me into a hunter. I was actually on a plane ready to go off with him to become some kind of *canidae*-killing machine. He's my bogeyman. I don't see myself getting a good night sleep until he's good and gone."

Diana said, "That'll make two of us." She leaned across the console and kissed Dale's cheek. "Happy birthday, by the way."

"Thank you. You gave me a pretty great gift."

"It'll be hard to beat next year, but I'll find something." She winked, patted Dale's hand, and got out of the car. Dale waited as Diana unlocked her own car, got Ari's clothes out of the backseat, and brought them back over. "Call if you need anything. *Anything.* Understand?"

"Understood."

Diana nodded and went back to her car.

Dale let her leave first, then followed her back out into traffic. Hayden arrived at the hospital with men dressed in suits. Ari said the hunters by the stadium were dressed like commandos. She tried to think about what that meant. There was a chance Hayden dressed up so he would look respectable when he showed up to collect Milo. But if they'd found her, and knew where she was, why had the men in black still been out searching? Had Hayden not contacted them to call off the search?

She decided the who and why wasn't important. The facts were that one group of hunters was out trying to abduct wolves in broad daylight, while another group had Isaac Hayden leading an assault on police officers.

She knew which one of those groups she considered most dangerous but, until they had more information, she was just going to consider them both one big scary thing to be on the lookout for.

The Washington Park Arboretum was two hundred and thirty acres of woodlands, gardens, and walking trails between downtown Seattle and Lake Washington. Ari was very familiar with it from runs as the wolf; she had a few stashes buried there and she knew how easy it would be for someone to get lost. Or for someone to hide, as the case might be.

Eva said her sister had entered the Arboretum from Madison Avenue, and she'd picked up Marin's scent in the parking lot of the Japanese Gardens. Ari parked there and got out of the car, taking a moment to separate the natural scents before she started walking. She still had the shirt Eva brought her in the car, and she'd picked up enough from it to know what Marin smelled like. It wasn't just body odor, but a mixture of sweat, perfume, soap, shampoo, and a dozen other things she probably didn't even realize were part of the equation. Scent was as unique as a fingerprint, and she could tell Marin Cardoso had definitely been in this parking lot at some point in the past twenty-four hours.

She walked along the side of the road and looked for visual clues, evidence of a wolf's passage. There weren't many cars on the road into the arboretum, so she didn't have to adjust for exhaust and gas smells. The deeper she got into the woods, the clearer Marin's scent became. Everything else fell away and she focused hard on her target.

Ari was so focused, so tunnel vision in her search, that she almost missed the unexpectedly familiar thread underneath everything else. When she noticed it, she stopped and closed her eyes, letting everything else flood back in so she could pick through it and find what had tripped her alarms. Grass and trees and mold, mulch, flowers, dirt, mud. And there, underneath it all... she opened her eyes and looked around.

"Milo?"

It could be a remnant from that morning. It could have been her mind playing tricks on her. But it was definitely Milo. Identifying someone's odor wasn't like smelling the same brand of perfume. It was distinct to each person. Ari crouched down, leaning forward with her eyes closed, breathing in deeply and holding it. Marin had been here. Recently. She was certain of that.

And Milo had been with her.

But how long ago? Certainly not more than a day. Marin and Milo were entwined, which could only have happened if their paths crossed or they passed through this way together. But what was Milo doing out, and this far out? The arboretum was six miles north of where Milo had been picked up by the police. Had she started here, or even further away, and gotten to CenturyLink Stadium before she was spotted? It seemed unlikely that she could have walked that far barefoot. If she'd been in wolf form, and it was before sunrise, maybe...

Ari sat back on her heels and let her brain work. Milo was in the arboretum with Marin Cardoso before she was found by the police, and taken to the hospital. But Milo was found alone.

The first piece of the puzzle clicked into place. The hunters in black hadn't been looking for Milo, they were looking for *Marin*.

But Marin had only been missing for one night. She couldn't have been another prisoner. Had it been some kind of rescue attempt? But if that was the case, there had to be more to Marin than Eva told her. She needed more information.

When she left the woods, she planned to call Eva and interrogate her about who Marin was. By the time she got to her car, however, she realized there might be an easier way to get answers.

She drove to Dr. Frost's house, knocked, and let herself in without waiting for him to answer. Frost caught up with her just before she reached his office.

"Milo should rest, Miss Willow."

"I know, but this can't wait."

Ari went into the darkened room and took Marin's shirt out of the plastic bag she'd been carrying it in. She held it out, close enough to Milo's head that she couldn't help but smell it.

Milo breathed in once, then again, and then her eyes snapped open. She shot out her arm and shouted, "No! Run! Get out of here!" Her legs kicked at the blankets and she shoved herself back against the pillows. "Go! Run!"

Ari dropped the shirt to grab Milo's shoulders. "Hey! It's me. You're safe. It's me."

Milo's eyes focused on her, and her brow furrowed with confusion. "Ariadne? What's... what did you do to me?"

"I let you smell this shirt. Do you know Marin Cardoso?"

Milo thought, then shook her head. "It doesn't sound familiar."

Ari took the photos of Marin out of her pocket and held them up. "This is her."

Milo looked at both with the intensity of someone trying to memorize every detail. Finally she shook her head. "No. I don't know her."

"But when you caught her scent, you freaked out and yelled for her to run. I think you saw her this morning at the arboretum."

Milo's look of confusion deepened. "Okay. So I was at the arboretum with this Marin person, and then I was at the waterfront by myself a little while later?"

"That's what it looks like right now."

Frost cleared his throat. "Miss Willow, I don't want to remind you that trying to force her memory to return could do more damage~"

"No, I want to try," Milo said. "Gwen is still out there. If this helps..." She made a grabbing motion. "Give me whatever I smelled a second ago."

Ari picked up the shirt and handed it over. Milo pressed the fabric against her face.

"It makes me scared," Milo said after a second. "But I'm scared *for* someone, not of them. I think I was trying to protect this person."

"That makes sense if your first instinct was telling her to run."

Milo brought the shirt up again. "I don't know. I don't know how I know her, I just know she's in danger."

Ari said, "But who were you protecting her from? The hunters?"

"No," Milo said slowly. "I think I was trying to protect her from me."

CHAPTER FOUR

VALERIE BYRNE had literally no idea how long she'd been a prisoner. It didn't seem helpful to keep a running tally, but at this point it had to have been months. The nights she couldn't sleep, she wondered if she still had an apartment. If the prison was holding her job. Definitely not, to both of those questions. She knew that even if she got out of this mess, she would be homeless and unemployed. She had some savings, but nowhere near enough to start over. It didn't make her hopeful for escape.

So she used the lessons she'd learned from lifers she'd met in prison. She followed the rules. She kept quiet. She woke up when she was told and tried not to draw attention to herself. Her main task had been taking care of Milo and Gwen. She cooked their food, made sure they recovered from whatever medieval tortures the hunters had arranged for them, and saw to all their needs. The hunters didn't seem to think of them as actual people, so it was up to Val to keep them alive.

She knew the names of her captors, but she preferred Gwen Willow's nicknames for them. They were too apt not to use, and she was more than willing to reduce them to cartoons.

Val's cell was on the ground floor, not far from where Gwen was being held. Milo's cell had been on the other side of the building. They were all decorated the same: sink, shelf, bed, toilet. They all had windows, all of them barred and impossible to actually see through, but they let in weak milky light that was better than nothing.

At the moment Val was lying on her bed, staring at a water spot on the ceiling, trying hard not to think about Milo. She'd snuck into Milo's cell to take a look around but hadn't seen any signs of an escape. No broken window, no tunnel hidden behind a poster of Raquel Welch, nothing that would indicate a person had gotten out. But Milo was undeniably gone, and their jailors were horribly pissed. At the moment it seemed as if only Walrus and the Geek were present. She'd never seen so few hunters at the building.

Gwen could probably overpower them, even in her current state, she thought. *The odds would be even better if she had help.*

Val sat up and put her feet on the floor. Walrus looked tough, and was probably armed. The Geek wouldn't put up much of a fight. She gripped her blanket with both hands and considered what she was about to do. She had no idea what Silver Skull planned to do with Gwen, but she knew it was bad. And she knew that with both Milo and Gwen gone, their plans would be crippled. She got up off the bed and left her cell. They never locked her in because they knew there was no point. She had free rein to move about the building so she could see to their prisoner's needs.

Well, now the only remaining prisoner had a need she could take care of very easily.

The main room was huge, had probably started life as a shopping center's display room or a bank lobby. Any identifiers had been torn out long ago, leaving behind a spacious empty box that the hunters had turned into their own personal campground. Tents, a card table, metal folding tables, and a cooler were clustered together in the center of the space. Val had noted several times that she, Milo, and Gwen had nicer accommodations than the men holding them hostage.

She was halfway across the space when she heard a car door close outside. She cursed under her breath and stopped to watch the door. If it was just the Goons, she might still go through with the plan. She might have to fight, and they might take her down, but she had a feeling she could hold them off long enough for Gwen to get away. But Silver Skull wouldn't go down easy.

The door swung open and Goon One entered. Val took a step toward him, the fight already half-over in her mind by the time

Goon Two appeared.

He was carrying a wolf.

Val froze to the spot where she was standing and stared as Goon Two carried the hopefully unconscious *canidae* across the room, his face twisted in a mask of anger and annoyance. It wasn't Milo. She was positive of that, but she had no idea if that was a good thing or a terrible development. Goon Two carried the new prisoner past her without a second glance. When Val regained her senses, she turned and saw Goon One staring at her. His expression matched his partner's.

"Who the hell is that?" Val asked, her voice trembling.

"That's your new patient. Wanna go introduce yourself?" He turned and started walking away.

Val pursued him. "Where's Milo?"

"Forget Milo," he said without turning around. "As far as you're concerned, Milo is dead and buried, Milo never existed. We have a new doggie now. Go say hi. Her name is Marin."

Milo decided that she didn't need any more rest, despite Frost's protests. He went to his room and came back with clothes for her to borrow, since she was still in the hospital gown.

"You know, I'm married. I have a wife, and she has clothes, too."

"Men's clothes offer more options," Milo said. "They're a little more wear-and-tear, if you get my meaning."

"And they have pockets," Ari pointed out.

"That too," Milo agreed, taking the clothes back into the office to change.

Frost shook his head like a weary father. "Stubborn young women stealing my clothes and ignoring my advice. If I was ever curious what it was like to have daughters, you two have certainly taken care of that."

Ari smiled. "At least we won't ask to borrow your car." She nodded at the closed office door. "Is she really okay to be up and around?"

Frost gave another sigh and scratched the top of his head. "No. But it's also not going to be a dire situation. She needs more bedrest if just to make sure there are no lingering effects from her captivity. Her mental trauma alone is enough to make me wary, but there was clearly physical torture as well. But I also know keeping her here will be difficult, if not impossible, and she'll spend the time fighting with me instead of healing. So I can only ask that you and Miss Frye keep an eye on her."

"You can count on that. Do you know the Cardoso family?"

He thought for a second before shaking his head. "Doesn't ring a bell. But I obviously don't tend to every *canidae* in Seattle. It does seem a bit convenient that your client's sister just happens to be connected to whatever happened to Miss Duncan."

"Not really," Ari said. "She was specifically looking for a *canidae* detective. Unlike you, as far as I know I'm the only one of those available in Seattle."

He "hummed" and nodded. "And what about you?"

"What about me?"

"You've had an incredible day, Ariadne. Have you had a chance to sit down? Rest? Take a breath?"

Ari nodded. "Dale made me eat lunch."

He smiled. "She's a good one. But it's just a good start, not actual rest. Take the rest of the night off."

"The night?" Ari said. "It's barely mid-afternoon. There's a woman missing~"

Frost held up a hand to stop her. "Your day started early. You were immediately hit with the emotional fallout of being reunited with a loved one you thought was dead. You will be much more useful to the missing woman if you don't burn yourself out on the first day of the search."

Ari wanted to argue, but she couldn't deny he had a point. So instead she nodded. "I'll do my best."

The office door opened and Milo came out. She'd changed into Frost's slacks but was topless and barefoot.

"I can't change."

"I might have a smaller shirt if you~"

"No," Milo snapped, staring at him with wide, unblinking eyes. "I can't *change*."

Ari said, "You tried to transform?"

"I started to have a panic attack about Gwen," Milo said, staring at the backs of her hands. "Sometimes changing for a few minutes helps. The wolf calms me down. But when I tried, I... I didn't..." She balled her hands into fists. After a second, she smacked herself in the chest with them. "Nothing is happening!"

Ari grabbed Milo's wrists to stop her from further blows. "Calm down. We don't know why your wolf brain took over this morning. You've been through something awful. Maybe it affected the wolf, too. Maybe it just needs a little time before it's ready to come out." She looked at Dr. Frost. "That happens sometimes, right?"

"Yes, of course. You probably experienced it yourself, following the transfusion from your mother."

"Right!" Ari said. "There were days when I felt like it was brand new. You just need time."

"What if it's that drug? The one you got in prison that kept you from changing?" Her eyes were full of tears.

Ari had never seen Milo looking so scared. She looked at Frost, who was shaking his head.

"I took your blood this morning. I would have seen evidence of that. Ariadne is right. You need time to get back to anything close to normal."

Ari said, "If it will help, I can have Dale get in touch with Dr. Byrne. She can tell us if there's a chance you were exposed to the drug."

Milo nodded, still looking at her fists. "I think that would help." She glanced down and realized she was topless. "Shit. I should probably finish getting dressed."

Ari smiled. "I never looked below your shoulders, I swear."

Milo grunted and shoved Ari's shoulder, then turned and went back into the office. Ari turned to Frost and raised her eyebrows. He raised his back at her.

"How concerning is that, really?"

"One to ten scale?" He shrugged. "Given everything she's been through and the unknowns we're dealing with, anything unusual should be treated like a potential symptom. I would call it a seven on the scale. Something else for you and Miss Frye to keep your eye on. If you're interested in hiring someone who can help out with the task, there are a few nurses I occasionally use. I can give you their numbers."

"Thanks. Every little bit will probably help."

Milo came out of the office, still tucking the shirt into her pants. She looked between them. "Talking behind my back?"

"Yep." Ari held her arm out and drew Milo close to her. "Come on. Let's go get you something good and greasy to eat." She aimed a finger at Frost. "No lecturing about junk food."

He shook his head. "Absolutely not. In fact, given her malnutrition and what she's obviously gone through, I'd say she's more than earned a nice juicy hamburger."

"Oh god," Milo said, grabbing a handful of Ari's shirt. "Hamburger... yes. Multiple hamburgers."

Ari grinned. "I'll take you to Two Doors Down and you can have all the burgers you can eat."

"And then?"

"Then we're going to take you home, pup. You've been gone long enough."

Ari unlocked the door to Gwen and Milo's house and turned on the lights, grateful to see the switch actually worked. She and Dale sometimes came over to keep things from getting too dusty and keep the spiders from taking over. Every time they visited, she was certain they'd discover the power or water would have been shut off. Her mother had set up automatic payments for things like utilities and rent before they went to Europe, but her bank account wasn't a bottomless pit no matter how much she might act like it was sometimes.

Then again, Ari had recently learned the majority of her mother's money was stolen from hunter bank accounts, so maybe it really was an endless resource.

Milo hesitated in the foyer, scanning the living room like she'd never seen it before.

"Everything okay?" Ari asked.

Milo nodded. "Weird to be here without Gwen. That's all."

"If you'd rather stay with me and Dale..."

"No," Milo said. "No, it's still home. And it still feels really great to be back here. Just not as good as it should feel."

Ari went to the kitchen and opened the fridge. She and Dale had cleaned it out months ago, but there were still bottles of water. She took out two and carried them to Milo, who was now standing at the living room window. The yard beyond was overgrown and wild.

"We kept meaning to find a kid to mow this for you..."

"Mm." Ari tapped Milo's arm with the bottle, which seemed to snap her out of her trance. She took it and cracked the lid, then downed half the bottle in one swallow. They'd spent over an hour at Two Doors Down, where Milo had eaten four monster 420 Burgers with an enthusiasm that drew comments and admiration from both the waiter and the cook.

Ari waited until Milo finished the water before she spoke. "I'm not going to try pushing you. I don't want you to frustrate you, or pressure you about something you can't remember. I just want you to know that Dale and I are both here for whatever you need."

"Just find her for me," Milo said, still staring out the window. "Do that for me, pup?"

"I'll do everything I can."

Milo nodded. Then she growled and spun on her heel, stalking to the couch and throwing herself down onto the cushions. "I feel like such a waste of space. Gwen's out there somewhere and all I'm doing is eating burgers and napping."

"Hey, you got away. You let me know she's out there to be found. That's more than enough for right now. You've earned a little rest."

Milo tilted her head to the side. "Isn't that what Dr. Frost told *you* earlier...?"

"Yeah, well, do as I say, not as I do."

"Sure," Milo chuckled. She looked up at Ari, trying to read her face. "You gave up on us, didn't you?"

Ari considered lying. Decided there wasn't a point. "Yeah. You were completely gone. Radio silent. No one knew where you'd gone. I thought if there was any chance you could send us a message, you'd have found it by then. It was easier for me to just make peace with it rather than clinging to hope."

Milo said, "I understand. I would've done the same thing. Hope can be a pain in the ass."

Ari went and sat down on the couch next to Milo. They stared at the wall in silence, drinking their water.

"You know, there's something from before my memory goes all~" She waved a hand next to her head to indicate a mess. "It might not be something you want to hear."

"Oh boy," Ari said. "Might as well pull off the band-aid."

"When we were in Germany, Gwen let people assume we were married because it was easier than defining what we actually are to each other. You know what I mean?"

Ari nodded. "Dale and I don't like girlfriend, either. You explained this at Dr. Frost's."

"I know, but what I didn't tell you was that after a while, it stopped feeling like a cover story." She picked at the label of her water bottle. "I've always looked for the next one, you know? Even when a relationship is good, at the back of my mind, I'd think, 'next time I live with someone, she's got to be a little tidier' or something like that. I don't know when I stopped doing that with Gwen, but I haven't thought of the next one in a really long time. I don't think I want a next one."

"For what it's worth," Ari said, "I don't think she does, either."

Milo didn't say anything to that, but Ari could sense she was struggling to keep her emotions in check. She looked around the living room, remembering things she spent years trying to forget. Her childhood, the first transformations, learning about who she was. The betrayal, the vow to never return...

"I spent a long time trying to get away from this house," Ari said. "My mother and I lived in the same city but I didn't see her for a decade because I was so betrayed by what she'd done to me. Mom's never really been my favorite person. But I understand her a lot better than I ever thought I would. And I know she's aware that she's made mistakes, and she's trying to do better. You make her happy, Milo. You make her want to be better."

Milo stared hard at her water bottle. "Which is ironic," she said, her voice lower than normal, "since she originally hired me to break up you and Dale."

Ari laughed. "Yeah. Funny how that worked out, huh?"

"How is she doing? After the whole book fiasco. We kept wanting to reach out, make sure she was okay, but we didn't want her to think we were worried."

"She's fine." They had also discussed this at Dr. Frost's, but Ari had a feeling Milo's memory still wasn't quite recovered. "Back to normal. She's more nervous about a relapse than I am."

"I think she's right to be." Milo held up her hands to hold off Ari's defense. "This isn't about Dale as a person. Her strength, dedication, fortitude, none of that comes into it. But when we were in Germany, Gwen and I learned a lot about these fucking essays and the horrors they've caused. They woke up a whole generation of hunters, and they've even managed to turn some wolves against their own pack."

Ari shook her head. "I don't get that. It's just words on a page. I've seen the book, it's like this thick." She held her thumb and forefinger up so they were almost touching. "How can one book so much power?"

"You ever heard of the Bible?" Milo said. "Some people don't even bother reading that one before they go off to do horrible things in its name."

Ari rolled her eyes. "That's not the Bible's fault. Those people started out with their own sets of beliefs that they use the Bible to justify. You and Mom had that book all those months and you never even peeked? Not even once?"

Milo sat up, grunting quietly. "We saw what it did to Dale. Dale Frye, of all people. It made her someone neither of us recognized, scared the shit out of both of us. We weren't about to play with something that could do that to a person like her. So no, I haven't read any of the essays. I have no desire to know exactly what they say, or to understand how they could make our sweet Dale into a monster. The evidence spoke for itself."

Ari wanted to argue, but she knew it wouldn't help. "Okay. I'll take your word for it, for now. I'm going to go back to the office and check in with Dale. Will you be okay here?"

Milo looked around, obviously wary of the empty space. "I'll call if I need to arrange a sleepover."

"Dale and I are on-call. Take a long bath, put on your own clothes, get back into your own skin. The wolf will be waiting when you're ready."

"Thanks, Ari."

Ari bent down and kissed the top of Milo's head. "Feel better soon, Millicent."

She left the house and was reaching for her phone to call Dale when it started ringing. She knew instinctively it was Dale even before she looked at the screen. Whether it was because they had such a close connection, or just due to the general insanity of the day, she couldn't have said. She swiped her thumb across the screen to answer.

"Hey, what's up?"

"Hey." Dale sounded breathless. "Are you close to the office?"

"I'm at Mom's house. Are you okay?"

Dale exhaled sharply. "There's... I... I need you to get here. I don't want to tell you this over the phone. Get to the office, puppy, please."

"I can be there in ten minutes."

She beat her estimate by four minutes, risking a ticket but willing to pay the price if it meant Dale didn't have to be alone for whatever fresh hell was rearing its head now. She parked in front of the building and ran inside, half-expecting to see Hayden behind the desk with a gun to Dale's head. She was alone in the office, staring at the computer with a look of anguish that was almost as bad as what Ari had imagined.

"What's wrong?"

Dale hit a button and motioned for Ari to come around the desk. "I have an alert for the word 'werewolf' and '*canidae*' on social media. I get a lot of ads for urban fantasy books, TV shows, things like that, but this went up about half an hour ago. Links started popping up all over the place about ten minutes later."

The screen showed a site with the words FULL MOON FIGHTERS scrawled across the top in blood-red letters. A video player was embedded underneath the title, a blank square until Dale tapped the button to start it playing.

A man stepped into frame. He wore a black turtleneck and a rubber mask of what looked like George Washington, leaning in close to the camera as if checking to make sure it was recording. When he stepped back they could see he was in a cinder-block room with no windows. The only exit must have been behind the camera.

"We are the Full Moon Fighters," he said, his voice muffled by the mask. "The purpose of this video is to spread the word about a scourge which has run amok in our world. There are creatures masquerading as people living in our neighborhoods, eating in our restaurants, shopping in our stores. They look just like us but they're *not*. They're monsters."

Ari said, "Is he outing werewolves?"

"Keep watching." Dale sounded like she was about to throw up.

"I know," George Washington continued, "that most people watching this will claim it's a hoax. But I also know there are people out there who know the truth, who will rise up to prevent humanity from being overwhelmed by these creatures.

"I'm talking about *canidae*, werewolves, skinwalkers. Don't be fooled by the fact they can look like us. They're animals. And we're going to prove it."

He stepped back from the camera and motioned someone forward. Two more men, dressed identically with different Presidents as masks, dragged someone into the center of the room and dropped her on the floor. A steel bar rested across her shoulders, and her elbows were bent so that her wrists could be shackled to either side. It made her look like a bird pinned to a display case. She was dressed in a thin white T-shirt and sweatpants, barefoot. Ari held her breath, only able to see the back of the woman's head but knowing in her gut exactly who she was looking at. One of the other men, with an Abe Lincoln mask, pulled the prisoner up into a kneeling position.

It was Marin Cardoso.

George Washington leaned back into frame. "Ladies and gentlemen, I present you with a real... life... werewolf. Looks like your neighbor, right? Your best friend? The girl who makes you coffee every morning. But twenty minutes ago, she was a wolf."

A pre-recorded clip began playing. It showed a wolf, the wolf Ari recognized from the photo Eva had given her, backed into a corner. She was growling, hackles up, snapping at the men who had surrounded her. She snapped and lunged at them, but it was clear she wasn't going to come out victorious. The scene snapped back to the Presidents. Lincoln and the third man, John F. Kennedy, had stood Marin up and was attaching the steel bar to chains hanging from the ceiling.

"We know very little about these beasts, but there are some hard and true facts. These monsters can't go more than four weeks without reverting to their true state. And that, my friends, is what you're going to see. The monster you see before you transformed back into her human disguise–" He checked his watch. "Seventeen minutes ago. At some point in the next twenty-eight days, she *will* change back. We are going to be filming her and streaming the footage *live* so you can see the transformation as it happens. No trick photography, no CGI, no bullshit. Just a woman becoming a wolf in front of your very eyes."

He stepped closer to the camera.

"And then the world will know the truth. The beasts won't have anywhere to turn, nowhere to run or hide. You will be exposed. Click the link below to go to the live video. Share the link. Make sure everyone is watching when the truth is exposed."

Dale reached past Ari and clicked on the link. A new page opened with a new video showing the same room, but now Marin was alone. A radio sitting in the corner was playing music.

"That's so people can confirm it's live," Dale said with a quiet, shaky voice. "It's KNOC. It's real. I checked. So far everyone online seems pretty sure it's a prank, but I don't know how long that will last. But Ari, that's not all."

Ari closed her eyes and braced herself. "God, what else could go wrong?"

"I tried calling Val. To ask her about the drug, if Milo could have been dosed with it. Her phone number was disconnected. I called the jail to see if I could get a message to her, but they said she's no longer an employee there."

Ari turned to look up at Dale. "Don't tell me."

Dale's eyes were full of tears. "She's missing. No one has seen her for months."

Chapter Five

"Talk to me, Ariadne."

Ari continued staring at the screen. Dale put her hand on the back of the chair and spun it so she had no choice but to look away.

"I full-named you, puppy. You can't ignore that."

"I know." Ari's voice was strained. "But she's..." She twisted to look at the computer again.

Dale hooked her finger under Ari's chin, turning her back around. "I told you everyone online thinks this is a hoax. The cops will probably get involved before too long, but there's one person who knows it's a hundred percent real and who has been hired to find that girl." She poked her finger into Ari's chest. "You, puppy. You're the only person for the job right now, and I know it's been a heavy day, and I know it's weighing on you, but you need to push past the horror and fear you're feeling right now. It's going to be hard. It's going to hurt. You're going to crash eventually. But I want you to know that when that happens, I'm going to be waiting to catch you and take care of you and get you back into fighting shape. Because that's my job. This..." She nodded at the computer screen. "This is yours."

Ari cupped Dale's face in her hands. "You're my pack, Dale."

Dale smiled, though her eyes were still pained. "And you're

mine." She turned her head and kissed the inside of Ari's wrist. "Do what you have to do, even if it hurts. I'll be here to patch you up. I swear."

"I love you."

"I love you, too."

They kissed again. Ari stroked Dale's hair when they parted, and she turned to look at the screen. "There's no way this actually goes the full four weeks. I mean, come on. They're live-streaming a hostage situation and giving proof they're in Seattle."

"They also made another mistake," Dale said. "A big one."

"What?"

"Come on, Ari. I know you'll see it."

Ari examined the room on-screen. She saw Marin, her head hanging down. She looked back at Dale, who nodded encouragingly. Ari looked at the screen and focused. It was like trying to solve one of those "Find Six Differences" pictures but there was only one thing in the room now that the Presidents had left. That's when it clicked.

"They explained their plan while she was in the room," she said.

Dale squeezed her shoulder. "There you go."

"So she knows exactly what they're planning to do. She won't transform until she has absolutely no choice."

"Right. And you've told me that you can push it if you absolutely have to. She's going to hold out as long as she can." She moved her hand to the back of Ari's neck. "But she won't have to. You're going to find her, puppy. I know you will."

Ari pushed away from the desk and went to her office. "Might as well get started. Can you put the names of the missing women on the board? I have to make a phone call."

"Eva?" Dale guessed.

Ari sighed and sat down. "Yeah. Not looking forward to it."

"Have her come down, hear it in person. This isn't the sort of thing you tell anyone over the phone, let alone a family member."

"Right." Ari dialed and watched Dale pinning notecards to the bulletin board. The phone buzzed twice before Eva answered. "Eva? This is Ariadne Willow. I'm–"

"I know." Eva sounded as if she'd been crying. "Is it real?"

Ari sighed. "We think so. We don't know anything specific yet. But the good news here is that they have to keep her safe if they want to follow through on the threat. We have a chance to get her back safe and sound, just a little banged up."

"Our parents always warned us about hunters." She sniffled. "I thought they were just made up. I thought they were just stories."

"Yeah," Ari said. "They've been pretty quiet for a while. Hopefully we're going to make them rethink making all this noise."

"Are you sure I can't pay you?"

"Absolutely sure," Ari said. "This is personal for us, too. We're going to keep you in the loop as much as possible. If you hear anything, or if anyone reaches out to you, call us. Let us know."

"I will. Thank you, Miss Willow."

"Don't thank me until this mess is all over. We'll talk again soon."

When she hung up, she stood and went over to look at the progress Dale made on the board.

The first card: GWYNETH WILLOW, MISSING SIX MONTHS.

The second card: VALERIE BYRNE, MISSING APPROX SIX MONTHS.

The third card: MARIN CARDOSO, MISSING ONE DAY.

She was adding a new card under Gwen's name with the information they knew about her disappearance. Taken with Milo, most likely from Germany, brought back to the States, kept somewhere presumably within Seattle city limits.

"Why here?" Ari said. "Why would they bring Mom and Milo all the way back here?"

Dale didn't stop writing. "Because you're here, puppy. If Isaac Hayden is involved, he has reason to be especially pissed off with you. This is also where wolf manoth almost happened last time." She straightened and tucked her hair behind her ears. "And it seems like Seattle has a pretty healthy wolf population. Has anyone ever actually done a census?"

"Kind of hard to pull one of those off," Ari said.

"Right." She moved to Val and brought up the pen, then stopped. "Fuck. I can't believe she's been missing all this time and we didn't even realize. I feel like shit."

Ari rubbed Dale's back. "We'll make it up to her by finding her."

"As terrible as it sounds," Dale said, "Val being taken is another silver lining."

"How so?"

"She's a doctor. Specifically, a doctor who knows about *canidae* anatomy. It means Gwen and Marin have access to medical care."

Ari considered that. "Yes. Or they took her because she's the daughter of a hunter." Her mind settled on that fact, rolled it around as she went back to her desk. "Which is probably how they found her."

Dale watched Ari bend over the keyboard and rapidly start typing. "What are you thinking?"

"They wouldn't just randomly grab a doctor who happened to be related to a hunter, even if they were estranged. They had to target Val specifically. I doubt they knew she had experience treating *canidae*, unless they had someone working at the prison. Which... now that I think about it, isn't impossible. But right now, I'm running with my theory."

"Which is?"

"I think Val's father put a target on her back. I'd like to have a conversation with him and find out for sure." She grunted, frustrated. "I don't think I'm going to get very far online, though."

Dale came over and waved Ari out of the chair. "You don't think she has him in her Facebook friends?"

Ari let Dale take over the computer. "Considering the man was a racist hunter who tried to raise her to be a carbon copy of himself, no. I don't think so." She dropped down onto the couch and took out her phone so she could text Diana, to see if there had been any updates on Hayden or the men from that morning. "I honestly don't even know if Byrne is his last name. She might have taken her mother's maiden name or a name she just came up with because she liked how it sounded."

"That's why you keep me around."

"Well, that and the fact you don't mind driving more than your fair share."

"Wow! I'm good for two things?"

Ari said, "I'll try to think of a third."

Dale winked at her. "Really rack your brain, puppy."

Ari watched her work. Her eyes darted over the screen, she typed and then chewed her lip as she scrolled through the results.

"Still enjoying your birthday?"

"Immensely." She glanced over. "I wish I'd gotten to spend a little more time with you, but we're ending the day together. That's enough for me. This is why I don't like putting much weight on the day."

Ari said, "I like putting weight on it. It's the day you were born.

It should feel special."

Dale smiled. "Aw, puppy."

"Milo told me that she and Mom didn't actually decide to start telling people they were married. It just sort of happened, and they started going with it, and they were both surprised by how right it felt."

"I'm sure it did," Dale said.

Ari leaned forward. "What if from now on, we don't remember today because it's the day you were born? What if it's because today's the day we finally stopped saying 'one of these days'?"

Dale's fingers hovered over the keyboard. Her head slowly turned to look at Ari. "What?"

"Don't 'what' me. I'm tired of stumbling over what to call you. Wife is easy. We don't have to do a whole thing, ceremony and name-change and all that. But I want to spend the rest of my life with you, and it's stupid not to make it official."

"We can't just run out and get married. Your mom would kill us if we do it without her. And we need a license, and there's a three-day wedding period... w-waiting period." She rubbed her temple. "We'd need to find an officiant..."

"How do you know that about the waiting period?"

"I've looked into it."

Ari smiled. "Yeah?"

Dale looked at her and sighed. "Yeah, Ari, of course I have."

"Did you come up with any details?"

Dale started to speak, then looked at the computer screen. "We... we should focus on the case."

"Are you close to finding Val's dad? Or any information that can help us find her?"

"No. Not really."

"You and Dr. Frost both told me to take the night off. Rest and relax. So if you want me to step back, this is what I want to do."

"Get married."

Ari nodded. "Whatever that looks like for us. I'm tired of putting it off."

Dale sighed, looked longingly at the computer, and then pushed the keyboard away. She stood and faced Ari.

"There is one idea I kept coming back to."

Ari grinned.

A generous person might have described it as an alleyway. The space between buildings was wide enough for a car to pass through, barely, and it was relatively devoid of trash. It was almost sunset, and the buildings on either side had bright security lights shining down over their delivery entrances.

Dale led the way, turning to make sure Ari and Milo were following her. Ari looked up at the buildings and then turned to look back out at the street where they'd parked.

"I know I said it didn't have to be romantic," she said, "but I think we can come up with something a little better than this."

Dale stopped next to a loading dock and held her arms out. "Here it is."

Milo looked at the almost-invisible logo on the wall. "Dennis Laurens and Associates?"

"What?" Dale looked at the faded paint. "Oh. No, I don't know what that is. This..." She pointed at the ground. "This is where a girl who was planning to drop out of college found a bunch of teenage pricks abusing what she thought was a stray dog. This is where she sacrificed the last cheeseburger she could afford to gain the dog's trust so she could take it home where it could be safe."

Ari looked around the alley with more reverence now. "This is where we met? I thought that was... I don't remember it being an alley..."

"I don't think this building was here. Or at least... the whole place was under construction. Either way, this is it. This is where I rescued you. I know it's not the most romantic or the most picturesque, but I've thought long and hard about it and I couldn't imagine marrying you anywhere else. If you have another idea, I'm willing~"

"This is perfect." Ari walked forward and took Dale's hands in both of hers. "This is right for us."

Milo came closer. "So, if everyone's ready?"

Ari nodded. They'd picked up Milo to act as their witness, even though they acknowledged nothing about the wedding would be official. Milo agreed to come with them before she even knew what the plan was, but her expression changed on the drive as Dale explained what they were doing. When she finished, Milo said, "Why don't you just do a *canidae* ceremony? We don't need all that license bullshit."

"This is a bit late to break it to you," Dale said, "but I'm not *canidae*."

"Bollocks," Milo said. "You're more wolf than anyone I've ever met."

Ari had twisted in the seat. "Do you know the ceremony?"

Milo had shrugged. "Well enough for whatever unofficial thing you two are doing, sure."

Now she took out the items she'd retrieved from the trunk of Dale's car. "Normally, we'd be doing this in the woods somewhere. But I guess the middle of a major city is close enough. And you'd both be naked, but that's just to make transforming at the end easier. I think we can skip that part. We ready?"

Dale's hands were shaking, so Ari brought them to her lips to kiss the fingers. "We're ready."

Dale nodded. "Yeah."

Milo smiled. "Okay, then. Now forgive me, this isn't going to be the most accurate thing in the world, but I'm going to do my best. And there are a lot of references to the pack, since this is really a ceremony to bring someone from one pack into another, but we can just consider that, um, symbolic. Okay, let's get this started."

Ari and Dale faced each other.

"Ariadne Willow, daughter of Gwyneth and none, member of no pack. Dale Frye, daughter of none, member of no pack..." She regarded them for a moment, then smiled. "This is actually better than most *canidae* unions. There's no history, no weight, no expectations of twenty other wolves to worry about. This is just about two women who found each other and decided... yeah, this is who I want. This is the family I want. I've seen packs with dozens of wolves, and they're not as strong as the bond I see when the two of you look at each other. What you have found here is truly a new family, a bond that connects you beyond your histories or species. You are human, you are *canidae*, and now you are one.

"Dale, now you swear to her."

"Ariadne," Dale said, "I swear to be faithful to you, to support you, and to be the pack you never had. My heart is yours, and I will stand with you forever."

Ari blinked back tears. She moved her hand up to Dale's wrist, to the bracelet she'd been wearing for years. It was threads of Ari's hair intertwined with fur from the wolf, symbolic of both sides of Ari and Dale's acceptance of her as a whole person, not just the human side of her.

"Dale," she said, when she trusted her voice again. "You've always been the only pack I ever needed. As long as you stand with me, I'll earn the right to have your faith. I love you."

"Shit," Dale said, "I love you, too. I can't believe I didn't say that."

Ari laughed.

Milo said, "I think we can ignore the slip-up. Ariadne Willow and Dale Frye, members of no pack, by the power vested in me by… no one, really, I pronounce you mates."

Dale said, "Do we~" and was cut off by Ari kissing her. Milo laughed and took a step back. Ari cupped the back of Dale's head and pressed close to her.

After an appropriate amount of time, Milo cleared her throat, looking past them at one end of the alley and then twisting to look back at the other end.

"Ladies, I understand getting swept up in the romance, but we *are* technically in public right now."

Ari smiled and ended the kiss, but brushed her hand through Dale's hair. "Now what?"

"Now," Milo said, "we trade keys and I stay at your place while you and Dale have a little honeymoon at ours."

Dale said, "You just got back. We can't kick you out of your home."

Milo was still smiling, but her eyes became pained. "I can't stay there without Gwen. Maybe tomorrow or in a couple of days, but…"

"We'll be happy to let you housesit for us," Dale said.

"Thanks." Milo cleared her throat. "So, um, we should probably go before anyone asks what we're doing here." She stepped between Ari and Dale and put her arms around their shoulders to guide them back to the car. "And let me be the first to congratulate the happy couple."

Despite the ceremony, Ari didn't plan on having sex that night. She didn't think Dale did, either. But the temperature plummeted as soon as the sun went down, and there was a fireplace in the living room. Ari figured out how to start a fire, then watched as Dale did it safely, and they stretched out on the floor in front of the hearth with all the lights out. Cuddling turned to kissing, and clothes started to come off amid the kissing. Ari knew they'd reached the point of no return when Dale was on top of her, alternating between nipping at her earlobe and kissing her neck.

"So…" Ari kept her eyes closed and licked her lips as Dale kissed her chest. "We need to work out some details."

"Okay." Dale nuzzled Ari's stomach. "Shoot."

"Keeping our own names?"

"I think so, but I'm open to debate."

Ari shook her head. "No, I agree. And, um... the, um..." She repositioned her hips and lifted her feet. Dale kissed the inside of her thigh. "Word. The word. Wife? We're okay with wife?"

"What are the options?"

"Partner," Ari said, "spouse, um..."

Dale said, "No." She pressed her lips to Ari's skin. "You're my wife."

Ari gasped and writhed and considered the matter settled.

When Dale kissed her way back up Ari's body a few minutes later, resting her cheek on Ari's chest to feel it rise and fall as she caught her breath, Dale whispered, "Wife. Yeah. I like that."

Ari stroked Dale's hair with one hand while the other explored Dale's curves. Part of her thought it was awful to be doing this considering the state of their friends. Gwen and Val, missing in action. Marin in imminent danger. Milo traumatized. It felt frivolous and wrong to be having this moment for themselves. Dale took Ari by the wrist and guided it between her legs.

"There," Dale whispered, craning her neck so she could brush her lips against Ari's.

"Right here?" Ari asked.

"Mm-huh," Dale put her head down on Ari's shoulder, and Ari began to stroke. Ari closed her eyes and pressed her face into Dale's hair, breathing deeply, listening to the sounds Dale made to set her speed and rhythm.

As she listened to her wife, her partner, her pack moan through her orgasm, Ari realized this was exactly what they needed. They had spent the entire day standing on a cliff, looking down, seeing how far the drop was. In the morning they would have to jump. These were the last few minutes they had to themselves, and she was grateful they were making the time count. Tomorrow they were going to save their family and be heroes.

Tonight was theirs.

Dale's lips trembled against Ari's collarbone when she came, and she turned it into a nuzzle as she sank down. Ari accepted her weight, bending her knee and rolling so they could lay side by side. Dale pulled her head back and bumped her nose against Ari's.

"That felt different."

"Yeah?" Ari said.

"Don't ask me why. It's like…" Her eyes searched Ari's face. Ari remained silent, grateful to be the object of such intense concentration. Dale's eyes were very, very green in this light. "It's like waking up and knowing it's Christmas or the first day of summer or something."

"I get that." She brushed some hair away from Dale's face. "I'm happy being your Christmas."

Dale shuddered and lightly kissed Ari's lips. "I love you, wife."

"I love you, wife."

Dale shifted her weight and curled against Ari's side so they could both watch the fire. They hadn't built a very big fire, so there were no leaping flames, but the logs were smoldering enough to cast a yellow glow over them. Ari kept her arm around Dale and idly brushed her fingertips up and down her shoulder blade. Dale used the tip of her middle finger to draw designs on the sweat on Ari's stomach.

"I have a confession to make," Ari said after a few minutes.

"You're thinking about Milo?"

"Val, actually," Ari said. "Being preoccupied by another woman isn't the best look on tonight of all nights."

Dale said, "Tonight is a special case, in a lot of ways."

Ari nodded. "I feel guilty. I sort of suspected she didn't have much of a personal life. But I can't believe she could go missing and no one noticed. How could someone just disappear? I didn't even see a story about it on the news."

"Yeah," Dale said. "I've been thinking about that, too."

"She deserves better than that. She's kind and she's beautiful. She deserves to have people who care about her, who would notice when she doesn't show up. I can't believe the only people who…"

Dale lifted her head to see why Ari trailed off. "The people who what, puppy?"

Ari blinked at the fire. "The people who rely on her at the prison. The wolves."

Dale pushed herself up on one elbow. "You think they'll have information about who took her or where she is now?"

"I don't know," Ari said. "But she was open with them about being a hunter's daughter. They still trusted her with their secret. They must have investigated her somehow. Maybe they have someone on the outside who looked into her, who confirmed she was on the level."

Dale's eyes widened. "They might have done all the work for

us."

"If there's something to be found, I'm willing to bet they found it already." Another thought occurred to her, one that was much more chilling. "If Val has been missing this long, every wolf in that prison could be at the tail end of a dose. We have to go talk to them anyway, find out what they need and figure out how to get it to them."

Dale grinned and cupped Ari's cheek. "Good thinking, Ariadne."

Ari said, "Looks like taking the night off really was good for focusing my mind."

"I wonder what other epiphanies you can have if we focused it even farther."

"Hard to say," Ari said, pulling Dale down to her, "but I'm willing to spend the better part of the night finding out."

Dale chuckled and rolled back onto Ari.

CHAPTER SIX

GWEN PACED by the window, a bit amazed that there wasn't a dip in the concrete to mark her passage. She'd watched her shadow stretch and shrink and then fade completely as the sun went down, but all her attention was focused on the sounds coming from outside. The hunters had brought someone in. Gwen could smell her; it was another wolf, but beyond that she didn't know anything. Activity throughout the building had increased tenfold. She estimated there were at least twenty hunters in the building at the moment with even more somewhere outside. How they were masking such a presence in the middle of Seattle was a mystery for another time.

She only snapped out of her trance when she heard the door unlocking. Val came in with a bag of fast-food, which she held up apologetically as she closed the door behind her.

"Sorry. It's been a hectic day. They forgot to feed you."

"What's happening out there?" Gwen asked, taking the cheeseburger.

Val sighed. "They have a prisoner. A *canidae*. She's chained up, and they're filming her so they can livestream someone transforming into a wolf live on the internet."

Gwen suddenly lost her appetite. "How'd they capture her?"

Val looked away.

"Don't chicken out on me now."

"Milo found her."

Gwen narrowed her eyes. "Milo would never lead hunters to another wolf."

"You don't understand what they were doing to her. Your experiences here have been very different. You know the saying about how there are no bad dogs, just bad owners? They found ways to force her to transform. Electroshock, mainly. They tried medication. Sleep deprivation. They were using her like a lab rat."

Gwen's hand trembled with the urge to grab Val and slam her against the wall. "You knew about this and didn't stop it?"

"I'm the one who kept her alive. I'm the one who brought her back from the edge when they went too far. I'm..." She cut herself off and looked at the floor. "I'm the one who told them they needed a control group. Otherwise they would have been experimenting on you at the same time, more than what they already were. I thought if I couldn't save you both from that, I should at least save one."

"You chose wrong."

"And you know Milo would say the same thing." Val went to the window and wrapped her arms around herself. "By the end, she was basically hypnotized and highly susceptible. They told her they wanted a wolf, and she went out and found one. But that's where the hope comes in. Milo found the other wolf, a girl named Marin, but stopped herself from leading her into the hunters' trap. She attacked them so Marin could get away."

"That's what this morning was all about?"

Val nodded. "They managed to tag Marin with a tracker, but Milo got away clean. As far as I know, she's safe at home."

"But still suffering the effects of whatever these monsters did to her."

"It's better than nothing," Val said.

Gwen said, "I suppose so. What the hell do they have on you? You told me there was nothing on the outside for you."

"Sure, now. After six months of being locked up in here, I'm probably homeless and unemployed. But when they first took me, there was hope. They threatened my job. They said if I escaped, they would leak a story that I'd been smuggling drugs into the prison where I worked. I would've lost my job and gone to prison."

"You're in prison right now."

"Yeah. Didn't really think that one through until it had been a couple of weeks and I realized there was really no winning.”

“You could have argued that the drug smuggling charges were bogus.”

“Except they weren’t. The hunters would have made something up, and I’m sure whatever lie they concocted would have looked legit, but the truth is, I *was* smuggling drugs into the prison. I was providing the means to create the drug that kept *canidae* patients like your daughter from transforming.”

“I didn’t think the hunters knew about that.”

“I don’t think they did. It was a fucking bluff, and they happened to get lucky.”

Gwen sighed and hung her head. “I’m tired of the bad guys getting lucky.”

“We have to hope we’re getting lucky, too. Milo is out there. That’s a big win for us, even if she is at less than a hundred percent. And if she managed to find Ariadne and Dale, you know they’re going to do everything in their power to make this right.”

“True.” She looked at the window. “I wish I was out there helping them right now.”

“Well, for now, the hunters want to keep you alive. Probably so they have a backup wolf in case anything happens to Marin. Not the most comforting thought, but it’s something. And they’re still willing to feed you, which I wasn’t entirely sure about. They have a freezer full of frozen dinners, but I convinced them to go an extra step. I thought you’d appreciate the fresh meat even if it is a little greasy.”

“I do. Thank you, Val. I appreciate everything you’ve done for me and Milo during this whole damn ordeal.”

Val nodded. “It’s the least I can do. And I’m glad I can be useful.”

“Keep me updated as much as possible. I don’t know what exactly I can do from here, but...”

“It’s good to have information,” Val said. “I get it. I work in a prison, I know how powerful the right knowledge can be.”

“Thank you,” Gwen said.

Val left, and Gwen heard the lock click on the door as soon as she was gone. The burger was already gone, so she stood up and went back to the window to start pacing again.

She didn't know if it would be possible to actually make a dip in the concrete, but she might as well keep trying until another activity presented itself.

The waiting room was full of families, a few lawyers, and a single private investigator sitting at a table next to the vending machines. She'd woken up that morning before the sun was up, but stayed in bed until Dale was also awake to avoid a lecture. She even allowed herself a leisurely breakfast before she called Eva Cardoso with an update about what she planned to do to find her sister. Dale had taken the time to call Milo and see how she was doing.

"Better naps," Dale had reported when she hung up. "She barely slept all night and feels achy, but not worse than yesterday. She's taking the morning to rest and hopefully heal."

Ari had promised to check in on her later in the day. At the moment, she was at the prison as early as possible, within ten minutes of visiting hours beginning, fingernails tapping on the table and one foot bouncing underneath as she waited for her guest. She was about to check her watch when a door at the far end of the room opened and a guard emerged with the prisoner Ari had asked to see. Gladys Celestin raised an eyebrow when she saw Ari waiting for her, then smiled up at the guard as she took her seat across the table from her. Ari had bought a bag of chips and an orange soda and pushed them forward.

"I remember you liking these when I was in here."

"Good memory," Gladys said, taking the snack. "And a good sign I should prepare for the worst when a meeting starts with a bribe. So make me feel like you actually want to see me. Give me a little chitchat first. How is Segura doing?"

Ari smiled. "Segura's doing great. She and her partner moved upstate a few months ago. They're still getting settled, but they're really happy."

"As long as she keeps that probation officer happy, too." Gladys popped a chip into her mouth. "And you? Staying out of trouble?"

"As much as I can," Ari said. "I got married yesterday."

Gladys made an indescribable sound of happiness. "Oh, I love to hear that. The human you mentioned? She still being good to you?"

"Better than I deserve."

Gladys laughed and winked. "Good for you, sweetie."

"How are things in here?"

"Kunz has been living up her big bad hero reputation. She thought she liked people being scared of her, but after she saved you from being killed, she realized respect is better. So she's made it clear she's watching out for everybody."

Ari said, "It's good to know my time here had positive consequences."

"Mm-hmm." She popped another chip into her mouth. "Okay. I feel less cheap now. What brings you back to the old bricks-and-bars hotel? Something to do with the fact Dr. Val has been missing for the past couple months, probably."

Ari said, "Yeah. Dale and I just found out about it. I'm so sorry it's taken us so long. As near as we can figure, she's been missing for about six months. That means you and the others in here are probably at the very end of your last dose. If you tell me where I can get the ingredients, I can find a way to get it inside."

Gladys tilted her head to her side. "Aw, here I thought you were being selfish and just coming to see how I could help you. But you thought we were in trouble. You're a good egg, Ariadne. We appreciate you thinking about us, but you don't have to worry. Once Dr. Val had been missing for a month, we knew we were on a deadline. We already found a new source. We're all good in here."

Ari's shoulders relaxed. "You're sure?"

"Positive, sweetie." She folded her hands on the table in front of her. "But I think you were trying to kill two birds with one stone again. You need to get your hands on the stuff?"

"Not necessarily," Ari said. "We were thinking that if you trusted Val to be in charge of getting what you need, despite knowing she's a hunter, you probably did a fair amount of background research on her to make sure she could be trusted. I thought that research might help us find her. It could at least give us a place to start looking."

Gladys opened her soda. "Makes sense. I'm not sure you'll like what I have to give you, though."

"Well, *I'm* not sure I'm in a position to like it or not."

"Fair point. To start with, you're absolutely correct. We weren't just going to trust this little huntress who came in here saying she wanted to help. As far as we know, hunters don't even know the drug exists and we'd like to keep it that way. So we found out everything we could about her. We have ways of getting information even in here."

Ari cocked an eyebrow. "I bet you do."

Gladys smirked proudly. "So I won't bore you with the how and get right to what you need to know. Val's father is named Gabriel Roemer. He's apparently one of the big-time hunters. His line goes back generations. The kind of person who would be pissed off if he had a daughter instead of a son to carry on his mighty line. We found evidence that he tried to make her the son he never had. She trained in archery and sharpshooting before she was ten. There are photos of her as a ten-year-old in bright orange jackets holding rifles taller than she is. But it never stuck. The thing that sold us is when we found out what finally made her cut ties with him."

Gladys stopped talking and rolled the edge of her soda can on the table. Ari gave her a moment before she glanced at the clock and held out her hands. "Don't leave me in suspense."

"I'm not. I just don't like this part of the story." She breathed in deeply and let it out through her nose. "Gabriel finally decided it was time for a trial by fire. Either Val was going to be his successor, or she was going to be useful in another way. He, um. He captured a *canidae* and locked it in a cage. He lied to Val to get her to go into the cage, then locked the door behind her."

"Fuck," Ari said. She was surprised Val had never brought this up, but she also understood it wasn't exactly the kind of story you told unless you were extremely comfortable with a person. "What the hell was his thinking on that?"

"Either Val would kill the wolf, or the wolf would bite Val and infect her, and Gabriel could examine her to see what happened after a *canidae* bite."

Ari tried to keep her breathing steady. "Experiments."

"Oh yeah. Old Gabe considers himself a scientist. Like Mengele, I suppose. Inhumane medical tests on living patients. I guess he thought he would find a *canidae* gene he could cut out."

"Did Val... I mean, I assume she..."

"She's never actually brought it up," Gladys said. "Unsurprisingly. And the place where we found the story, which is just a journal kept by one of Gabriel's assistants, didn't reveal how it ended. But we can see that she wasn't bitten. So we can assume whatever happened wasn't great."

Ari fought back her nausea. "Yeah."

"He's always been one of the holdouts. Most hunters have pretty much gone to seed, but not him. I admit, when we found out Val had Roemer blood, we almost turned our backs on her. But then, one of us got sick. Her name was Elena. You didn't meet her; she passed away, despite Val's best efforts. But we saw how hard she fought. We watched her fight to save our friend and we watched her shut down when she failed. That's when we knew we could trust her."

Ari said, "So you know how to find him?"

Gladys stared at her, twisting her lips as she considered the question. "What exactly do you think he'll give you?"

"Val isn't the only person who's missing. My mother, and a *canidae* named Marin Cardoso have also been taken. I think tracking down Roemer will lead us to wherever they're being held."

"You think he's trying to start the war again? Wolf manoth?"

"I think he has bigger plans this time. But if I can find him in time..."

Gladys exhaled sharply and drummed her fingers on the table. "I have a real problem sending a fellow wolf to that man, for any reason. Especially a wolf that I'm sorta fond of."

"Aw, sweet talker."

Gladys crossed her arms over her chest. "I would warn you to be careful, but I remember you picking a fight with Kunz specifically so she would break one of your bones. So I don't think you and careful are ever in the same carpool. But I will say that I hope you have someone to watch your ass."

"I do," Ari said.

Gladys considered it another moment before she finally spoke. "We got all our information on Roemer from a wolf on the outside named Conrad Rigas. He's also the one making sure none of us go wolf while inside. I'll get in touch with him and let him decide if he wants to reach out to you."

Ari wanted to argue. Time was of the essence, but she also understood caution. If she was Gladys' contact, she wouldn't want her number to be handed out to someone she'd never met. She nodded reluctantly and leaned back.

"Tell him we're up against the clock here."

"I will." She watched Ari's face. "Bigger than wolf manoth? You're not just exaggerating?"

Ari shook her head. "I really wish I was, but it could be a lot worse than the wolfsbane incident from a few years ago."

Gladys shuddered. "I'll get some phone time and call him as soon as I can. He'll be in touch, I'm sure. And be careful."

"I thought you weren't going to say that."

"You might not listen, but I'm the one who has to look at myself in the mirror. So I've still got to say it. Get through this, Ariadne Willow. Come back and buy me more snacks and soda pop."

Ari smiled. "Will do, Gladys. I promise. You stay safe in here, too."

Gladys laughed and said, "Honey, from the look on your face, I'm a little worried we're all better off than you are."

Val's cell door wasn't locked or guarded, but she was as much a prisoner as Gwen or Marin. She'd spent the night lying on her cot and staring at the ceiling, fighting the urge to get up and rush the door. She would only have done it if she could have warned Gwen to use the distraction for her own escape. So instead she tossed and turned and eventually got out of bed when the window was brightened by the sun. She washed up using a large bowl and water from the bottle that was left outside her door every morning. She dressed in this week's T-shirt and slacks. Her captors decided it would be easier to just give her a new outfit every Sunday rather than creating a laundry schedule, apparently.

It was shocking how quickly a person could get used to a wholly new set of circumstances, but here she was. She needed a haircut, but she just pulled it back and tied it as well as she could before she went out into the main room.

There were already a half dozen hunters present, the late crew at the end of their shift. A few looked up when Val came out of her cell but none of them gave her any real attention. They were exclusively male, mostly in their thirties. Most were seated around a card table with their phones out, but two of them were leaning near the main exit. The sentries looked bored and half-asleep, but she knew they'd snap to attention if she got anywhere close to them. They were all dressed identically in tactical clothes: black cargo pants with matching turtlenecks. She thought they looked like washed-up college athletes hoping for one more shot of glory.

"Is Miss Willow awake?"

"If you want to take her out for a walk, leash is by the door," one of the hunters said.

Another chuckled and said, "Don't forget the pooper scooper."

Val rolled her eyes and walked past them. The other wolf... the *girl...* was being held on the second floor. Her cell had four guards standing outside, two of them armed with shock sticks. The other two had holstered pistols on their hips. They tensed when they saw her, but she refused to shrink away from their laser stares.

"I need to check on her."

One of the guards seemed to have been elected as spokesperson. He shook his head, remained where he was, but swiveled his head to face her. "Boss said at the top of the hour."

Val looked at her watch. "It's close enough."

The guard shrugged. "Take it up with him. No one's getting in here until both hands are pointed straight up."

"I'm amazed you can read a timepiece without Mickey Mouse on it."

He didn't react in the slightest, just kept staring at her.

"Is this how it will be?" Val asked. "There's a real person in there. She's been in there overnight. She needs to eat, she needs to go to the bathroom, she needs to sleep."

The guard furrowed his brow and turned to one of the other men. "Did you see a person in that room? All I saw was a dog wearing a girl suit."

Val bit down hard on her tongue. "If she dies, then all of this will be for nothing."

"If she dies," the guard said, his impatience starting to bleed into his words, "we have a spare downstairs. And you've been keeping that one nice and healthy, right? So no big deal." He fixed a phony smile on her. "Now why don't you get out of here, sweetheart?"

She resisted every initial impulse she had, turning her back on him and storming off instead. She went up, to the fourth floor. It was the top floor of the building, and it was a single room with boarded-up windows on all sides. The stairs ended next to the gaping maw of an elevator shaft, its door missing and the forty-foot drop blocked by a haphazard lattice of rotted wood. A desk had been placed on a rug in the center of the space, complete with walls formed by bookshelves and a trio of plush armchairs for guests. It could have been transplanted from any hundreds of downtown offices except for the tall floodlights arranged in a square so the "office" would still be lit up after dark.

The man Gwen and Milo had called Silver Skull was at the desk, leaning back in his chair and staring at his laptop. His chin was resting on one fist, and he looked almost bored. She knew what he was watching even without being able to see the screen.

"Why don't you go downstairs, get a live show? I'm sure all

your adoring internet trolls would love to see the man who made their snuff film possible."

He sighed and turned his attention to her. "What do you want?"

"You abducted me, held me prisoner here, to be a doctor. I *want* to be allowed to serve that purpose. Your goons downstairs won't let me in to see the wolf."

"Of course they will." He looked at his watch. "In seven minutes."

She put her hands flat on his desk. "I need to examine her. I need to make sure your boys didn't hurt her when they dragged her in."

"She's fine," he said, turning back to the screen.

Val slapped the laptop shut. "I'm the doctor here. I'm the expert. You might know how to kill a wolf, but I know how to keep them alive. Right now, it's in your best interest to keep that girl downstairs as healthy as she can be. Let me be a doctor. That means I make the schedule, I make the rules, and your goons answer to *me*. Otherwise..."

"Otherwise what? You'll walk?"

"I can find all kinds of ways to make myself useless to you," she said.

They stared at each other across the desk. Neither of them blinked. Finally, he screwed his lips into a wry smile and flipped his hands in surrender. He retrieved his phone and began tapping out a message.

"Fine. Sending the boys their new mandate now. The audio will be cut while you're in there, so don't try anything cute like trying to send a message about where we are." He looked up at her and smiled. "You get your pig-headedness from your mother."

She turned her back on him, raising her middle finger to him over her shoulder as she left. "Shove it up your ass, Gabe."

CHAPTER SEVEN

VAL STARED at her watch, waiting for the second it clicked over to nine. She was on the landing as far from the guards as possible while still being on the same landing, ignoring their stares and attempts at conversation. It was easy to tone them out, harder to keep her patience as the second hand swept around the dial at an excruciatingly slow pace. When it finally clicked over to nine, she walked forward, only to have her way blocked by the same guard who had stopped her before. He was almost a foot taller than her, but the doctor side of her brain had a wide catalogue of ways she could hurt him using minimal effort. She stared at him without blinking.

"Move," she said.

He smiled down at her and held up a rubber mask. "Orders are orders. Don't want her to be able to identify you, right?"

It wasn't worth arguing with him so she grabbed the mask and pulled it on without bothering to see who it was. The guard moved out of her way, and another one unlocked the door to let her into the cell. Marin didn't look up, didn't even react to someone coming into the room with her. Val stood in front of her and bent her head down so she could see the girl's eyes.

"Marin?" Her voice was muffled, made ridiculous by the mask.

"My name is Valerie. I'm a doctor. I'm not with them, I'm here to help you."

Marin raised her eyes without moving her head. "You're not a wolf."

"No. But I have a lot of experience with them." She checked Marin's pulse. "My only goal is to make sure you stay as healthy as possible."

"Good hunter/bad hunter? Disappointingly cliché."

"Give me a sniff," she said. "It should be painfully obvious I haven't had a real bath in a really long time. You think a hunter would do that just to trick you? Trust me. Let me keep you alive so we can both get out of this shit."

Marin looked at her again, this time with a bit less certainty. "I have to go to the bathroom."

Val turned to look at the camera, then at the door. "Yo, Nixon. Get in here and block the camera."

"Boss says we record twenty-four sev~"

"You can move if she starts transforming, just get your fat ass in here and block the damn camera."

After a moment, someone came in and stood behind her.

"And face the wall," she said. "This isn't a fucking peep show."

The guard sighed and slowly turned his back on her. "You might want to watch your tone, Doc. Boss says we have to keep her in tip-top shape. Didn't say anything about you."

"Yeah?" Val said as she helped Marin. "How exactly do you plan to keep a *canidae* in 'tip-top shape' without a doctor?"

He didn't answer that.

Marin made a quiet exhale that, under the circumstances, might have passed for a laugh. "Okay. You better not be lying, because I think I'm starting to like you."

Val smiled sadly behind her mask. "Not lying. Just not the best ally in the world."

"Right now I'll take all the friends I can get."

"You and me both, sister," Val said.

Ari went from the jail directly to the office, where she found Dale wrapping up a phone call with Diana. "Hold on, Ariadne just came in." She turned her head away from the phone. "Anything Diana needs to know?"

"Big bad hunter boss is named Gabriel Roemer. Other than that, nothing." She raised her voice. "Good morning, Diana."

Dale smiled. "Did you hear the first part? Yeah. Okay. Bye." She disconnected the call and put the phone down on the desk. "The two men she arrested yesterday at the hospital have lawyered up."

"Great," Ari said, slumping into her office. "So much for getting information from them."

"Oh, ye of little faith." She repositioned her chair so she could type on the laptop. "They lawyered up, which means Diana can't talk to them. But it also means that two people associated with Isaac Hayden hired a lawyer, so by the transitive property, we have the name of a lawyer connected to the hunters."

Ari came back to watch over Dale's shoulder. "Dale, you genius. I ought to marry you."

"Leave your name and number, and I'll give you a call when I'm single again." She nodded at the screen. "Here's our hunter lawyer. Donald Keech."

"Ugh, Donald."

"Yeah, that name is going to be ruined for a couple of generations, isn't it? But it looks like he's a legitimate attorney. What about you? Who is Gabriel Roemer?"

"Val's father. Apparently he's the guy using Hayden and the book to get the hunters all riled up. He's probably the one who came up with the video torture."

"Oh, about that." Dale opened a new window and waved Ari over. "I checked out the footage after you left to talk with Gladys. First, they apparently set it up so that the video archives itself every twelve hours. The live feed continues uninterrupted, but you can look back at what streamed before. I've been looking at the usual suspects - Facebook, Twitter - but it doesn't seem to be picking up much traction."

"How is that possible? It's a video of a woman literally being held prisoner."

"Some people think it's a YouTube prank, most people are saying it's a hoax. The ones that really disappoint me are the people who are positive that it's viral marketing for a horror movie. They say it looks like the movie will have terrible special effects."

"I don't know whether to be relieved or horrified."

"That's pretty much where I fell, too."

Ari looked at the screen, where Marin was still hanging from her restraints, head bowed, face shadowed. She wanted to reach through the screen and break the iron bar with her bare hands.

Instead, she asked, "See anything interesting?"

"Just after nine o'clock, this happened." Dale clicked on an archived video and scrolled along the bar to the right time. "Watch."

Marin's head twitched as the light in the room changed slightly. The glow of an exterior hallway fell on her before it was blocked by someone coming into the room. The new arrival was a woman in a dirty T-shirt and slacks. She was wearing a rubber mask of John F Kennedy that concealed her entire head, but Ari recognized her immediately.

"Val."

Dale nodded. "I was pretty sure, but I wanted a second opinion."

"Audio?"

"It cut out right before she went in and stayed off. I assume they don't want to give any hints about where they might be. Airplanes going overhead, trains going by..."

"Right," Ari said. "Damn."

Val stood in front of Marin and gently raised her head, apparently examining her eyes as her hand moved to Marin's throat.

"At least the bastards are letting her get some kind of medical attention."

"They don't want the star of their twisted little show to die before the big reveal," Dale said.

On the video, Val turned and motioned for someone to come closer. A body appeared at the edge of the frame before stepping to the side and blocking the screen entirely.

"What's happening?" Ari said.

"I assume they're giving her privacy to use the bathroom."

Ari said, "Geez, what swell captors she has."

"Aren't they just?" Dale said. "Did you see Val's clothes...?"

"Yeah," Ari said.

Dale shook her head. "We're not going to leave them there a whole month, are we, puppy? Please tell me we're going to get them out long before that."

"Oh, hell yeah." She kissed the top of Dale's head and started into her office. "We're going to get our girls back. I have a plan and everything."

"A plan?" Dale turned her chair around and leaned forward. "Oh, what a relief. Tell me this great plan."

Ari glared at her from the office doorway. "When you say it

like that, it sounds like you're mocking me."

Dale batted her eyelashes. "Wow me, Willow."

"Gladys told me about a *canidae* named Conrad Rigas who provides them with information. He's the one who set up the supply line to make sure they kept getting their drug when Val disappeared. If he decides to get in contact, I'm going to convince him to give me everything he has on Roemer. Then I go undercover."

All the humor evaporated from Dale's face. "The hell you do."

"It's our best option."

Dale stood up. "The hell it is! Ari, this is a guy who arranged to kidnap four women without breaking a sweat. He got the drop on Mom *and* Milo. No offense, but if he can take them out, you're not going to stand a chance. I'm not going to risk losing you, too."

"Someone has to get close enough to gain his trust. It's the quickest way to finding Mom, and Val, and Marin."

"You're probably right. And someone probably should go undercover."

"Well, who do you sugg~" She stopped herself, eyes widening as she realized. "Oh, fuck no."

Dale said, "I'm the best~"

"Fuck. *No*," Ari said again. "There is absolutely no way I'm letting you~"

"Oh, 'letting' me?"

Ari shook her head. "Don't turn this into that. I'm the private investigator here, Dale. I'm the *canidae*."

"We're partners, Ariadne," Dale said. "This isn't a case. It's not private investigator business, so it doesn't matter if I have a license or not. I've bled for wolves in the past. I'm part of your pack now. And the simple truth is that the second you walk into a hunter's lair, you're going to have a target on your back. What if they have a way to identify you? What if they know you're a wolf as soon as you're in the door? What if they know you personally?"

Ari clenched her jaw and looked past Dale out the window.

"You know this is the best option. I'm... I'm not just a human. I'm also a hunter."

"You're *not*~"

Dale put her finger on Ari's lips. "We both know that book did something to me. Just like we both know that I've overcome it. But if anyone is going to risk being exposed to hunters, it has to be me. Let me protect you. Let me save our family."

Ari met Dale's eyes. "I'll be there, seconds away, the whole time. If *anything* happens to you...”

“You’ll swoop in and save me like the perfect wife you are.” She cupped Ari’s face and pulled her in for a kiss. “That’s the only reason I feel brave enough to do it, you know. I’m scared to death. These guys are monsters. The only reason I’m offering to do this is because I have faith in you. My parachute and my safety net.”

“Always,” Ari said.

“Always,” Dale repeated, and kissed Ari again.

Ari put her arms around Dale. “So. First fight as a married couple. Still want to stick with it?”

Dale rested her hands on Ari’s hips. “Well... I *do* have a backup plan for when we call it quits. A really sexy lady from work made an offer.”

“I knew it was trouble letting my woman work.”

Dale kissed Ari’s cheek. “Let me see what I can find on Roemer and Keech. Maybe I can connect them somehow and find a link that shows us the right place to look.”

“That would be nice.” Ari stepped out of the embrace. “I’m going to go see Eva Cardoso. Maybe there’s a reason the hunters targeted Marin, something that can lead us to where they’re holding her.”

“It’s worth a shot,” Dale said.

“Before I do that, I thought I’d run over and check on Milo. Take her something to eat, see how she’s doing.”

“Oh, good idea. Give her my love.”

“Will do. Call me if you find any dirt, or if anything happens in the video.”

Dale saluted, already back at the laptop.

Ari drove home, making a quick stop to pick up another greasy burger and fries, and let herself into the apartment. She expected to find Milo in their bed but instead she was in the living room, curled up in a ball on the floor next to the couch. She’d made herself a nest out of blankets and pillows, her knees pulled up to her chest, one arm over her head. Ari froze in the doorway, terrified she’d had a relapse.

“Milo...?”

Her shoulders twitched and she lifted her head, staring at Ari until her eyes focused. “Ari,” she said, and the tension faded from Ari’s posture. Milo sat up and stretched. “Your couch sucks.”

“It inspires me to not fight with Dale before bedtime.” She held up the bag of food she’d brought. “Want some lunch?”

Milo growled low in her throat and practically pounced on the bag. Ari let go before she lost a finger and went to the offending couch. Milo took her bounty to the dinner table and sat down, tearing the paper bag to get at the food inside.

"How are you feeling," Ari said, "other than starving?"

"Bad sleep," Milo said, then took a bite. She chewed, swallowed. "Weird dreams..."

Ari leaned forward. "Weird how? They could be your memories trying to resurface."

Milo narrowed her eyes and stared at a fixed spot on the wall. "Dark room. There were flashing lights, and someone was talking to me but I couldn't see her."

"Her?" Ari said. "Val?"

"I don't think so. This was one of the hunters."

Ari was surprised by that. All the hunters they'd seen so far, or at least the ones she could remember, had been male.

"Pretty sure it was a her, anyway. Everything is kind of jumbled." Milo rubbed her arms. "I remember being really cold and really hot. Pain." Her expression hardened, like she was trying to solve a really complicated crossword puzzle, but eventually she shook her head. "I don't know. I... I don't think I saw Gwen the entire time we were being held together."

"But you know she was in the same place? That she was okay?"

Milo nodded. "I felt her there. Even though they kept us apart, I knew she was there."

Ari gave her a moment with her emotions before she spoke again. "We're going to get her back. We already have some good leads."

Milo perked up. "Leads? What do you have? Do you know who took us?"

"Not so fast," Ari said. "Even if we had an address and map with a big X on it, you wouldn't be getting anywhere near the place."

Milo got to her feet. "Ariadne..."

Ari also stood. "Millicent."

They stared at each other across the room. Milo was breathing hard, her hands balled into fists at her sides. Neither of them spoke, neither moved, but Ari could feel the tension between them.

"We can fight," Ari said. "You'll probably kick my ass. Or maybe not, considering you aren't exactly in top shape. No matter what happens, you'll still have to convince Dale to let you go along, and there's no way you're getting past her. You're not going to do the prisoners any good by rushing in there when you're still recovering from your last visit."

Milo worked her jaw. "If Gwen doesn't see me there…"

"She'll know you're somewhere safe," Ari said, "and that you were smart enough to let someone else take the first wave. What would you do if she was the one who got away, and you saw her come running in a few days later?"

"I would be relieved!"

Ari glared at her.

"And… I'd be furious at her for being so stupid." She dropped heavily back into her chair. She looked at the to-go bag and then swatted it away, spilling fries across the floor. "*I hate this!*" she bellowed, then put her head in her hands, shoulders rising and falling with ragged breaths. Ari sidestepped the spilled food and rubbed Milo's back. "I hate being useless."

"You're not useless. You're healing. Mom will appreciate you taking care of yourself when she wasn't around to do it."

Milo sniffled and wiped her eyes. "Thanks. I'll, uh, I'll clean up the floor and vacuum."

"We'd appreciate that." She kept rubbing Milo's shoulders. "How's the… Have you tried transforming again?"

Milo held up her hand. Her fingers twitched a little. "A couple of times. Still nothing."

Ari crouched down and laced her fingers with Milo's. "Whatever's going on, we're going to figure it out."

"How'd you deal with it in prison? And afterward, when you knew you wouldn't be able to change until the drug was out of your system?"

She remembered those days, the insomnia, feeling the wolf inside of her but knowing it was hibernating and wouldn't come out no matter how much she tried to force it. She remembered the really bad days, when it felt like she wanted to claw her skin off. Unfortunately the only advice she had to offer, the thing that had gotten her through those sleepless nights and anxious days, was Dale.

"It was having her, wasn't it?" Milo said, looking up with a wry smile.

"Sorry."

"Don't be." She stood up and clapped her hand on Ari's shoulder. "I'm going to take a shower and try to sleep again. Thank you for the food. It was just what the doctor ordered."

Ari said, "Text me if you need anything else. Dale and I are your personal Postmates for the duration of this thing."

"Appreciated. Can you at least tell me you have a target to go after?"

"We have a couple," Ari said. "Really good leads. Promising."

Milo nodded. "Okay. After all the miracles I've seen you and Dale pull off over the years, I'd be stupid to start doubting you now. Keep me in the loop."

"Promise," Ari said.

Milo went past her to the bathroom, and Ari crouched down to start picking up the fallen fries. Maybe the effort she'd put into convincing Milo there was hope would help convince herself of the same thing. Because at the moment, despite the leads they'd already gathered, she felt incredibly daunted by the forces stacked up against them. She couldn't help but worry that no matter how fast they moved or how much intelligence they gathered, their enemy could just crush them into dust.

CHAPTER EIGHT

ONCE MILO was in the shower and the mess had been cleaned up, Ari left the apartment and went back to where she'd parked. She was almost to her car before a voice from behind her stopped her in her tracks.

"I hope you appreciate the fact that, just by being here, I've proven that I could cause all sorts of headaches for you and Miss Duncan."

Ari slowly turned to watch Isaac Hayden come down off the front porch of the house. He held his hands out to either side to show he was unarmed. He wore a sweater vest over an Oxford shirt, both of them tucked into a pair of dark slacks. Ari kept her guard up. She wasn't about to be the first person in history killed by someone in a sweater vest. She turned to face him fully.

"I can't smell you."

He smiled. "That's almost like a compliment, but I don't think you meant it as one."

"I couldn't smell those hunters at the waterfront, either. You guys start using a new cologne?"

"Yes, Wolf Blind, by Calvin Klein." He chuckled. "I was hoping we could talk."

"Talk?" Ari said. "That's weird. Because the last time we saw each other was pretty hectic, but I seem to remember you yelling about how you were going to kill me this time."

Hayden sighed and looked down, the portrait of shame. "Yes, I admit, I allowed my emotions to get the better of me yesterday morning. I hope you can forgive me. It had been a very stressful night and I lost my composure."

"Yeah, it's always rough when the women you're holding prisoner get away from you."

He pressed his lips together. "I've obviously found your home," he said. "I know Miss Duncan is staying there. I've always known where your office is. I came here to demonstrate that I don't want to be a threat to you."

"By lurking outside my house? By pointing out you can get to me at any time you want? Some people might consider that a threat in and of itself."

"You are... the most frustrating woman I've ever met."

"Aw, you're just saying that."

Hayden stepped forward but Ari held out a hand to stop him.

"How about we keep this gap, Mr. Non-Threatening? I can hear you just fine from over there."

"The hunters want to kill you. They want a genocide. All wolves dead, skinned, wiped from the face of the planet. I don't want that. I don't want to kill an entire species even if I thought it was possible. Forced extinction is a heinous act. I'm the one who convinced our boss to go with this plan."

"Kidnapping and torturing a college student?"

Hayden said, "Exposing *canidae*. Revealing the truth to the world."

Ari said, "You think that's a better plan? You think the world would just accept that we exist? There's centuries of folklore calling us monsters."

"Vampires were called monsters for centuries, too. Now they're sex symbols."

Ari rolled her eyes. "Okay, what do you want, Hayden? Do you want my help? Because you kidnapped my mother and her partner, you're holding an innocent *canidae* hostage, you tried to abduct my partner the last time we met. You don't have a very good track record, bud."

"I only want..."

A police cruiser pulled up to the curb. Ari stared at it, then turned back to the house when she heard the front door open.

Neka Teller, skilled Duwamish boat builder, very understanding landlady, and Ari's current favorite person in the world, stood on the porch with her phone in her hand, staring daggers at Hayden.

"Everything okay, Ariadne?" she asked.

"Everything's fine," Ari said. The officers were coming up the lawn now, and she raised her voice so they could hear. "Mr. Isaac Hayden was just leaving."

"Mr. Hayden was loitering on my property for most of the morning," Neka said.

The cops struck their typical hands-on-belt intimidation pose. One of them said, "Sir, why don't you move along and leave these ladies alone?"

"That sounds like a great idea," Ari said. "Run along, Mr. Hayden. Isaac Hayden." She spelled it. One of the cops smirked and ducked his head, wiping his fingers across his lips.

Hayden was already moving toward the curb. "We don't have to be enemies, Ariadne. Think about what I said. I won't come back here, and I won't come to your office, but we will talk again."

"I look forward to it," Ari said, waggling her fingers in farewell.

When he was well off the property, the lead cop looked between Ari and Neka. "Everything under control, ladies?"

"Yes, officer. Thank you," Ari said.

The other officer, the one who was now smiling openly, hooked his finger over his shoulder. "We're going to follow him for a bit. Make sure he doesn't just circle back around. You ladies have a good afternoon."

The police left, and Neka crossed the lawn to stand next to Ari. "Are you okay?"

Ari squeezed Neka's arm above the elbow. "Yeah. I don't think I really needed the backup, but I'm really grateful they were here."

"Who was that guy? Is he dangerous?"

"Not to you," Ari said. "But if you see him hanging around, you might want to go ahead and call the cops again."

"In a heartbeat. Take care of yourself. And remember, if it happens on my property, I'm part of it. Whoever that dude is, he's on my shit list, too."

Ari smiled. "I appreciate you watching our backs."

Neka saluted and headed back in the house.

Ari looked down the street, half-expecting to see Hayden doing a slow drive-by. She couldn't help but wonder about his motives. She didn't trust him an inch, but he had been right. He got the drop on her, and he could have grabbed her before she even knew he was there. He didn't. He knew where Milo was, so he could have recaptured her. He didn't do that, either. She wasn't naïve enough to believe he was sincere about wanting to help, but he was definitely working an angle that might run counter to what the hunters had in mind.

Whatever he really wanted, Hayden had just confirmed just how dangerous he was. She turned around to go back in the apartment. He could claim all day that he had no intention of taking Milo back into custody, but she wasn't about to trust his word on that.

***

Eva Cardoso and her sister lived in a condo in Eastlake, comfortably settled between the I-5 and Lake Union. Ari had always liked the neighborhood, though the students and tech gurus who populated it made her feel like a geriatric refugee whenever she risked venturing into its bohemian borders. But it had unbeatable views of the water or downtown, depending on which part of the hill you were on, and some of the streets were bona fide cobblestone. It was a lovely place to visit, spend an afternoon, but if the constant traffic on the I-5 overhead didn't eventually drive you out, the prices would.

Ari was surprised to see there were no parking spaces available in front of Eva and Marin's building; she had to park at the end of the block and walk back. When she knocked, the door was almost immediately answered by a very short, very dark woman in a sleeveless dress, her feet planted shoulder-width apart as if she expected Ari to try rushing past her. Her center-parted hair hung down well past her shoulders, long enough that the curled ends might brush the carpet if she bent her knees.

"State your business."

Ari was taken aback. "Uh. Ariadne Willow. I'm the~"

The woman's demeanor immediately changed, as if an unseen director had yelled cut. "Oh, the private investigator. You're okay, she said you can come in." She stepped aside. "I'm Mickie. Eva's in here with the rest of us."

"The rest...?" Ari followed Mickie into the living room and saw *canidae* in human form taking up every available surface. Two were on the coffee table, three on the hearth, one in each of the armchairs, and two on either side of Eva who was sitting on the couch. The only one standing was a woman at the window, who held up her phone and snapped a picture of Ari.

"You don't have to do that, Hazel. She's a friend."

"As far as we know." Hazel glared at Ari. "Spell your name for me."

Ari did. "Eva has my contact numbers, too. I'm happy to be on your suspect list in the interest of completion. Is it everyone who has come by the house since Marin went missing?"

"Yep," Hazel said.

"I'd like a copy of that, if it's okay."

Eva didn't give Hazel time to answer. "Absolutely. Hazel will email it to you."

Hazel didn't look too happy, but turned away and peeked through the curtains at the street. Back on sentry-duty, it seemed.

Eva squeezed the hands of the girls next to her, then stood up and went to Ari. "I assume you'd prefer to speak to me in private?"

"It's really up to you."

"Probably be fewer interruptions if it's just the two of us." She put a hand on Ari's shoulder and guided her into the hallway. "Sorry about Hazel and Mickie..."

"I assume their attitude is the main reason they're on guard duty. I understand."

Eva nodded. She led Ari into a kitchen, the counter still cluttered with breakfast dishes. She immediately started gathering the plates and glasses, moving them to the sink where she ran water over them. Ari had been around enough people with nervous energy to know it wasn't really about doing a chore. She found a towel and went to stand next to Eva to help her.

"They've probably been keyed up by watching the feed."

Eva sighed heavily. "One of the boys has been. I ca~ I can't see her like that. It hurts too much and I just shut down. They tell me if anything happens. There was a woman on the video this morning... a doctor, I think? She looked like she actually cared about Marin. That was a bit of a relief."

"Dale and I think we know who she is. If we're right, she's a prisoner, too."

Eva shook her head. "And they call us monsters."

"Has Marin mentioned anyone hanging around, anything suspicious the past few days?"

"I don't think so." She paused scrubbing to think. "She doesn't really date, so there aren't any evil exes who might have set her up. She mostly just goes to school and to work. I gave you her work address and class schedule when I hired you, right?"

"Yeah. To be honest, I'm just covering my bases by asking about stalkers. I think it's more likely the hunters just grabbed the first *canidae* they saw."

"How would they even tell the difference between a *canidae* and just a big dog?"

Ari shrugged. She didn't want to confess about Milo and her germ of a theory that the hunters had somehow used her to track and capture Marin. She caught movement from the corner of her eye that, combined with a scent she recognized from the foyer, told her Mickie was eavesdropping.

"I'm glad you have a pack to help you through a time like this."

"It's killing them that they can't help more. I'm sure you know what it's like when a member of your pack is in danger."

Ari cleared her throat. "I... I do understand. But not from personal experience. I've never really had a pack."

Eva stopped scrubbing a plate and turned to look at her. "Are you serious? I don't think I've ever met a wolf without a pack before."

"I didn't have the most traditional childhood," Ari said. "I have someone now."

"One person?"

Ari said, "She's enough."

Eva considered that, then accepted it with a nod. She went back to the dishes. "They help keep me busy. Focused on the right things. I don't know what I'd be doing right now without them. Probably curled up in a ball at the foot of my bed."

"There's something to be said for doing that at times like these. As long as you have someone to pull you out of it after a few hours."

"I'll keep that in mind. It helps to have you on the case, Miss Willow."

"Is there anything you can tell me about Marin that can help? I'm not even sure what would be helpful. But I think knowing a little bit more about her as a person..." She sighed and rested her hands on the counter. "Honestly, I just want to see her as more than a victim. These people are also holding two people that are very close to me. They're my priority because I know them and I care about them. I want to care about Marin the same way."

"I want that, too," Eva said. "She works at a... a... store." She laughed and shook her head. "God, I don't even know what to call it. They buy stuff from estate sales, but they also showcase work from local artists and crafters. I guess it's like a slightly fancier version of Goodwill. The hours are flexible and let her work around her class schedule."

"U-Dub?" Ari asked.

Eva nodded. "She's studying museology."

Ari turned the word around in her head for a few seconds before she raised a helpless eyebrow.

"Museums," Eva revealed, smiling. "She wants to work at the aquarium."

"Wow. Must be pretty clever."

"She's a genius," Eva said, her voice cracking. They washed dishes quietly as she composed herself. "I hate the water, like most wolves. You?"

Ari chuckled. "Oh yeah."

"Mom and Dad, too. But not Marin. We can't keep that girl out of the water. She absolutely loves fish, so around sixth grade, she figured out everything she needed to work with them and made herself a roadmap. Ever since then, she's been following it. Until now. These assholes." She sniffled. "She's missing classes. I called and told them she's sick, but it's only a matter of time until that video starts getting traction and someone recognizes her."

"We're doing everything in our power to stop that from happening. At the moment, everyone seems pretty convinced it's a hoax. But the longer it goes on, the more attention it will attract."

Eva stared into the soapy water and nodded. "The only good thing about it is that I know she's alive. She's really badly hurt, she's in a horrible situation, but she's alive. That's something, right?"

"That's definitely something." She heard a brush of a shoe against carpet in the hall. She looked but didn't see anyone. She raised her voice so that the eavesdropper would be sure to hear. "And I know that if I drag my feet, I'm going to have a whole wolf pack on my ass. So I have extra motivation to find her as quickly as I can."

"Damn right," Hazel said without showing herself.

Eva lowered her voice. "Don't mind them. They love Marin as much as I do, and their love language is to punch the thing that's hurting their friends."

Ari said, "I understand the urge. I won't hold it against them. Marin's lucky to have such a loyal family." An idea occurred to her, and she considered how to frame it to Eva. "You might want to think about giving your wolves a chance to process her situation as well. Sometimes you have to turn off the human brain and just let the wolf deal with something. I suggest the whole pack transform tonight and go for a run. For Marin. Even if she can't transform and join you, I think her wolf will know you're out there for her."

"That sounds like a really nice idea," Eva said. "And honestly, it sounds like exactly what I need. I'll bring it up."

Hazel came into the kitchen. "Bring her home, Miss Willow. And if you can't... if these bastards hurt her before you're able to save her, then do us all a favor and bring us their names."

Ari held eye contact with Hazel and nodded.

"You have my word."

CHAPTER NINE

GABRIEL RAISED an eyebrow when Val dropped a flattened and grease-stained fast food bag on his desk. The blank side of the bag had been filled with rows of Val's tight, sloppy handwriting. Gabriel sat up straighter and picked up the bag, angling it toward his desk lamp as he attempted to decipher the scrawl.

"What exactly am I looking at here?"

"Demands."

He laughed and put the bag down. "Demands? Who the hell do you think you are?"

"I'm the woman keeping your prized prisoner alive. That list will go a long way toward helping me achieve that. Don't tell me Gwen Willow is your backup plan, because you spent most of a day scouring the city looking for Marin when she got away. You want her, specifically. Probably because a young, cute college student gets more views than a woman in her fifties. Chauvinist. Maybe because it would ruin your narrative to swap out the guinea pig once the livestream has already started. I don't give a shit about your reasons. In the end, the only thing that matters is that Marin Cardoso remains healthy and comfortable." She gestured at the bag. "I offered to email you the list, but for some reason your guys refused to let me use an iPad. They have trust issues, I guess."

Gabriel picked up the bag again. "A bed. Hygiene products." He laughed and waved the bag when he saw the next item. "A *privacy* screen? Do you not understand the purpose of this whole endeavor?"

"It doesn't have to be big enough for her to hide behind completely," Val said, "but the woman needs to use the bathroom. She needs toothpaste, tampons, soap. If you're worried about her escaping, you have a non-stop live feed of her on your computer so you can see what she's doing every second of every damn day. She's not going to dig a tunnel or build a transporter to get out of the room. She deserves to have a little comfort, otherwise this is just a slow murder."

"I obviously wasted a lot of time finding this place. I should have just booked a few rooms at the Crowne Plaza."

Val put her hands on the desk and leaned down to look him in the eye. "She won't survive a month being strung up the way you have her. A malnourished or sick *canidae* won't transform in order to conserve energy. Treat her well or this whole *endeavor* will be nothing but a waste of time and resources."

Gabriel pursed his lips and put the bag down, drumming his fingers on it. "You're turning out to be a lot more trouble than you may be worth."

"Then I guess I'm doing my job right, then."

He stared hard at her, but she thought there was some amusement in his expression as well. She was conflicted by that; she didn't want this asshole to like her.

"Fine," he said. "I'll have the guys improve our *guest's* accommodations. Are you happy now?"

Val's smile was maniacal, cartoonish. "Absolutely *thrilled*, Daddy, thank you ever so much."

The smile collapsed as she turned and walked out of the room. It was a small victory, and she wouldn't celebrate it where he could see, but she was still thrilled to have achieved even that much. It meant Gabriel could be reasoned with. It meant there was hope, however small, that they could all get out of this in one piece.

Dale was at her computer when Ari came in, but she stood and motioned for Ari to follow her before the door was even shut behind her.

"Busy day?" Ari said.

"Always is, when I'm doing your job as well as mine."

Ari followed Dale into her office. The bulletin board had been populated with multiple photos and new index cards filled with information about each major player. Ari obviously recognized Hayden, whose picture was obviously a headshot from some online profile. The photo next to him, labeled Donald Keech, showed that the hunters' lawyer was a man who somehow managed to look gangly and squat at the same time. He was long-limbed and his suit was somehow misshapen and baggy on him despite the fact he was overweight. He had salt-and-pepper hair that had been turned into a tangled mess by the wind.

"I guess he's not using his big hunter retainers for a tailor. Or a stylist."

"Now, now, don't body-shame him. Focus on the other reprehensible parts of his personality." Dale hung up another photo, this one of a man with sharp cheekbones and slicked-back grey-white hair. He might have been handsome if it wasn't for his heavy brow and almost black eyes. He was smiling in a way that said he'd already won at a game his opponent didn't even know they were playing. "This guy, though. Say whatever you want about this creepy dude."

Ari thought for a second. "Vegas magician, but way off the Strip, with a bunch of mysteriously missing assistants."

"Wow, spot-on. Well done. That's Gabriel Roemer."

"Ah, my nemesis. Nice to put a face to the skin-crawling feeling I get when I hear his name."

Dale said, "Yeah. So should I go first, or do you want to tell me how your errands went?"

"I'll go first, since I don't have a whole lot to report. Eva's hunkered down with her pack, worried about her sister. Milo still hasn't remembered much but she seems to be doing better. She still can't transform."

"It's going to take time," Dale said. "I can't imagine how it feels for her, though."

"Yeah." Ari braced herself for the next part. "Hayden was outside the house."

Dale spun away from the board, moving closer to Ari. "What? *Our* house? He was at *our* house? What did you do? Did you talk to him?"

Ari held up her hands. "Slow down. He was just waiting there. It was strange. I couldn't smell him."

"You're having a hard time with your sniffer this week," Dale said.

"No, that's not it. I can definitely smell you."

Dale said, "Hey…"

"In a good way. But it's the hunters. It's like they found a blind spot. It's weird. But not as weird as what Hayden had to say. He claims he wants to help *canidae*."

Dale laughed. "Good one."

Ari narrowed her eyes. "I kind of believe him."

"You can't be serious. You do remember the plane, right? The gun?"

"I remember *you* holding the gun on me, because he left it on the seat when he came out to talk with me. He says the hunters are looking to kill all the *canidae* they can. Genocide. It's basically been their goal for a thousand years. Hayden says he just wants to expose the truth. He claims the video evidence is his idea."

"So he doesn't want to kill wolves, he just wants to torture one. Not to mention that exposure is just as deadly for you as an all-out war."

Ari said, "I'm just reporting, babe. Looking at every angle. He clearly knew where Milo was and didn't even knock on the door. He could have attacked me, he chose to have a conversation. And he could have come here at any time since we took Milo from the hospital, and he didn't."

"Or it's intimidation." Dale looked at the window. "He wanted you to know you wouldn't be able to smell him coming."

"Point," Ari said. "But he could also be sincere. If there really is a divide between the hunters, the ones who want us dead versus the ones who just want the world to know we exist, we might be able to use that to our advantage. I'm not sure how, but it's worth thinking about."

"True," Dale said.

"Okay, so, wow me with your genius."

Dale cleared her throat and pointed at the board. "Hayden's goons lawyering up is the best thing that could have happened to us. I did some digging and found out Keech was a very low-level attorney at Gilles Girard and Moreau."

"So he knew Cecily Parrish."

"Well. He probably knew *of* her. We're talking really low-level here, puppy. He barely scraped by, but apparently he built up enough of a client base to start his own firm. Real classy. We're talking ads on bus benches in Roxhill."

Ari whistled sarcastically. "Classy."

"Classy," Dale said once more. "Somewhere between leaving GG&M and this year, he started building up a reputation as the go-to guy for hunters. He's smart enough to serve as a competent lawyer for them, but shady enough that he doesn't mind working in the grey areas for them. I found some interesting names connected to him. Remember Adam Beck?"

"Celebrity chef. He was part of Keighley's group. Whatever happened to that guy?"

Dale said, "He got #MeToo'd and the show was canceled. That's part of what Keech was helping him with. Not a lot of success there, thankfully."

"You used to watch that show."

"Don't remind me. Going down the list..." She poked her finger at another picture, this one of a man Ari recognized from a few years ago. "Colin Vance. Tech twerp. Worked for Microsoft and also was part of your sperm donor's little cabal. He could definitely afford someone light years more reputable than Keech, so it's pretty damning that he's on the client list for such a bargain-basement lawyer. Any lawyer with an ounce of credibility wouldn't touch him."

"Is everyone from Keighley's group a client?"

Dale said, "As far as I could tell. Keighley used him, too." She bit her lip and then looked at Ari. "You never talked about what happened to him."

Ari shrugged, examining the board instead of looking at Dale. "What is there to talk about?"

"He killed himself after he was arrested."

"Right. Because Mom bit him, and he decided not to wait around to die horribly. Not to mention he was about to be tried for rape, along with all the other shit he did during wolf manoth. I figured he wasn't worth our attention."

Dale said, "Sure. I get that. And I know he wasn't really your father. But at the same time... it's like the bogeyman disappearing from under your bed."

"Plenty of other bogeymen to take his place," Ari said, gesturing at the board.

"Yeah, I guess. If you want to talk about it–"

"I don't," Ari said, as gently as she could muster. She finally looked at Dale. "I appreciate the offer. But if I had any emotions about it, I would have brought it up when I first found out. I'm fine. Really." She squeezed Dale's arm. "Thank you for worrying, though."

Dale didn't look convinced. "Okay. But the option is on the table if you change your mind."

"Noted."

Dale cleared her throat and looked at the board to get back on track. "So we know the guys with Hayden are clients of Keech. We can assume they're connected to Roemer, and that he's the key to finding where Gwen, Val, and Marin are." She tapped the board with her Sharpie. "This is my way in."

"How?"

"I have a relapse. Turns out you didn't really cure me, you just confused me for a little while, and now that I know Hayden is back in town, I'm looking for a way out." She bit her bottom lip again and faced Ari. "This plan might be a little scary for you."

"It would only be scary if I had any suspicion that was actually happening," Ari said. "That's less of an issue than Keighley's suicide. Are *you* worried about it?"

Dale sighed and walked away from the board. "Honestly? Yes. I've woken up in a cold sweat worried about it."

"You said those nightmares were about the circus."

"Some of them are," Dale said, sitting on the edge of Ari's desk, hugging herself. "I don't have any of those feelings. When I think back to those days when I was under the book's influence, it makes me sick. But I also worry about how easy it was to break that hold. Like... what if it was just a band-aid? What if there's some germ of it just waiting to pop back up? And then I walk into a den of these assholes and start talking like them, using their language, convincing them I'm like them. What if that flips a switch?"

"Then I'll be there to flip it back," Ari said.

"What if it's not as easy the second time?"

"Then I'll fight as long and as hard as necessary to get my wife back." She took Dale's hands, unfolding her arms. "It'll be my full-time job, if it has to be."

Dale relaxed and stepped forward, resting her head on Ari's shoulder. Ari wrapped her arms around Dale and held her.

"You know I don't like this plan," Ari said, "but I think it's a good plan, and I think you're incredibly brave for doing it. Thank you."

"Will you come save me if things go bad?"

"In a heartbeat. Always."

She kissed Dale's hair. Her lips happened to land on a scar from a bullet, inflicted years ago during their first really big case. She always shuddered when she thought about how close she'd come to losing Dale that night, and how much her life had changed since then. She doubted she would have gotten through the past ten years without Dale at her side, and had no intention of seeing what the next ten would be like without her.

"Marry me."

"Are we going to have to do this every night? That sounds exhausting."

Ari leaned back. "But worth it...?"

Dale smiled up at her. "So worth it. You were kidding, right...?"

"Yeah."

"Okay. But I would."

"I would, too," Ari said, pulling Dale back to her. "You know what would be nice right now? A massage. Just like the old days."

Dale laughed. "Oh, you're going to put me to work?"

"Who said anything about you?" She put her hands on Dale's shoulders, turning her around to guide her to the couch. "You must have rubbed the aches and pains of transforming out of me a couple hundred times. And since you're doing my job, maybe it's time I do yours." She kissed Dale just above the ear. "Take off your shirt and lay down."

Dale licked her lips and started unbuttoning. "Is it still sexual harassment if we're married?"

"Only if you don't like it."

"Then I think you're okay." Dale stretched out face down on the couch, and Ari straddled her waist. She folded her arms to make a pillow. "We should do this more often."

"I'm game if you are. Better than paperwork."

"You still have to do the paperwork," Dale said.

Ari squeezed Dale's bicep. "Hey, who's the boss here?"

"Who do you think?"

Ari grinned. "Okay, fair."

She was midway through the massage when her phone rang. Dale groaned and Ari patted her on the hip as she twisted to take the phone from the back pocket of her pants.

"Unknown number. Should I chance it?"

"Live dangerously for once in your life," Dale said.

Ari smiled and swiped, assuming a professional tone as she

brought the phone up. "This is Ariadne Willow."

"I took part in the Howl Around the Sound."

Ari furrowed her brow. "Pardon?"

"My pack heard that the *canidae* who wiped out wolfsbane needed us to howl for her, so I left work early and did it from my garage. Hope it helped."

"I'm sorry, who..." She realized who she was talking to. "You're Conrad Rigas."

"Ah, you are a detective. Well done. I hear from a mutual friend that I might be able to help you out again."

Dale tapped Ari's knee. Ari shifted to let her get up and retrieve her shirt. "I definitely hope so. We're hoping you can give us information on Gabriel Roemer."

"Which one?"

Ari was thrown. "Uh. I only know of one."

"There have been fourteen or fifteen," he said. "Only two are still alive, and I'm pretty sure you're looking for the youngest of those. His family goes way back. One of those lineage things where the patriarch tries to gain immortality by giving his name to his kid. Always feel bad for those kids. Like their whole life is just a chapter in someone else's book..." His voice trailed off.

"Uh," Ari looked at Dale. "Sure..."

Conrad snapped out of whatever mental distraction he'd suffered. "Our mutual friend says you're good people. She doesn't say that often, even about her friends. So I'll help you out."

"That's great. When do you want to meet–"

"We won't meet," he said, "at least not yet. I'm a wolf who spends most of his free time hanging around hunters to find out their deepest, darkest secrets. Agreeing to work with you doesn't mean I trust you enough to set up a meeting."

Ari grunted. "I guess that makes sense. I'm not terribly interested in his past unless it directly affects what he's doing now."

"Define now."

"The past year or so."

There was a pause. She assumed he was making a note. "Understood. I was led to believe that you think he's involved with this *canidae* exposed video that's making the rounds on social media."

"Yeah," Ari said.

"Is your involvement common knowledge or should it be treated as confidential information?"

She hadn't considered that. "Well. I'm a *private* investigator, so I guess~"

"Noted." Pause. "Anything else?"

"Yeah. Do you keep an ear out for general *canidae* information as well as specific targets?"

"Of course. You never know what piece of knowledge could become vital."

"Right," Ari said. "In the past two days, I've encountered two hunters and a man who might as well be one. I didn't pick up the scent of any of them."

One more pause, this one longer than either of the others. "They didn't smell like hunters, or...?"

"They didn't smell like anything," Ari said. "They all snuck up on me because I didn't realize there was anyone around. It was like they'd blocked their scents somehow."

"Interesting," he said. "I'll see what other wolves are reporting. Although it is hard to ask someone to recall an absence of something, to know when a thing has not been seen requires more attention than most people are willing to be pay."

Ari wondered if he was high. "Okay," she said. "Well... stay in touch, and let us know what you find. The clock is ticking." She listened for a response. "Conrad? Mr. Rigas...?" She looked at the phone to see the call had disconnected. "I guess you'll be in touch."

"The clock is ticking louder than you know."

Dale turned her monitor so Ari could see the screen. It showed a column of tweets, all of which either had a link or screenshot of the video along with hashtags about werewolves next to a string of content warnings.

"You said people were ignoring it."

"They were. But I guess someone with a blue checkmark and a million followers must have found it and started spreading the word."

"So what does that mean?"

"I think it means Marin Cardoso is about to go viral."

CHAPTER TEN

THE VIDEO still hadn't made it to any mainstream news sites, but it was spreading like wildfire across every social media platform. The people who thought it was clickbait viral marketing were growing quieter, giving way to discussions about how sickening it was to use images of a woman being tortured to sell a movie. Some were starting to worry that it wasn't a prank, although no one seemed quite ready to believe it was real. It was only a matter of time before the police got involved, which was a double-edged sword. More people looking for Marin, Val, and Gwen could only be a good thing. But if Marin's imprisonment was proven to be authentic, people might start looking at the "werewolves are real" part of the equation.

The worst part was that they were essentially helpless against it. The site was up, and it was spreading around from tweets to Facebook posts to blogs, and she didn't think it was humanly possible to stop something once it had that kind of momentum. The only thing they could do was hope something big, flashy, and controversial took over the news cycle before Marin gave in and transformed. The internet had a very short memory and, without the spectacle of someone literally becoming a wolf in front of them, the video would easily be forgotten by the masses while the police would keep looking. The best of both worlds.

Ari spent the rest of the afternoon trying to nap in anticipation of her plans for the night. She hated that she'd misled Eva, even if it was well-intentioned and her plan wouldn't have worked if she was upfront about what she was trying to do. The poor girl was worried about her sister and Ari couldn't help but feel like she was manipulating Eva's grief. But if a little manipulation was what it took to get Marin back...

It was almost dark when she woke up. She had dinner with Dale, who had spent the past few hours creating new accounts so she could spread the word that the "werewolf rumor" was very clearly fake. She pointed out tiny details in the video - "Look at that break, they obviously cut something" and "oh please, it's on a LOOP!" - and retweeted herself enough times that strangers started picking up on it.

"I'm glad it's working," Ari said, "even though it's also depressing and terrifying that people can be manipulated like that."

"Yeah," Dale said. "I feel a little like an evil genius."

"So..." Ari poked at the bowl of chicken and rice Dale had made for her. "Are you, um... are you ready for... for tomorrow...?"

Dale reached across the table and put her hand on top of Ari's. "We can push it back if you want. See if there's another angle."

Ari shook her head. "Sending you in is a good plan. And time is crunching on us, so waiting would just leave them in danger for no reason. But I feel like all I'm doing is sending one more person I love into the fire while I sit back and chase my tail."

"It's a great tail," Dale said with a smile.

Ari smiled back at her. "You have to do something you don't like tomorrow, I have to do something that makes me feel dirty tonight. We're really coming out of this smelling like roses."

"Well, lie down with dogs, you're going to get fleas." Her eyes widened. "Oh, god."

Ari laughed. "Hey..."

"I'm so sorry."

"It's a common saying," Ari said.

Dale was blushing bright red. Her eyes were shining with tears. "This is like what I did when I started reading that fucking book."

Ari got up and came around the table, crouching next to her chair. "Babe, look at me. I remember when you used slurs against me. I remember it *very* well. Because they weren't just words, there was a tone and a venom behind them that I felt deep inside. People slip up. It happens."

"I'm still sorry."

Ari leaned in and kissed Dale's cheeks. "I forgive you. And I love you."

"I love you, too." She kissed Ari's lips. "Go on. They might leave early."

"Yeah," Ari said. "See you by morning."

"Be safe, puppy."

Ari promised by kissing two fingers and touching them to her heart as she went to the door. She undressed and slipped outside into the ditch of their stairwell, just low enough that her head was almost even with the grass. She put her hands on the steps and arched her back. She felt the bones along her back popping like a symphony, her shoulder blades sliding apart, her hips reforming. She watched as her fingers curled and the skin thickened from her elbow to wrist before sprouting dark brown fur. It felt like standing up to stretch after being seated for hours, only the blissful feeling was magnified by a million. The pain she'd once felt was not just manageable now, it was all but an afterthought. A vague memory of soreness and ache that was easily forgotten.

Ari trotted up the stairs before she shook out her fur. Her wolf brain wanted to run wild, to explore, to race and get into mischief, but she reminded herself that this was a work night. She huffed, hating how she gave herself Responsibilities while in human form. But it was Important, so she would do it and be rewarded with a free night later on.

She thought about Eva and her pack, the scents she'd picked up at the Cardoso house without even realizing she was doing it. She headed out, north, toward the lake. The lake, with all its wonderful smells, the highway! Oil and gas and exhaust, smelling like burning poison but also kind of good. Mixture of dirt and metal, perfect, her favorite, and she ran faster to get there so she could enjoy it before the Work started.

The cars were still parked in front of the house when she arrived. She sniffed the stoop and walkway that led around to the condo, but she didn't think anyone had passed by in the past few hours. Good good good, she was on time, not too late. She went to the end of the block and scoured around until she found a good place to settle out of sight. Her Job was Harder the unusual tonight, hiding from other wolves, following other wolves, without them noticing her or picking up her scent. She'd have to be Sneaky and

Very Focused.

Earlier she had planted the seed in Eva's mind: let the wolves out, let them process what was happening to Marin. She knew wolf brains, she knew they would take that Huge Grief and Sadness and try to make it useful. She knew that Eva and the rest of her pack were too distraught and stressed out to be in full control once they transformed. Ari hated taking advantage of that, but it was for the greater good. If the wolves came out, there was every chance they would be drawn to their missing member.

She was staring at a squirrel when she saw a shadow move near the condo. Ari lifted her head and watched as first one wolf slipped out onto the sidewalk, looked around, then darted across the street. She was followed by a second, then a third, fourth, fifth. Ari tried to remember how many wolves were in Eva and Marin's pack. She had a hard time remembering numbers. The wolves moved furtively down the street. Ari let them get a lead and then followed.

They went to the lake, Ari loved the lake, she loved the smells and the animals and the sound of the water, even though she stayed well away from the water. She'd been dunked in the water too many times and didn't want that to happen again, no, on purpose or on accident, she didn't want the risk. Eva's pack was also cautious. They stayed as close to the water as possible, using foliage to conceal them when possible and hiding in the dark silhouettes of buildings the rest of the time. Ari found it difficult to see them sometimes even when she knew they were there.

This pack is good, she thought. *Clever, sneaky, quick.*

When they reached Fairview, they used the walkway to avoid being seen by traffic. Ari hated it. Too exposed to follow them, but too dangerous to follow from above, and it was too close to the water. She gave them more of a lead, let them get almost all the way across the walkway before she went out onto it. She stayed low, her belly scraping the surface, ears flat, heart pounding, but she made it across safely.

Soon they turned south, sometimes cutting east or west to avoid traffic but always returning to a southern bearing. Ari was starting to worry she'd set this whole pursuit up just to be led back to the remains of the viaduct, which would take her right back to square one. But at least then she would know for a fact that Roemer and his people were stationed in that area. Lots of empty buildings due to the construction, lots of places for the hunters to set up their little house of horrors.

Because she was over a block behind Eva's pack, the men who slipped out of a black van to follow them didn't see her. Ari's ears pricked up as the men spread out, one near the side of the building with the other walking along the curb. The one by the building pulled something out of his pocket that Ari couldn't see, but she didn't need to see anything else to know they were a threat.

She sped up and aimed herself at the men like a bullet. A growl brewed in her chest, building and rattling against her ribs until she was right behind them. The man next to the building raised his arm, and Ari let out a mighty bark-howl that echoed up and down the street as she threw herself hard into the attacking man. He collapsed hard against the pavement, crying out in pain as his elbow bounced off the pavement in a way that couldn't have been healthy.

A member of Eva's pack launched himself at the other man, who was already retreating back to the car. The man Ari had tackled got onto his feet, cradling his arm to his stomach. It was twisted at a very unnatural, clearly painful angle. He jabbed out his other arm at the wolf who had jumped into the fray, and its body convulsed with electricity discharged from the sparking tip.

Fortunately the man with the taser was only interested in escape. He ran, and Ari pursued. She saw a wolf watching her and recognized it was Eva. They watched each other for only half a second, but it was more than enough for a full conversation to pass between their wolves. Eva dipped her head, yipped to the rest of her pack, and darted across the street. The other wolves followed.

The van peeled its tires as it pulled away from the curb. Ari let it pass and then gave chase. The world narrowed down to the back of the van, its lights and empty license plate holder, the dents and dings that would identify it from a million other vans if she happened to lose track of it. Everything on either side of the street became a blur. The other cars on the street were just ghostly shapes of light and noise. She heard honking horns and tires screeching, either in response to her or the fleeing van, but they were non-entities to her.

At the next red light the van screeched to a halt. The driver, who was still uninjured, leapt out and charged her. Ari braced for his attack, head down, teeth bared. *Don't bite, don't bite, don't bite.* She recognized him now. He was one of the men who had attacked her the morning after the hospital. He was carrying a shock stick like his partner, and he waved the tip of it in her face.

"I think I know you," he said. "I think you're the same bitch we saw by the viaduct, huh? You want to see your friend? We can take you to her, no problem..."

The offer was tempting. She would at least have confirmation about Gwen, Val, and Marin. But getting herself captured was a horrible plan. When he got close enough, she ducked under the stick and snapped at his leg. She timed her lunge perfectly so that her teeth plucked the fabric without getting close to the skin, but it was enough to make him back off. Even that close, she couldn't smell him at all. Not even a hint of cologne or shampoo.

"Should've just thrown the van in reverse and smeared you all over the damn road. Fucking mutt."

Sirens filled the air and both Ari and the thug turned toward the sound. Being rounded up by animal control was only slightly more appealing than being taken prisoner, and the goon didn't seem interested in explaining what he was doing or how his friend had been hurt. He glared at Ari and retreated back to the van, climbing behind the wheel, slamming the door. Ari, wary of his threat, ran to the sidewalk just in case he decided to make good on it.

She watched him go and then looked around to see where they'd ended up. She wasn't far from Denny Park, so that's where she went at a more leisurely trot.

Eva and the rest of her pack were waiting for her there, in one of the more tree-obscured areas. Eva was the only one in human form, arms crossed over her chest in a half-hearted attempt at modesty. The rest of the pack gathered around her in a protective circle, every eye locked on Ari as she joined them and changed into her human form.

"What just happened?" Eva asked.

Ari sighed. "I'm sorry. I used you because I thought your pack might be drawn to wherever Marin is being held. I should have told you, or asked you for permission to follow you, but I honestly thought it might not work if you tried to force it."

Eva tightened her jaw and looked away. Ari gave her all the time she needed.

"We probably would have gone out tonight no matter what you said to me," Eva finally said. "And if you hadn't been following us, those jerks might have actually gotten the drop on us. So rather than accept your apology, I extend our thanks." She furrowed her brow and shook her head. "Even after we knew they were there, we couldn't smell them."

"Yeah, I've noticed that. I'm looking into it."

Eva pressed her lips together and nodded. "Did you learn anything, at least?"

"Confirmed, more than learned," Ari said. "I think I have a general idea where they're located. You were heading there, and the goons went in the same direction when they drove off. So I'm going to assume that Marin's being held somewhere down by the waterfront. That's where I'm going to focus my search."

"Keep us updated, please?"

Ari nodded. "Again, sorry for the manipulation."

"If it leads you to my sister, manipulate me any way you want."

Ari cleared her throat. It was an odd thing to hear while standing naked in a public park, but she chose not to be embarrassed by it.

Eva transformed first, and the rest of her pack filed out of the clearing. Eva was the last to go, looking over her shoulder at Ari. She gave a nod, and Ari saluted back. A moment later, Eva and the pack were gone, lost in the darkness.

Ari stretched her arms out to either side, then worked her shoulders. It was still early, and she was pretty wide awake after the fight and her nap earlier. She could let the wolf get a bit of running-around time down by the water, and it could double as reconnaissance. She might not be able to smell the hunters, but her mother, Milo, Val, Marin, they would all leave some kind of trace that she might be able to pick up if she was in the general vicinity.

She crouched and put her hands flat on the ground. She slipped back into the wolf, thanking it for letting her work for a little while.

Now she was going to let it play for a few hours.

***

Dale reached for the phone before she realized the sound that woke her up was the front door opening. She rolled onto her back and watched as Ari slipped into the bedroom, still naked, shoulders hunched as she tiptoed like a cartoon character trying to sneak past a prison guard. The moonlight caught her outline, shining off the sweat that coated her like a second skin. She didn't look at the bed as she crept by, closing the bathroom door before she turned on the light. A few seconds later, Dale heard the squeak of the faucet and the powerful spray of the shower.

She pushed back the blankets, checked the time, and undressed as she crossed to the bathroom. She could see Ari's outline through the curtain and smiled, biting her lip. It was her turn to creep as she crossed the cold tile and eased the curtain back.

Ari was already looking at her, hair plastered to her skull. "At least I can still smell *you*."

"Again, that's not quite the compliment you think it is." Dale got into the shower and pulled the curtain shut behind her. "Although I do take it in the spirit you intended. Turn around."

Ari faced the wall. Dale retrieved the soap and the loofah that Ari insisted on calling the "shower flower" and began to wash her shoulders. Ari put one hand on the wall and explained what had happened during her run. After the encounter with the goons, she'd spent another few hours letting the wolf run around the area between Pioneer Square and the stadium.

"I even sniffed around a few of the homeless encampments in the area, but I didn't pick up anything. I might head back down there when I can actually talk to people. See if they've noticed any suspicious activity. Abandoned buildings that are suddenly occupied again, you know, that sort of thing."

"Detective shit," Dale said.

"Detective shit," Ari confirmed. She rubbed Dale's arms. "Turn around. I'll do your back."

Dale did as she was told. Ari stepped closer and ran the shower flower down the curve of her shoulder, back up to her neck, and then slowly dragged it down her spine. Her other arm went around Dale's waist and pulled her closer. Ari's hand pressed flat against Dale's stomach and she gently stroked with her fingertips. Dale chuckled and arched an eyebrow.

"Is this sharing a shower, or is the wolf feeling a little frisky? Not that I'm complaining, but if you~"

Ari pressed her lips against Dale's ear and started to whisper.

Dale's smile slowly faded as she listened. Soon it was a frown, and she twisted her head to see Ari's face. Ari returned the stare. Dale started to ask a question, but Ari shushed her. She repositioned her head so her lips were against Dale's ear again. More whispering. Dale's frown deepened. She put her hands on top of Ari's and stared at the far wall of the shower.

"Okay?" Ari asked. "Can you do that?"

Dale's jaw was tight.

"Dale."

"Yeah," Dale said, "okay."

Ari stroked Dale's hair. "Are you ready?"

Dale nods. She will be. She has to be.
For Gwen. For Val. For Marin. She'll be ready.
No matter how much it will hurt.

Chapter Eleven

Dale tried to dress like it was any other day, even though her mind was swimming with the details of what had to be done. Ari had already left, out the door while her hair was still wet so she could go check on Milo before she found Diana to ask about sightings of the hunters' black van. Dale appreciated having the time to prepare for what she had to do. But if the plan worked, there were good odds that she might not see Ari for a while.

She finally chose a concert tee under an unbuttoned shirt and jeans. It wasn't the sort of thing that she would wear to work, but it felt appropriate for the task ahead. She took a look around the apartment, trying to believe she would be back there soon, but memorizing everything just in case something went wrong. Finally, unable to delay any further, she braced herself and left.

The address of Donald Keech's office hadn't inspired confidence and, when she arrived, she discovered that it shared a parking lot with a liquor store and a cigarette shop, both of which had bars on their windows. She parked next to a station wagon with the entire back end crammed full of plastic bags, clothes, and various trash. Its entire backend was covered with stickers for conservative political campaigns going back thirty years.

The front windows of the shop looked like they hadn't been

washed in Dale's lifetime. A bell over the door chimed when she opened it. The waiting room was poorly-lit and smelled like mold, cheap carpeting, and cigarette smoke, all of which was joined together by a flowery fug of room freshener. She wrinkled her nose and tried to imagine a *canidae* trying to come into this place. Maybe that was the point of the stench. Posters with cliché law advice were sloppily framed on the walls: KNOW YOUR RIGHTS!, THE LAW IS HERE TO HELP YOU, and DEFENDANT'S BILL OF RIGHTS.

"Be with you in a second!" someone called from the back office.

Dale stepped around the counter where a receptionist would have been seated in a more reputable establishment. The desktop was stacked tall with towers of files and loose paperwork that indicated no one had assumed that station in years. She continued back through a door marked PRIVATE and found herself in a store room with a desk crammed in among the filing cabinets. Donald Keech, looking far worse than his internet photos, jerked upright and blinked in surprise at her.

"You can't be in here, go!"

Dale examined one of the chairs in front of his desk and, deciding she could just throw out her jeans later, dropped down into it. She crossed one leg over the other and folded her hands in her lap.

"I want to speak with Isaac Hayden."

Keech blinked at her. "You can't be in here," he enunciated this time. "Go!"

"You want to call the police?" Dale asked, summoning every ounce of calm coolness she'd picked up from Ari over the years. "Bring them in here, give them a chance to look around? Because I'm pretty sure they could find a few interesting things laying out in the open. So I think you'd be more likely to call an unofficial security team. And to do that, you'd have to go through Isaac Hayden. Which, coincidentally, is exactly who I want to see anyway. So..." She held out her hands. "I don't see what the problem is."

Keech pressed his lips together like he was working a straw. It was an extraordinarily unappealing look for someone who was already on the very low end of the appealing scale. Dale had to fight the urge to look away and held his gaze.

Finally he reached for the phone and started dialing with one stumpy finger.

"Tell him it's Dale Frye," she said. "He'll know who I am."

Keech glared at her as he put the receiver to his ear. The phone seemed to ring for a long time before there was an answer.

"Hayden. I... no, look, I know." He wrinkled his nose and drummed the fingers of his free hand on the desk. Dale could hear the quiet buzz of Hayden's voice on the other end. "Hayden!" Keech finally snapped. "Listen to me. There's someone here who wants to talk to you." Keech looked at her. "Dale Frye. Yeah. I know. Yeah, she doesn't look like she's planning to leave. Right."

He hung up and leaned back in his chair.

"We know who you are," he said.

Dale widened her eyes. "Uh-oh. I'm in trouble, then. And all that trouble I went through putting together this cunning disguise."

"Hayden will be here in twenty minutes."

She checked her watch, nodded, and settled in to wait.

Keech stared at her for another minute and then sighed heavily and shoved himself up. "Would you like something to drink?" he said with false hospitality.

"Oh, sure," Dale said, chuckling under her breath. "Like there's any chance I would drink something a hunter's lawyer made for me." She looked around the office and curled her lip. "Actually, I wouldn't drink anything that came from this office even if you weren't related to the hunters. God knows what kind of diseases are brewing here."

Keech shifted his weight around the corner of the desk and went past her into the front room again. Dale waited until she heard him at the coffee station before she let out a long, slow breath and relaxed her spine. She didn't know how Ari pulled off this sort of thing on a daily basis. She seemed to have no fear, no trepidation. Maybe the wolf helped her hide the nerves.

She spent the time waiting for Hayden examining Keech's office. Diplomas were hung next to photos of Keech with famous clients, or maybe they were just hunters who kept him on retainer. Either way, Dale took note of their faces for any she recognized, or in case any of them showed up.

It only took twelve minutes before Hayden arrived. "Where?" he asked Keech, who had remained in the waiting room. Keech mumbled something and Dale heard Hayden's heavy footsteps on the carpet. She twisted to look up at him with a wide, friendly smile.

"Hello again, Mr. Hayden. You're looking well."

He narrowed his eyes at her. "Miss Frye. I must admit to being surprised to find you here."

"Really?" She stood up to face him. "You haven't been watching me and Ariadne since you got back to town?"

Hayden tilted his head to the side. "Know thy enemy, right?"

Dale laughed. "Right. Well, I'm here because I know more than enough about Ariadne Willow and those m-mutts." She wrinkled her nose and shook her head.

"I thought you made your decision on the plane."

"Why, because I didn't murder someone in cold blood? I'm not a monster. No book could make me that kind of psychopath. I went with Ari because it seemed like the easiest course of action. It was very clear by that point she wasn't going to give up, so I surrendered. I thought maybe I could learn to love her, or at least tolerate her, but now that I know the hunters are making a comeback..." She shrugged. "Maybe that's where I belong."

"As much as I would love to believe you, Miss Frye, there's—"

"Ari told me to come here."

He blinked in surprise.

"I'm supposed to pretend the essays still have a hold on me so I can operate as a mole in your group. Maybe lead her to Gwen and Milo, help her save the day. I'm offering to give her to you on a silver platter. Your friends get a new prisoner, you get an annoying bitch out of your hair, and I finally get away from her."

She took off her bracelet and tossed it into the overstuffed trash bin next to Keech's desk without hesitation.

"If your offer is still good, I'm ready to be done with Ariadne Willow once and for all."

A cot had appeared in Marin's room overnight. There was a privacy screen in one corner, blocking off a bedside commode that looked like a spider with a toilet seat on its back. Marin had been removed from the chains and was sitting up on the cot, back against the wall, dressed in what appeared to be cleaner clothes than what Val currently had on. The renovation was the second bit of good news Val had gotten since waking up. The other news was that sometime overnight, Goon Two and the Geek had gone out 'wolf hunting.' They came back without any new prisoners, and the Geek's arm was in a pretty serious looking cast. She'd asked if he needed a professional to look it over and was given a string of extremely inventive curse words in response. No one seemed willing to explain what had happened, but Val could guess a certain private investigator had a hand in it.

Marin looked up when Val came into the cell, offering a weak smile when she saw who it was. "I hear I have you to thank for the upgrade to the Presidential Suite," she said.

Val said, "They better not have forgotten the mint on your pillow. I was very firm on that."

Marin didn't laugh, but she did breathe out through her nose. Val assumed that was as much as she could hope for in the current situation. She sat on the edge of the cot and noted that Marin's left wrist was shackled to a pipe running along the wall.

"Any physical complaints?" Val asked. "They kept you in that crucifix position for a really long time. Your arms and shoulders must be killing you."

"No, it's good. It's a distraction. I like having something to focus on." She rested her head against the wall. "Can I ask you a question?"

Val glanced toward the camera. She opened the medical bag she'd brought in with her, prepared to administer some aspirin at the very least. "Sure."

Marin wet her lips. "This would all end if you killed me. Right?"

Val's hands went still.

"They want a spectacle. Let's give them one. Snuff film. You can probably figure out a way to do it slow, poison me or something, so you're not in the room when it happens. I'm being self-destructive, I don't want you to go to prison. You've been kind to me, and I think~"

"I think you're panicking," Val interrupted. "No one is going to kill anyone. Just take a few deep breaths. Try to remain calm. Right now all you have to focus on is not transforming."

Marin closed her eyes. "Yeah, try not to think of an elephant."

"I know." Val rested her hand on top of Marin's. "I'm going to keep doing everything I can do ensure they treat you humanely. I've already managed to get you a toilet and a bed. Who knows what's next? Maybe a TV. A laptop."

"I'd settle for a yoyo."

Val smiled. "I'll see what I can do. This isn't just about making you comfortable, although that would definitely be enough. The more they do for you, the more likely they are to see you as a real person instead of just some tool they want to use for their endgame. We might be able to turn some of these hunters around."

"You really think they can be reasoned with?"

Val shrugged. "I could've been like them, until I came to my senses. People can change."

"Well, hopefully they can change in a matter of weeks, or else I'm going to be the one changing." She looked at the camera. "Followed by the rest of the world, I guess."

"We're going to figure it out. There are people outside who are working to help us."

Marin sighed. "I kind of hope my pack is hunkered down and hiding. I don't want them getting anywhere near these bastards." She held out her uncuffed hand, and Val took it. "I'm glad you're here, though. No offense. I mean, don't stay on my account..."

Val laughed and squeezed Marin's fingers. "It's nice to be appreciated. I'll be back as soon as I can with something to eat."

"Okay."

Val got up to leave. At the door, she turned and looked back. "There's a wolf named Ariadne Willow. I met her when she was in an impossible situation like this. She got out. I know she's working on getting you home."

"How can you be so sure?"

"Because she cares about *canidae*. And if this video has gone out online, she knows about it, and she won't be able to ignore it."

Marin raised an eyebrow. "Sounds like a good person to have on my side. But will she fight for me? She doesn't even know me."

"No. But the other prisoner here is Ari's mother." Val winked. "Sit tight. Hold out as long as you can. Ariadne is coming. We just need to give her time."

Marin said, "Okay. If you vouch for her, I'll take your word for it. Oh, and Val?"

"Mm?"

"I can't do a yoyo. If you really do ask them for something, I'd take a deck of cards."

Val smiled and winked. "I'll see what I can find."

Dale went into the bathroom to wash her hands before they left Keech's office. Hayden looked around with a sneer that said he didn't blame her, so she was fairly confident he didn't suspect anything as she slipped into the small en suite next to the office. The pipes roughly rattled the whole sink when she twisted the taps, letting the water spray into the basin as she dropped to her knees next to the toilet and threw up with as little noise as possible.

She didn't think simply saying words could provoke nausea, but her stomach had twisted from the bullshit she'd spewed a few minutes ago. Throwing up became an urgent need when she took off her precious bracelet and threw it in the garbage. It didn't seem to matter that it was a decoy, fashioned earlier that morning, and that the real bracelet that Ari had presented to her all those years ago was safely tucked in her jewelry box at home. Just the ceremony of removing it and discarding it was enough to make her physically ill.

She went back to the sink and splashed some water on her face before turning off the tap. Ari had changed the plan that morning in the shower, whispering in Dale's ear. "*We don't know how long Hayden has been watching us. We don't know how much he's seen or heard. Act like you're going through with the plan, but then turn on me.*" Dale still couldn't believe she'd gone through with it, couldn't believe she'd done it well enough to convince the bastard she was still under the influence of the essays.

There'd been doubts in her mind. She'd stayed awake some nights wondering if it was just dormant, waiting for something to trigger that vileness again. But she could say, definitively, she didn't have anything to worry about. She cupped her hand under the water and brought it to her mouth, slurping it up and rinsing before spitting into the sink.

"Everything all right in there?" Hayden said from just outside the door.

"God, give a girl a minute," she snapped. She turned off the faucet and stepped out. "I'm turning my back on the past decade of my life. My job, my girlfriend, my home. Forgive me for taking a second to process the enormity of that, okay?"

"Of course, Miss Frye. My apologies."

Hayden gestured for her to lead the way out of the office. Keech was sitting where a receptionist would have been stationed, and he glared at her as she walked by. She winked at him, forcing him to look away. Once they were outside, Hayden put on a pair of sunglasses.

"You can come with me or follow in your own car. I don't mind taking you, but leaving your car unattended in this neighborhood for an extended period of time is... not advisable."

"Where exactly are we going?" Dale said.

"Well, obviously I'm not taking you to Miss Willow's mother. I don't trust you quite that much yet. But there's someone I'd like you to meet. I think you can help him see the light."

Dale was irritated but unsurprised. Hayden would have to be an idiot to take her to the prisoners so early, but she'd kind of hoped against hope he would do it anyway. They stopped next to his car.

"I like meeting new people. Who is he?"

"He's the man I was taking you to meet last time, when our departure was so rudely interrupted. His name is Gabriel Roemer, and I'm really hoping you can convince him not to commit genocide against the *canidae*."

Dale swallowed a lump in her throat. "No pressure."

"I told Ariadne that my goal isn't death. It's understanding. I'm hindered by the fact that the foremost authority on their species is also the group that's spent most of the past thousand years trying to kill them."

"Ari said you threatened to kill her."

"I was frustrated," Hayden said, a look of frustration on his face. "I want this to be a true partnership, Dale. And who knows, maybe there's a way you and Ariadne can still work together when all this is over."

Ari and I will be together long after you're gone, you putz, she thought. Out loud, she shook her head. "I tried. That ship has sailed."

"The book is really that manipulative?"

Dale said, "Look at the world we're living in. We have people willing to go full insurrectionist to support a failed reality show host because of something they read on Facebook. I don't know if the book has special powers or if it's just an example of very, very manipulative writing. Either way, I know I'm not the woman I was before I read it. I tried to be her again. I really did. But if I don't put some distance between me and Ariadne, I worry about what I'll do to her. And I definitely don't want to be that person. So come on." She gestured at the cars. "Lead the way."

Hayden nodded and got into his car. Dale got into hers, waiting for him to back out of the spot. When they were on the road, she took out her phone without looking down and dialed Ari's number without looking at the phone. She switched it to speaker.

Ari answered on the second ring. "Hey," she whispered. "Everything okay?"

"I love you, puppy."

"I love you, too," Ari said. "Are you okay?"

Dale blinked back her tears and breathed in deep. She let it out through her lips, then spoke without moving her mouth in case Hayden was watching in the mirror.

"I knew this would be hard," she mumbled, "but some of the things I have to say really fucking hurt. And taking off the bracelet..."

"I know."

"You're *positive* the real one is safe...?"

Ari said, "Cross my heart."

"Are you still at home? Can you please go look and make sure it's the real one?"

Ari chuckled. "It's not in the jewelry box. After you left, I took it out."

"Why?" It was suddenly hard to see the road until she wiped at her eyes.

"It felt wrong to leave it at home. It's been in my pocket all morning."

It felt like a rubber band around her chest had suddenly snapped. She took a deep, full breath and flexed her fingers on the steering wheel, suddenly revitalized.

"Smart puppy."

"I have my moments. I'll wait for a full update when you can speak freely."

"Okay," Dale said. "Hey, before you go..."

"Yeah?"

"Who am I?"

Ari was silent for a moment. "You..."

"*What* am I," Dale clarified.

Ari chuckled. "You're my wife, Dale."

"And you're mine. Be safe, puppy."

"Be strong, babe."

"Easier now," Dale said. "Love you."

"Love you."

Dale hung up and moved the phone to the passenger seat. Just a few days, with any luck. She could manage this for just a few days if it meant saving the lives of three women. She braced herself and focused on the back of Hayden's truck, preparing herself for her next performance.

CHAPTER TWELVE

ARI HAD a hand in her pocket to finger Dale's bracelet, only stopping herself when she realized touching it too much might cause the threaded hair to fray. She was sitting at Diana's desk, flipping through photos of mug shots, men who matched the description she gave of the hunters she'd encountered. She could barely focus on each photo since talking to Dale on the phone. Diana had gone to get coffee and finally came back, two cups in one hand and a file tucked under her other arm. She placed one cup in front of Ari as she sat down in the visitor chair even though it was her office.

"Anything?" Diana asked, hopeful.

Ari shook her head, eyes narrowed with frustration. "That's the downside of playing detective as the wolf. Sometimes I can recall everything with crystal clarity. Sometimes trying to remember a person's face is like... well, like most people trying to remember a dog's face."

Diana nodded. "I got a call back about the black van you described. It was involved in a fender-bender outside the Safeway on Madison." She tossed the file onto the desk. "Driver was named Earl Foster. Does he look like someone you know?"

Ari opened the file and looked at the DMV photo. "That's

him. That's the guy who broke his arm when he fell."

"Hey! Progress," Diana said. "We might be able to learn more of their names from this. Known associates, see when he arrived in Seattle and how. Pieces of the puzzle."

"I'd settle for just finding the box and seeing the whole picture at once. I don't have time to gather all these little pieces. Not this time." She rested her elbows on the desk and pushed her hands into her hair. "How are they masking their scent? When I'm the wolf, it should be impossible for them to cover up. And if they tried, I would smell *that*. I would smell whatever was covering them up. But it's a void. It's nothing. Eva and her pack couldn't smell anything, either. So I know it's not just that I'm getting a cold. But how the hell are they doing this?"

"You told me Roemer is from a line of hunters who have been doing this a long-ass time. Even if they haven't been actively fighting a war, they've probably been developing new weapons. Hell, that book of essays was written at a time when humans and *canidae* were technically in the middle of a truce, right? Apparently, they found a trick they've been keeping up their sleeve for the right time."

Ari grunted her agreement. Her phone rang and she quickly took it from her pocket, expecting Dale even though she highly doubted she would call again so soon. She saw it was an unknown number and answered it.

"Mr. Rigas?"

"Come outside. I need to talk to you."

"How do you know~" She heard the click of the line disconnecting. "Okay. I don't think I like that guy."

"What guy?" Diana asked, then held up a hand. "Forget I asked."

"Probably a good call." Ari stood up and let Diana have her chair back. "I guess I need to go outside and find him."

Diana said, "I'll look into the fine Mr. Foster and see if he has any known associates."

Ari paused in the doorway. "You have other active cases, right?"

Diana was already typing. "None with a girl being held prisoner live on the internet, no."

"Fair enough," Ari said. "Dale and I owe you and Lucy dinner when all this is over."

"You already owe us that for not inviting us to your wedding," Diana said, the corner of her lips curling into a smile.

"Congratulations, by the way."

Ari grinned and left the office. She wasn't sure which exit to use, but assumed Conrad Rigas had that covered.

She stepped out of the precinct and scanned the street even though she had no idea what the man looked like. She reached the sidewalk and stopped, scanning faces and subtly scenting the air to see if she could pick up a *canidae* scent. There *was* something, subtle and completely drenched in some kind of cheap cologne, but unmistakably wolf. She followed it around the corner, where she found Rigas leaning against a utility pole that was covered with peeling and faded flyers.

Conrad Rigas was surprisingly young, bald, broad-shouldered, and built like a football player. He wore baggy clothes that made him look bigger than he was, and he lazily raised an eyebrow as Ari approached him.

"Well, we can confirm your sniffer isn't broken," he said. "But I haven't heard anything about hunters being able to mask their scents. I'll keep digging."

"I appreciate that." She offered her hand. "I'm Ariadne Willow."

"I know," he said, pushing away from the pole. "Simon Lehner. Does the name sound familiar to you at all?"

Ari searched her memory. "No. Should it?"

"*Canidae* from the eighteen hundreds. Around the time Roemer's family got into the hunting business. He wanted to kill as many humans as he could, and he decided the Napoleonic Wars would be a good cover for widespread death and disappearances."

"Damn," Ari said. "What was the end goal? Eradicating all humans?"

Rigas shrugged. "He seemed to want a *canidae*-only territory. There was already a small village called Wolfsbau, but he wanted more. Think West Berlin. Hell, think Hitler annexing Poland."

"What stopped him? Wait." She closed her eyes and touched her forehead. "Wait. Simon Lehner? Agatha Westreich and Johanna Brion. The wolf and the huntress who joined forces to stop a *canidae* army from slaughtering humans. That story again?"

Rigas nodded. "The very same. Lehner had a book of his own, like the Magnusson essays but for wolves. The Book of Simon. 'We do as we must, we do as they do, we do what is needed to survive.'" He rolled his eyes and shrugged. "Got a lot of *canidae* to join his cause. Could have gone very badly if there wasn't that alliance."

"My mother tried to recreate that alliance the last time the hunters threatened to have a wolf manoth. It wouldn't have worked. The hunters would have agreed to a council just to slaughter anyone who showed up."

"Roemer obviously isn't looking for any kind of treaty," Rigas said. "Simon's book could be the secret weapon we're looking for. Fire with fire."

Ari frowned. "Wait, you want to find Simon's book?"

"The hunters have a book that make people want to hunt wolves. We have a book of our own that makes wolves want to go out and fight back. Seems like the perfect solution to the problem."

Ari sighed. "Going to war is not going to help anything."

"We're not going to war, we're answering a call," Rigas said, growing more animated. "They started this."

"What does victory look like to you, then?" Ari asked. "Kill every human in Seattle and declare it a *canidae* safe zone? You can't honestly think that will ever happen."

Rigas said, "The alternative is having the humans wipe us all out. That's a lot more plausible, because there are so few of us, comparatively. I'd rather go out fighting."

"Do you actually have the Book of Simon?"

He stared down the street for so long that Ari started to think he wasn't going to answer. Finally he took a deep breath and shook his head.

"No. But I have leads."

"Don't use it. Please, I'm begging you. If you try to go against the hunters, they'll just use it as an excuse to be more brutal than they've already been."

"I can't make any promises. A lot of my contacts are already looking for a fight, after seeing what Roemer is doing to that poor girl. They consider it a challenge, and the longer they don't answer it, the weaker they'll feel."

Ari nodded. "I know. I just need a little time."

"Well, the clock is ticking, Miss Willow. Eventually Marin Cardoso is going to be forced to transform, and thousands of eyes are going to see it happen live on their phone. The light will be shining on us then. And no matter what the truth is, no matter what heinous lengths Roemer has gone to in order to reveal the truth, nothing will change the fact that *we* look like the monsters from the fairy tale book. Once that genie is out of the bottle, it won't be easy to put it back in."

Ari closed her eyes, suddenly feeling very, very tired.

"So?" He shifted his weight and looked down the street as if he was waiting for a ride. "You need anything else?"

Ari opened her eyes. "Yeah. You know a good copy place?"

Dale parked behind Hayden on Third Avenue and followed him to Regrade Park. Dale hated this park; it was in a terrible neighborhood, and the ground was littered with broken glass and garbage from the homeless encampment nearby. It was billed as a dog park, but the ground was a combination of cement and gravel that would wreak havoc on sensitive paws. They were almost two miles from where Ari had encountered the hunters, and where Milo had been recovered, close enough that Roemer could get there quickly but not so close it would be in spitting distance of where the women were being held.

She tried to act nonchalant as Hayden led her toward a bony man with silver hair who was seated on a bench near the back of the park. He wore a green polo shirt tucked into khakis, looking like they'd just interrupted his golf game.

"Gabriel Roemer," Hayden said, turning to gesture at Dale, "meet Dale Frye."

Roemer stood up and examined her with far more scrutiny than she was comfortable with. He finally extended a hand, smiling through a thin gray goatee.

"It's a pleasure to meet such a unique individual. Hello, Miss Frye."

Dale ignored his hand. "Mr. Hayden tells me that the two of you are at an impasse when it comes to the wolf problem."

Roemer lowered his arm. His expression soured a bit at the slight, and he struggled to keep his voice upbeat. "Yes. Isaac seems to believe we can coexist with the beasts. I assume that's why he brought you along with him, someone who has been coexisting with one of them for over a decade. Hm. Perhaps it's better that you refused to shake my hand..."

Dale immediately clocked four things in her field of vision that she could use to take the bastard's head off. She killed the impulse and swallowed her initial response.

"You can't honestly believe it's feasible to kill every wolf in Seattle, let alone the world. Even they don't know how many *canidae* there are."

"You believe it's more plausible to coexist?" Roemer asked.

"You claim this even as you're fleeing the wolf you've been living with?" He raised an eyebrow and smirked. The urge to decapitate him grew stronger. "Let's be as unbiased as possible, shall we? There is no perfect solution. Do I think exterminating the entire species is possible? Of course not. But a little population control is very overdue, and it will be proof to the others that this world was made for *humans*, not the abominations. We will show them that humanity will defend its rightful place as the dominant species and, if they try to rise up against us, they will find themselves very swiftly reminded of their rightful place."

Dale's skin crawled, and she fought the urge to scratch at her arms. He was touching on themes from the Magnusson book. She didn't think she was still vulnerable to those heinous words, but it didn't make it easier to hear the tenets preached like this.

"You said that their numbers are great, and I believe that's true. I believe their population has grown unchecked for the past few centuries, a by-product of that damnable treaty, and that is why we must act now. People will learn about the enemy hiding in their midst. And whether that results in executions or merely running them out of society, I am not in a position to guess."

Dale could feel a scream building like a physical object lodged in her throat. It wasn't enough that humans were constantly finding reasons to persecute and kill each other, the country wasn't tearing itself apart enough already, this asshole wanted to dig up an old grudge to create a new group to discriminate against? She bit back the diatribe she had planned, focusing on a spot just above Roemer's head to avoid making eye contact.

"You don't think we have enough problems as it is?"

"That's exactly the reason we have to do this. Imagine humanity united against a common threat. Wolves are literally at our door, quietly infiltrating. Once people have been made aware, they can start fighting back. They can forget about silly separations like political affiliations and loyalty to a country when they see what a true enemy looks like."

Dale knew that wasn't ever going to be the case. But she had a part to play. She ran her hands through her hair and looked around the park. Roemer was standing there ranting about uniting humanity against a common threat, and no one in the park was even looking sideways at them. She guessed it was just that kind of a neighborhood.

"People don't even believe the video is real," she said.

"They're starting to." He sounded fully confident. "The longer it goes on, the more attention it will get. And the more attention it gets, the more people will look for evidence that it's fake. They won't find it. So by the time that girl finally gives in to her primal urge and transforms, we will have millions of eyes on us and everyone will be confident it's the real thing."

"The more attention it gets," Dale said, "the more likely you'll have police scouring the city because you *kidnapped a woman* and you're holding her hostage. If they don't find you, the website is bound to be taken down."

"We have a man on our team in charge of making sure that doesn't happen. We've covered our angles, Miss Frye. We know that we're up against a clock. We don't have to buy all the time in the world. Just a few weeks." His smile grew, becoming more sinister. "By then the damage will be done, and we'll have an army standing at our backs to defend us."

Dale raised an eyebrow. "So war. Your endgame really is an all-out war between humans and wolves here in the middle of Seattle."

"Seattle will just be ground zero. It will spread, believe me. The war will be fought wherever there are wolves. Hunters and uninitiated humans alike will join together. Wolves like your friend Ariadne won't stand a chance."

Dale looked at Hayden, who had remained silent throughout the sermon. "What about you? You still claim you just want to create awareness? You know that there will be people like him no matter what happens."

Hayden worked his jaw. "We can ask for... understanding. We can push for communication~"

Dale laughed and shook her head. "I just said that humans can't get along with each other for *believing* different things. Hell, we hate people who cheer for the wrong sports team. People find out werewolves are real, it's going to be a massacre. Maybe, *maybe*, after the first wave of violence, some cooler heads will start to prevail. But a lot of wolf blood is going to be shed before that happens."

Roemer clapped Dale on the shoulder and she jumped, tensing to avoid the urge to shake off his grip. She turned and saw his grinning face way too close to hers.

"The time is coming, Miss Frye," he said. "When Marin Cardoso finally gives in and transforms, the world is never going to be the same."

Dale forced a weak and unconvincing smile.

Hope you're making progress, puppy, she thought, *because the idea of faking who I am for this asshole is seriously going to give me an ulcer.*

Milo sat cross-legged in the living room of her own home, facing a window that looked out on their backyard. She was naked, calm, her mind clear. She'd come back home in the hopes that the familiar scents would trigger the wolf to come out. *You're home now. You're safe.* So far there still hadn't been an answer despite the change of location.

She had been trying to reach the wolf all morning with no luck. She couldn't remember being rounded up by the police, going to the hospital, or Ari taking her to Dr. Snow's. She didn't even know how she'd gotten to Seattle. The gap in her memory terrified her. There were months of her life she couldn't account for. And judging from Dr. Snow and the condition she'd been in when she was found, it wasn't a very fun time.

And Gwen was still suffering.

She opened her eyes and took another long, slow breath. The wolf was there. She would know if it was gone. She'd never had to work this hard to transform, and she doubted it would happen before Gwen was safe. Still, she had to try. So she rolled her shoulders, cleared her throat, lifted her chin, and thought back to Germany.

They'd stayed in so many inns, hostels, guest rooms, and cottages during the trip that every room combined in her brain until they were just a blur of generalities: a huge bed, an armoire that was older than both of them combined, exposed stone or log walls, windows straight out of a Gothic movie set, and views that made her feel like she'd been transported back in time. Everywhere they went, they had to be careful about who they trusted. Hayden had gotten the book somehow. He'd killed the wolves who had dedicated their lives to protecting it. Every ally they met was also a potential traitor.

And one of those traitors had ended up betraying them.

No, she scolded herself. *Only the nice thoughts.*

Like lying in bed with Gwen, a woman she never would have matched herself with. And it would be a lie to say it was love at first sight. Gwen was a terrible person when they met. Singularly focused on her goal, cold, calculating, the sort of person who would manipulate her own daughter to accomplish what she wanted. The Gwen she met was cruel, but she had a stack of money she was willing to hand over to Milo, and Milo liked the idea of never again worrying about where her rent would come from.

Gwen changed when she reconciled with Ari. They fought together during wolf manoth, and Milo started to see her in a new light. She started to understand Gwen was someone who'd been thrown into a life she never asked for and tried to do the best she could. She'd never really had a life outside of fighting hunters and, when peace was reestablished, she found herself adrift.

Milo decided she was attractive enough to be worth a night or two. Gwen claimed she was straight; Milo argued she hadn't really had enough experience to say for sure what she was. So they slept together. Then they slept together again. Gwen quickly realized that she was bisexual, and Milo had to admit that she was starting to hope whatever they were doing would last longer than a night, or a weekend, or even an extended holiday.

She didn't fall in love. She certainly didn't fall in love with Americans who were old enough to be her mother. Someone who actually *was* the mother of someone she considered a friend. But wolves aged differently than humans, so the gap between them wasn't all that big of a hurdle. Ari had found it uncomfortable at first but eventually she came around. When Milo introduced Gwen to the rest of her pack, a few of them had exchanged money to pay off lost bets, but they all agreed that being with Gwen was a good thing for her.

She hoped she was good for Gwen. She hoped she hadn't done something wrong in Germany and led the hunters to them. If she was responsible for whatever was happening—

The front door to the house opened and Ari came in. "Milo?"

Milo snapped out of her trance and relaxed her shoulders. "In here." She picked up the T-shirt next to her and stood up, wriggling into it as she walked to the kitchen. Ari was facing away from her at the counter, unloading one of three plastic grocery bags.

"Hey," Ari said without turning around. "I brought you some stuff. Cereal, pasta, milk, bread. The staples."

"I appreciate that," Milo said.

Ari finally faced her, but she wasn't wearing her own face. She looked like a man with a wide jaw and small rat eyes. His eyebrows were thick and knitted together over a broken nose.

Milo recoiled and slammed into the fridge, her teeth bared and her back arched and knees bent. She saw the face in flashes of memories: on a plane with a syringe, surrounded by darkness, the lines of his features blurred by pain... no, water, she'd been held underwater and looked up to see him looming over her, his hands a drowning pressure on her shoulders, and she heard his voice *fucking mutt* as she was thrown onto the floor.

"Hey, hey, hey." Ari's face was her own again, and she had her hands on Milo's shoulders. "Shit, what a bad idea. Hey. It's okay, it's me. Milo. Milo, you can relax. It's me."

"Where'd he go?" Milo whipped her head left, then right, trying to see where Earl - *fuck*, his name was *Earl* - had gone. "Where'd he go?" she asked again. Her heart felt like a wrecking ball against the inside of her ribs. "Ari, that was one of... he was here, he was right here, he was b-behind you or something."

"I know, pup, it was Earl Foster. Diana found a file on him." She picked up the mask she'd been wearing when she came into the house. It was Foster's face blown up to life-size. "I had this made because I wanted to try tricking your brain into remembering him. I didn't think it would work that well. Damn, I'm sorry."

Milo wet her lips and clung to Ari. The tension faded from her along with the rush of adrenaline. She felt like she needed to throw up.

"No, it's good. It's good. Shock to the system." She patted Ari's cheek, then slapped her gently. "Asshole. It worked. I remembered him. He's... he was..." She put one hand on her stomach, the wave returning. "Oh, shit... back up."

Ari took a step away from her. "What's wrong? Do you need a bucket?"

"I'm... I think I'm..."

Milo cried out in pain and dropped to her knees. Pain spread down the center of her face like someone was drawing a red-hot knife down the bridge of her nose, and her voice broke with the snap of her jaw. She felt hands on her and had just enough presence of mind to lift her arms so Ari could peel the T-shirt off of her. When she dropped her arms they had become more slender, furred, and her hands hit the ground as paws. Milo stretched out her neck and arched her back, then collapsed in a heap at Ari's feet. Ari knelt next to her, stroking her flanks.

"It's okay. You're all right."

Milo trembled violently, then rolled and tried to get to her feet. She slumped against the cabinets and hung her head. A mournful howl rumbled up from her chest and came out through barely-parted lips. She turned her eyes to Ari, who returned the stare with concern.

"Milo? You in there, babe?"

She got onto her feet and went into the living room. She was aware of Ariadne following her, could feel the concern flowing off of her like a scent, but she ignored it. She sniffed around to confirm Gwyneth wasn't there and howled again, nudging Gwen's reading chair before she turned and charged up the stairs. Into the bedroom, sniffing the sheets, over to the closet. Not only was Gwen gone, her scent was fading, almost gone now, she'd been gone so long. Milo walked in a circle, confused and scared. Where Gwen? How long gone Gwen? When come back Gwen?"

Ariadne was in the bedroom doorway watching her. Milo growled at her. Ariadne held up her hands, peace, and Milo began to pace.

She had seen Gwen not long ago. Gwen in a room. Gwen unconscious. Hurt? Asleep? Bad men, warning her, threatening. They had hurt her. Hurt Gwen. Pain. So much pain. She had heard Gwen cry out in the night and beat her fists bloody against the door trying to break it down. Hurt her shoulder, worried she wouldn't be able to change until that was fixed. She remembered sedatives. The doctor, Val, the nice one, helping. Soothing the pain.

Milo threw her head back and howled. Long, mournful, painfully loud in the confines of the bedroom. Ariadne was speaking... "If you're ~ a run ~ warning so ~ change and ~ with you ~ an eye on you" or something... but Milo was more concerned about how empty the house was. Gwen was somewhere. Gwen was close but also very far away because the Bad Men were all around her. The Bad Men who had taken them away in Germany.

She realized she remembered things that had been erased from her human memory. Something had happened to erase or block those memories when she was a person, but the wolf mind held onto them. She got back down on the carpet and went to Ariadne, looking up at her with hopeful eyes. Ari crouched down and returned the stare.

"~to help you, but~"

Milo turned away and jumped back onto the bed. She stretched her forepaws out, strained, and she watched her fingers unfurl like sprouting plants. The fur receded down her arms, her bones popped and snapped and her whole body jerked with the force of it. She whimpered and cried out, the animal sounds changing to "Ah!" and "Fuck!" She had a splitting migraine, but then relief spread across the base of her skull. She felt her hair fall across her forehead and flopped onto her side, panting hard, drawing her knees up to her chest as she shivered in the sudden cold of the room. She was covered with sweat from the quick changes, and from her frantic search of the house.

Ari pulled a blanket across her body, then rested a hand on her shoulder. "Milo? Are you... yourself?"

Milo rolled onto her back and clutched the blanket to her chest.

"I remember, Ari. I remember everything."

Chapter Thirteen

MILO HAD managed to put on sweatpants and a hoodie before she finally sat up and took the glass of water Ari offered her. She barely took a breath as she drained it, exhaling sharply when she handed it back. Ari took it to the bathroom sink to refill it.

"So I guess the transformation constipation has cleared up," Ari said.

"Ugh, don't say it like that," Milo said.

"It rhymes. When it rhymes, that makes it cute. Here." She handed the glass to Milo and sat down on the edge of the bed. She watched as Milo took a more leisurely drink. "So I don't want to press you too hard... but when you say you remember *everything...*"

Milo shook her head. "I don't think I ever saw the exterior of the building where we were being held. I was either unconscious or they put this bag over our heads whenever they had to move us somewhere."

Ari grimaced. "Damn. I didn't think we'd be that lucky, but I had to ask. So what *do* you remember?"

"Faces," Milo said. "I can recognize all the assholes who were holding me hostage. Everything they did to me." Her jaw tightened. "They tortured us, Ari. They tried to draw the wolf out. They did everything but cut us open to see what our organs looked like."

"As much as I hate the man, you probably have Hayden to thank for that. He claims he doesn't want to kill us, he just wants the world to know we exist."

Milo stared at her in disbelief. "This is the same guy who *slaughtered* the wolves guarding the Magnusson essays, right? You don't really believe that shit heel, do you?"

Ari shrugged. "I'm just trying to make sense of what's happening. How about this... do you know why I can't smell the hunters?"

"Yes," Milo said. "They did a whole battery of tests on how sensitive our noses are. They tried some godawful stenches. I don't even know what everything was. But after a few weeks of experimenting, they came in and I didn't smell anything. I mean *nothing*. It was like they walked in, flipped a switch, and all the smells in the whole building turned off. I think they found some kind of cologne that masks them from us. It's the only thing that makes sense. But I can't imagine how something that powerful wouldn't smell like absolute death to a human nose."

"Whatever it is, we need to start warning other *canidae*. We still don't know what Roemer and Hayden are planning, or if their plans are even complimentary. Until we know that, we have to act like there's another wolf manoth just around the corner."

"I can help spread the word."

"Are you sure you're up for that?"

Milo gestured at the room around her. "I can't just sit around here anymore, Ari. I know I need to heal, but I'm going crazy. I have my wolf back now. She might not be perfect, but she's close enough that I can contribute."

Ari nodded. She'd been on the opposite side of this argument enough to trust Milo's word but also knew to take her assertion with a grain of salt. She'd let Milo help, but she'd keep an eye on her.

"So, help. What do you remember about the day Marin got taken?"

Milo closed her eyes. "There was a drug they used. They came into my room... they kept me, and I guess Gwen, in these rooms that used to be offices or something. Not actual cells, but they might as well have been. It was before dawn. They dragged me off the bed and pinned me to the ground. They jabbed me with something and then things went... fuzzy." She opened her eyes but looked at the floor, seeing the past instead of what was in front of her.

"Did they ever..." Ari cleared her throat. "I know it's, uh..."

"No," Milo said. "We were spared that, at least. The drug knocked me out and, when I woke up again, I was in the back of a van. We were driving. One of them... I think, um, I think he was the one who was always hanging out with..." She gestured in the general direction of the kitchen. "The guy whose face you borrowed. I'd... I had..." She put her fingers to her temples. "I can't even remember if I was the wolf or not."

"Given how they found you, I'm not surprised."

Milo nodded. "At some point I must have changed. I don't remember getting undressed in front of them. I might have become the wolf at the prison, but I don't know for sure. We got to the park and one of them took me out. He said my friend was out in the woods. Go find my friend and bring them back to the van. They said if I wasn't back in an hour, they'd take it out on Gwen." She swallowed the lump in her throat. "I'd heard her scream, Ari. I don't know... I didn't... I've never he-heard Gwen scream like that. I don't know what they could have been doing, but I..."

"It's okay, Milo," Ari said softly. "You went into the park, and you found Marin Cardoso?"

"I guess. I remember running. The drug was messing me up. And the wolf. You know how it can be. Gwen was in trouble. I had a clear line to keep her safe. All I had to do was find another wolf." Her lips curled into a sly smile. "To be totally honest, I was kind of hoping to run into you."

Ari smiled sadly. "You have no idea how much I wish I'd gone for a run that night, believe me."

"Kinda glad you were with Dale." Milo rubbed a hand over her face. "So I find Marin. Got her to follow me to the van. When she realized I was trapping her, she panicked. And I had a moment of clarity where I realized what I was doing to this poor girl and fought back. They got us into the van and headed back. On the drive, I was conscious enough to know Gwen would never forgive me if I put another wolf in danger just to save her. Hell, I wouldn't have been able to live with myself. So even with the drug making me loopy, I made one last effort to get us both free.

"Marin and I hatched a plan. We communicated, the way we do, and I told her to go for the door. When she made her move, I attacked the goons. Marin got the door open and jumped. One of the goons got his hands on the drugs and gave me a dose. A huge, drop-you-in-a-second dose. Pushed me out onto the road and went after Marin. Shit. I really thought she'd gotten away."

"The drug," Ari said. "Is that what made you so rattled?"

Milo nodded. "I guess. I still don't really remember anything about that morning. Makes sense if I was high as a kite and my brain was cracked. I don't even know how I had the presence of mind to find clothes, but thank goodness for small favors. Still, I think... yeah. I think my body and brain weren't talking to each other right. They still might not be. I only transformed because you scared the bejesus out of me. Thanks for that, by the way."

"My pleasure."

"And... thanks for getting me out of the hospital before Hayden got there. And getting me to Dr. Frost." Her eyes shimmered with tears. "Thank you, Ariadne."

Ari got up and put her arms around Milo, hugging her tightly. "We're family," she said into Milo's hair. "I'd burn down the world for you. Always."

Milo hugged her back. "I love you, Ari."

"I love you, too." She kissed the crown of Milo's head and leaned back. She brushed the hair out of Milo's face and looked into her eyes. "The building. You don't remember anything about it?"

Milo sniffled, shook her head. "Like I said, we were never taken outside unless we were masked or drugged. Inside it was just... blank. Bare drywall, concrete floors, no carpeting. Lots of windows covered by plastic. Loud, loud construction noises."

Ari said, "The viaduct demolition. You were found wandering down there. Could you have been trying to get back to Mom?"

"Maybe," Milo said.

Ari stood up and retrieved her phone. She opened the map as she went back to sit next to Milo on the couch. She reverse-pinched the screen to zoom in on the proper area.

"Marin was taken from the arboretum. You were found wandering by CenturyLink Field. We can work with that. How loud was the noise?"

"Loud," Milo said. "A lot of times, the hunters had to shout to be heard over all the noise."

"We can work with that," Ari said. "You were being held for months. Was the noise of demolition louder when you first arrived or did it get louder over time?"

Milo closed her eyes again. "Worse over time. It was bearable when we first got there, I think, but it kept getting worse and worse every day."

"It was getting closer." Ari looked up a timeline of the demolition. "Okay, we can~" Her phone interrupted her by ringing, blocking the map. She was about to dismiss the call when she saw it was from Diana. She swiped to answer, putting it on speaker for Milo's benefit. "Diana?"

"We're starting to take it seriously." Diana's voice was a whisper, and there was the unmistakable echo that told Ari she was calling from a bathroom.

"Who is taking what seriously?"

"Seattle PD," Diana said. "The video has gotten enough attention, and enough people have said that it looks authentic, that we're officially opening an investigation on it."

Ari said, "Well, that's good news, isn't it? The more people looking for Marin, the better."

Diana said, "Sure. But it also lends credence to the claims. If the police are actually looking into the werewolf video..."

"Oh, come on," Ari said. "It doesn't matter what some idiot in a mask claims. The bottom line is that a woman appears to be in danger. The cops would be interested in that even if the kidnappers said she was a space alien."

"Be that as it may," Diana said, "the internet has gone into overdrive. It looks like we're legitimizing their story by believing any part of it."

Ari groaned. "I hate the internet. Okay. Thanks for the heads up. I think I'm making progress, but I can't promise anything."

"The best thing for you would be if the whole thing looked like a hoax," Diana said.

"That's the goal. I'll call you back when I have something for you." She disconnected the call and looked at Milo. "Any bright ideas?"

Milo raised an eyebrow. "Actually, yeah. Pretty simple one, actually."

"I'm all ears."

Dale insisted on Hayden following her when they left the park, grateful for the solitude of her car. What she really wanted to do was drive home and take a scalding shower to get the dirty feeling off her skin. She didn't know where she would lead Hayden so at first she just drove aimlessly through downtown while she got her thoughts in order. She realized she had driven to the Space Needle when she saw the Science Center and decided that was as good a place as any to have a conversation with Hayden.

He smiled at her when they parked, tilting his head back to look up. "You know I never actually made it here on my last trip."

"Yeah, I'm sure you were busy," Dale said as she crossed the street. "Come on."

"We're going up?"

Dale answered him by not stopping, and he was forced to follow. They rode the elevator up with a group of students and their laser-focused teacher. Hayden watched out the glass like any other tourist as they ascended. When they reached the top, the field trip went one way and Dale went the other. Hayden followed again, seemingly willing to go wherever she wanted. She wondered how long his obedience would last.

She went out onto the observation deck, which was shockingly uncrowded, and looked out over the city. Hayden stood next to her, crossed his arms over his chest, and waited patiently. They were looking out over the Sound, a gorgeous view under any circumstances, even if her present company was pushing the limits of that beauty.

"You need to tell me everything," she said at last.

Hayden looked at her. "What do you mean?"

"I mean," she said, turning to face him, "you claim that you want to expose wolves, not kill them. But you killed a lot of them in Germany to get your hands on those essays. I mean that you were involved in kidnapping Milo and Gwyneth Willow and letting Roemer do god-knows-what to them. You were fine with Marin Cardoso being kidnapped as well. So I need to know exactly what you did and why you did it, or I'm walking away. I don't need your help to be done with *canidae*."

"Oh, you don't?" Hayden said, his mood suddenly darkening. "Unemployed and homeless? Cut off from all your pals? You need me more than anyone needs you right now."

Dale clenched her jaw and stared at him. Finally he forced a smile.

"But I suppose," he said in a measured tone, "in the interest of full disclosure, you do deserve to know the whole story. Yes, I killed the wolves who were guarding the book. It was the only way I could leave with it. The wolves who told me about its location are still alive, I can assure you. I paid them. I paid them very well because I'd convinced them the book was just an artifact that couldn't hurt anyone. I could have tortured the information out of them, but I didn't. But the pack guarding it... they were more relentless. They wouldn't even listen to me. My intention was to wound them, but they were relentless. I had to take fatal action to ensure my own survival."

"Self-defense," Dale said, her voice flat.

Hayden nodded. "Yes. Exactly. As for the Willows, my intention with their imprisonment is entirely academic. As far as I can tell, there are no legitimate physicians capable of tending to wolves who might need medical help. Ariadne and her ilk are forced to find back-alley clinics when they require treatment. If we can better understand their physiology, we can better serve them as patients in the future."

"Right," Dale said. "Saint Hayden."

"You don't have to believe me," he said. "My motives remain the same. I admit that I lost my cool with Ariadne in the hospital. She... she has been a pain in my side ever since we met."

Dale bit the inside of her cheek to keep from smiling proudly, looking away before he could see it in her eyes.

"Roemer was putting this together long before I came to him with the book. There are other methods we could have taken, but this is the most expedient."

"And all it costs is the safety of four women," Dale said. "What a bargain."

"In the long run, yes! I despise my part in what's happened to the Willows, to Valerie and Marin. I'm going to do everything I can to ensure they come out of this in one piece."

Dale laughed. "Roemer's going to let Marin transform live on the internet, and then he's going to put a bullet in her head."

Hayden grunted and looked down. "That's his plan. He hasn't said in so many words, but yes. He has no intention of letting her leave that building. I'm doing everything in my power to ensure all three of them get away just like Millicent did."

"She got away in spite of you."

Hayden leaned closer. "She got away *because* of me. Roemer and his goons gave her a drug that made her susceptible to their orders. I watered it down. She still followed their orders enough that they wouldn't become suspicious, but it gave her just enough freedom that she could do something like, I don't know, escape from their custody."

Dale looked into his eyes, trying to find any sign of deception. It would explain how Milo managed to escape. And futzing with a mind-altering drug might also explain why the wolf brain had still been in control even after Milo transformed back into her human form.

"I went to the hospital on my own, to take Millicent somewhere safe, away from Roemer. Why do you think it was just me and two men? Roemer had no idea she had been picked up. I had a very small window in which I could spirit her away. When Ariadne and that detective got in my way, I was frustrated. I wasn't thinking straight. Of course it's better for her to be at home, with friends. You know I could have taken her prisoner at any point over the past few days. You haven't exactly surrounded her with armed guards."

Dale had to admit that was true. "Okay. Prove you really want the best for everybody."

"Name it."

"Free Gwen."

Hayden laughed. "There's no way I can do that."

"Of course there is," Dale said. It nauseated her to be negotiating like this when actual lives were on the line, but if she could keep playing the part while also saving one of the hostages, she had to power through. "Roemer would never let you free Marin, so she's not an option. And Valerie needs to stay there in case of a medical emergency. Gwen isn't necessary to the plan anymore. You said you wanted to save Milo, and you did that. Now you can prove to me that your intentions are pure by getting Gwen out as well."

Hayden sighed heavily and rocked on his heels. Dale watched him and hoped she wasn't betraying her eagerness.

"If I prove myself to you," he finally said, "you'll agree to work with me to expose the wolves, protect the girl, and stop Roemer from committing mass murder."

"Absolutely, I will," Dale said, never breaking eye contact with him.

Hayden chewed on his lip and considered the proposal. Finally he turned to face her.

"Okay, Miss Frye. I'll go back and help Gwyneth Willow escape to prove you can trust me. I'm confident I can get her out tonight, barring any unforeseen complications. But I want *quid pro quo*. I need to know beyond a shadow of a doubt that I can trust you as well."

Dale sighed. "What do you want me to do?"

He took his phone from his pocket and tapped the screen a

few times. When he found what he was looking for, he held it out to her. Dale took it and saw a picture of a handwritten page. She tried to cover the panic in her eyes as she looked up at him.

"I want you to read the essays."

"You know I've already read them."

His smile didn't waver. He shrugged. "Then reading them again should only strengthen your resolve. There's no real reason *not* to refresh your memory, right? I can't think of a good reason you shouldn't read them again."

The hell of it was that Dale couldn't think of one, either.

CHAPTER FOURTEEN

THEY MOVED quickly to implement Milo's plan. When they called Eva, she was immediately on-board with what she had to do in order to protect her sister. The press conference was scheduled so it could be aired live on the local news, and they arrived at the police station just before the fleet of trucks carrying reporters and camera equipment filled up the street. Ari and Milo escorted Eva into the building, found Diana, and were taken to a briefing room on the second floor.

A blonde woman whose name Ari didn't catch took command of their group. She was wearing the fanciest uniform in the room, so it seemed like it was safe to follow her instructions. Ari remained at the very back of the room, next to the exit, while Diana and Eva went to the front with the boss lady cop. When the reporters seemed to have settled, the blonde cop stepped up to the podium and quietly cleared her throat. The room snapped to attention.

"Good evening," she said. "Thank you all for coming. We wanted to address this, ah, viral video that's going around on social media. Obviously a lot of people seem to think it's a joke or a hoax, but we take this sort of thing very seriously. I'd like to hand this over right now to someone who can express just how serious this situation is. Eva?"

She stepped aside and let Eva come forward. She had a prepared statement, which she laid down on the podium.

"My name is Evangeline Cardoso. The woman in the video is my sister, Marin Cardoso. I don't know why these men chose her, or why they're making such ridiculous claims on their video. My sister is..." Her voice broke and she ducked her chin to compose herself. "My sister is just a normal girl. She goes to the University of Washington. She wants to work at the aquarium. She loves fish." She laughed quietly, though her eyes were about to overflow with tears. "What is happening isn't a joke or a hoax. I'm grateful to the Seattle Police and Chief Collins for taking this seriously despite how it's been portrayed online. These men are delusional and they're dangerous, and I'm terrified of what will happen to my sister at the end of their deadline. Please stop sharing this sick video. Stop giving them a platform to make my sister's horrible ordeal into some kind of joke. Thank you."

She stepped back and the blonde woman, apparently Chief Collins, stepped forward. "We will not justify the, uh, ridiculous claims made by the men who made the video by referring to them here. The only pertinent information is that we have reasonable evidence that the kidnapping of Marin Cardoso is, in fact, real. We believe she's being held here in Seattle, and as of now, our top priority is getting her home safely. Thank you."

Collins left the podium without taking questions and ushered Eva out of the room so she wouldn't get swarmed. In the hallway outside, she looked at Diana and Ari.

"I want to make one thing clear, Miss Willow. The police are in charge of this investigation. Your input will be welcomed, but if I get any indication you're interfering with our work~"

Diana cleared her throat. "With all due respect, Chief, Ariadne was working this case long before any of us even knew Ms. Cardoso had been abducted. I don't think we should be blocking her from continuing her momentum as long as she promises to keep us in the loop with anything she finds. I'm willing to be her liaison with the department so we can share progress going both ways. I'd take full responsibility for her until the matter is resolved."

Collins considered the request. "You have a reputation, Miss Willow."

"Good."

"I didn't say if it was good or not."

Ari shrugged. "Either way, a reputation means I'm not sitting on my ass."

Collins looked at Diana. "She's your responsibility. She keeps you in the loop, and you report everything directly to me."

"Understood." Collins left, and Diana turned to Ari. "Don't get me fired."

"If I do, I'll hire you at Bitches. I've missed having Shae around to help out."

Diana scoffed and guided Ari and Eva to the elevators. "It would look great if you could give me something immediately."

"Milo's memory is coming back," Ari said. "We think we have a location narrowed down. Somewhere by the south end of the viaduct demolition."

"That's not a big area," Diana said.

"Especially not for a wolf. I was going to go check it out tonight."

"Keep me updated." To Eva, she said, "Thank you for coming today. That couldn't have been easy."

Eva nodded. "I'd do it a hundred times if it helped my sister. Please let me know if you need anything else."

Diana gestured for a uniformed officer to come over and escort Eva back to her car.

"You need backup tonight?" Diana asked. "If the hunters find you sniffing around near their base, they might grab you."

"At least then I'd know for sure where they are," Ari said. "And so would you. I think it'd be best if I went solo, but I'll call if I find anything."

"I'll keep my phone handy," Diana said.

"Thanks, Diana. For everything."

Diana shrugged as she backed toward the stairs. "We're family, Willow. So don't make your sister look bad in front of her boss."

Ari saluted, then turned and headed out past the throng of reporters who were still hoping to get a statement from someone.

***

Val and Gwen sat across from each other on the floor of Gwen's cell, playing a card game called Skirmish. It was similar to War, but with just enough strategy involved to keep it from becoming monotonous. Tonight's dinner had pizza, the box sitting to one side of their game board. Val played a three card, Gwen countered with a seven. She sighed and leaned back, rubbing her face as Val considered her next move.

"There had to be some kind of progress," Gwen said. "Milo is out there somewhere. The video has been online for over a day. Ari has to know what's going on by now. There was that scuffle last night, but today it seems quiet again." She nodded at the door, indicating the hunters in the rest of the building. "Have they been acting any differently today?"

Val shrugged and held up a nine of clubs. "They let me have two decks of playing cards. Other than that, nothing. Still the same smug, paranoid bastards as always."

Gwen lost the round by playing a five, discarding it. "Something has to happen. I can't believe--"

She stopped talking when she heard the rattling lock of the door. Val turned as well, sitting up straighter as the door swung open to reveal Isaac Hayden. He smiled brightly at Gwen, then gave Val a look of surprise.

"Are we bonding, ladies?"

"What do you want, Hayden?" Val asked. "We're busy."

"Don't be rude to me. I'm offering kindness." He returned his gaze to Gwen. "I have permission to take the doggie here for a run."

Gwen and Val looked at each other, then went back to playing.

"I expected a bit more of a reaction than that, honestly."

"We don't waste energy on bullshit," Val said.

Hayden stepped closer. "No bullshit. Roemer is pissed that the guys can't find Milo. I convinced him that we need to bring in the big guns. You."

Gwen said, "You want me to track down my partner so you can drag her back here to be tortured some more."

"We need wolves to examine. The more we know about you beasts, the better we can fight you."

"You're not helping your cause."

"I wasn't finished," Hayden said. "We need wolves. We have you, and you will be invaluable. But Milo is younger and in better shape."

"Hey, now," Gwen said. "Just because you're a sadistic bastard doesn't mean you have to be rude, too."

Hayden's voice hardened. "What I'm saying is that we need a young wolf. We can't use Marin because she's currently serving her own purpose. The guys have proven inept at capturing other wolves. So that only leaves one option." He looked at Val, holding the stare until she looked back at him. He smiled and raised his eyebrows.

"I'm not *canidae*," Val said.

"Not yet."

Gwen's blood went cold. "You bastard."

Hayden showed her his palms. "Invaluable research. We can infect her with your curse and examine her over the coming month to see what happens to her body. To see if there's a way to prevent the infection from taking over. And yes, it's highly unlikely Dr. Byrne would survive the procedure~"

"She's his *daughter*," Gwen snapped. "He would really approve of that being done to his daughter?"

Val spoke very softly. "Oh, come on, Gwen. That's the most believable part of anything happening in this room." She threw down her cards and unfolded her legs, standing up to walk away. She faced the wall, head bowed.

Hayden said, "It's no different than you trying to break up Ariadne and Dale for the greater good. This is a war. Sacrifices must be made."

Gwen glared at him. "I'll go."

Val said, "Gwen, don't."

"We'll figure something out."

"*Gwen*," Val said.

Hayden motioned for Gwen to stand, and she complied. "Don't fight me on this, Valerie. Milo being taken prisoner again is a thousand times better than a death sentence for you. It's not even a question." She started unbuttoning her blouse, glaring at Hayden as she did. "Don't think I'm going to make this easy for you."

"That's what I'm counting on." His voice was so soft that Gwen could almost believe she hadn't heard it. Before she look at Val to see if she'd heard it as well, he said, "If you do fight, just don't do anything permanent, okay? Not until you can see the whole picture of what's happening. Can I trust you on that?"

Gwen looked at Val, who seemed to be just as confused as she was. "Okay. Fine."

"Okay." His voice was louder again, and he checked his watch. "Best we get this show on the road. Go ahead and transform and we'll go see if we can find your lady."

Gwen and Val shared another look before Gwen dropped into a crouch and transformed. Part of her still expected some kind of a trick, though there was something in Hayden's voice... She didn't trust him, not by any stretch of the imagination. But she was willing to play along, at least for a little while, until she had a better idea of what cards he had up his sleeve. The wolf took over her easily, like shedding an extra layer of clothes to reveal her true self. She stretched her paws out in front of her and felt the muscles rippling up and down her sides as she settled into her new form.

Hayden crouched to fit a muzzle over her face, securing it behind her skull. When he stood, he looked at Val.

"I promise you, everything will be clear soon."

"It better be."

Hayden guided Gwen out of the cell, one of the very few times she'd actually left the room without being taken somewhere to be tortured. She hesitated at the threshold but after a moment, prompted by Hayden, continued out on a path that would take her to the front of the building.

A hunter coming downstairs stopped. "Hey, where do you think you're going with that?"

"Bloodhound duty."

"Boss know about this?"

"Assume that he does. Or better yet, assume it's none of your business what I chose to do with our prisoners because I don't answer to you."

Gwen could see the hunter was torn, clearly wanting to run upstairs to confirm with Roemer, but after a minute his posture relaxed. "Fine. Fuck do I care what you do with the damned thing."

Hayden led Gwen to the door, pausing to take off his jacket and drape it over her head. She suffered the indignity, and the stench of his cologne, because immediately after her eyes were covered, she was led Outside. The smell of dirt and concrete and grass rose up from beneath her paws. She smelled Water, Salt, Mud, Sea Air. The wind ruffled her fur like a friendly hand as Hayden led her across a cracked street and then into a car.

"Just stay calm," he said. "I'd tell you where we're going, but I doubt you'd believe me. So it's best if you just see for yourself."

She huffed air out through her nose, still blinded by his coat, and settled on the seat. Hayden started the car and pulled away from the curb.

Over the next few minutes, she was very aware that they were driving in circles in an attempt to disorient her. Eventually, though, he seemed satisfied that she wouldn't be able to find her way back to the building and began driving a more direct route. Five minutes later, he slowed and came to a stop. Gwen could smell lots of cars: a parking lot. He pulled the coat off her face, unfastened the muzzle, and pulled her out of the car without excess force. The sudden brightness of multiple security lights blinded her, and she squinted to make out anything but blurry silhouettes.

"As promised," he said.

Gwen turned toward the sound of approaching footsteps. A dark shape slowly sharpened as it approached. The smell gave her away before Gwen could actually see her, and her hopes suddenly soared.

Dale crouched down next to her and cupped her face. "Hey there," Dale whispered, looking into Gwen's eyes. "You okay?"

Gwen huffed and threw herself against Dale, the closest thing she could get to a hug in her current form. Dale accepted the hug, squeezing in a confusingly impersonal way before she stood up and faced Hayden.

"I'm taking her home."

"Do you believe me now?" Hayden said. "I don't want to kill anyone. I don't want anyone to die."

Dale made a face and looked away from him. "Sure. You're a prince. Uniting the species. We'll be in touch." She started to turn away.

"Wait, one more thing." Dale sighed heavily, and Hayden took out his phone. "I want a photo to prove she's leaving with you."

"Why?"

"Because if I go back without her, Dr. Byrne is going to assume the worst. She'll think I took her out and put a bullet in her head or something. She'll refuse to help us if she thinks Gwen here is buried in a shallow grave somewhere. I want proof that Gwen is safe so she'll keep cooperating."

Dale sighed. "Fine." She knelt next to Gwen and put an arm across her back.

Hayden aimed the phone. "Would it kill you to smile?"

"Just take the damn picture," Dale snapped.

Hayden snapped the picture and slipped the phone into his pocket.

"Wait. Give me the coat."

"What?"

Dale gestured at Gwen. "She's going to need something to wear."

"You didn't bring anything?"

Dale shouted, "Just give me the damn jacket!"

Gwen flinched and looked up at Dale, sweet and funny Dale, the kind of woman she never would have expected to snap at someone like that no matter who it was. Hayden rolled his eyes and handed over his coat. Dale didn't bother thanking him, but she snapped her fingers for Gwen to follow her back across the parking lot. Gwen fell in behind her, turning to make sure Hayden was really letting them go. Sure enough, he remained where he was. He even lifted a hand to wave goodbye. Gwen turned away from him and followed Dale out of the parking lot to her waiting car. Dale opened the back door for her and Gwen hopped in.

By the time Dale got behind the wheel, Gwen had changed back into her human form. She pulled on Hayden's coat. It was big enough that she could hold the collar closed, and the tails reached to mid-thigh. She watched Dale's profile.

"Hello, Dale."

Dale's jaw tightened. "Hi." She looked in the rearview. "Are you okay?"

"As okay as I can be, given the circumstances. Ariadne? Milo?"

"They're fine." Dale's voice was worryingly flat. "Milo had a rough time of it right after she got away, but she's improving. Ari's... Ari. She's always good."

Gwen said, "Dale is everything... are *you* okay?"

Dale's shoulders tensed. She flexed her fingers on the steering wheel. After a pause long enough that Gwen assumed she wasn't going to answer, Dale finally said, "Not really."

They continued the ride in silence. Dale, her daughter's lovely partner, was unrecognizable behind the wheel. She was cold and businesslike, an Uber driver ferrying a passenger from Point A to Point B with no emotional involvement at all. Gwen wasn't afraid of her, she wasn't giving off a dangerous energy, but there was certainly something wrong with her.

Gwen recognized the route to Lake Washington, and soon she saw the familiar sights of her own street. Hope welled in her chest and her eyes burned with tears that she refused to shed. She'd assumed she would die in that cell, that she was doomed as soon as the hood dropped over her head in Germany. Seeing everything again felt like a gift, a miracle, and she couldn't stop herself from sobbing quietly when Dale pulled into the driveway. The living room curtains were open on a dark room, but she could see through to the fully-lit kitchen.

"Milo's really okay?"

"She's right inside."

Gwen got out of the car and crossed the lawn. Her hands shook as she opened the side door into the laundry room. She heard a voice suddenly stop speaking. She looked around and saw a pair of slacks on the dryer. She didn't know who they belonged to, or when the last load had been done, but she stepped into them so she would be slightly less naked during the reunion. She had just fastened the button when the door flew open to reveal Ariadne with a frying pan raised over her head.

Ari froze in mid-motion. Her eyes widened and she lowered her arm. Gwen hadn't seen her daughter in almost a year, and now she hallucinated a vision of Ariadne at all her ages. The confused young girl, the angry homeless wolf, the strong private investigator. Now a mature and powerful woman ready to fight against an invader.

"Mom," Ari whispered.

Gwen stepped forward and hugged her daughter. Ari dropped the frying pan to pull her tighter, backing up into the kitchen as she gasped in surprise. She cupped the back of Gwen's head, kissed her hair, and alternated between whispering, "How..." and laughing incredulously. Gwen burrowed her face into the crook of Ari's neck, breathing her scent, fully appreciating the feeling of being in her daughter's arms again for as long as she could.

"Gwen?"

Gwen's heart seized. She turned and looked toward the voice. If Ari had looked like a warrior, Milo looked distressingly vulnerable. Her hair was unwashed, she wore clothes that didn't fit, and the bags under her eyes indicated she hadn't slept. But when their eyes locked, Milo got to her feet as if she'd suddenly become completely weightless. She crossed the kitchen with a magnetic pull. Ari sensed her approach and wisely stepped out of the way so Milo could take over the embrace.

"Penny," Gwen whispered, burying her face in her beloved's hair.

Milo let out a surprised laugh, and her arms tightened around Gwen's shoulders. "Oh my God. Penny. *Penny.*" She laughed again and put her head on Gwen's shoulder. "I'm your lucky Penny."

"I'm not against taking your name," Milo said from the passenger seat of a car cutting through a dark German forest at 2am. Gwen could barely keep her eyes open, but the inn was just a few miles away. She could make it as long as Milo kept talking. "I'm for it, actually. Never really had much attachment to Duncan if I'm totally honest. But my problem is that my first name doesn't go with it. At all."

"Millicent Willow?" Gwen said.

"Too many Ls." Milo fought a yawn. "And every nickname has the same problem. Millie, Lissy, Lizzy, Lily."

Gwen closed her eyes then snapped them back open. "What about... Mill. Liss. Cent. Cent." She smiled. "Penny."

Milo snorted. "Penny Willow." She hummed. "I don't hate it..."

"You really want to change your entire identity just to take my last name? Penny Willow is a huge shift from Milo Duncan."

"So maybe it'll just be for us. You'n me. Everyone else will still call me Milo. But I'll be Penny to you."

"My lucky Penny," Gwen said.

"Hum," Milo said, then chuckled. "Lucky Penny Willow... Growing on me."

Gwen wanted to know everything the bastards had done to Milo over the past few months, wanted to know what she needed revenge for, but there would be time for that. She stepped back and cupped Milo's face in her hands.

"I love you."

Milo kissed Gwen's lips. "I love you."

Ari said, "How are you here?"

"Hayden. I don't know what... um..." She furrowed her brow and suddenly realized someone was missing. "Dale. Dale picked me up. She drove me here."

"Dale's here?" Ari said, already moving to the laundry room.

"She was," Gwen said. "I don't know why she didn't come in with me..."

Ari was already out the door. Gwen brushed her fingers over Milo's face, watching Milo's eyes as they took in the woman before her.

"There's so much I want to say to you," Gwen said. "I just don't know any of the words or which ones should be first."

"There'll be time for that," Milo said. "For now, there's only three that are important."

Gwen said, "Three...?"

Milo smiled. "Welcome home, love."

Gwen closed her eyes and kissed Milo again.

CHAPTER FIFTEEN

ARI SAW the dark silhouette behind the wheel of Dale's car and approached cautiously, even though she had no doubt who it was sitting there. She walked over to the driver's side and knocked on the window.

"Uber for Ariadne?"

Dale opened the door and got out, not replying with her usual response that she was there for someone named Adrian. They were far enough away from the side of the house that the porch light didn't reach her face. She slumped against the side of the car and kept her head down, arms crossed over her chest, and Ari's mood darkened dramatically.

"Dale? What's wrong?"

She reached out, but Dale cringed away from her. "Don't! Don't..."

"You're scaring me. What happened?"

"I read it again." Dale's voice broke. She brought a hand up to her face. "I read the fucking essays again, puppy. Hayden needed me to prove I was telling the truth, needed to trust me, so he made me read the essays off his phone in front of him. I'm so sorry. It was the only way to get him to free Mom."

Ari swallowed the lump that had risen in her throat. "How...

um, how do you feel?"

"Sick. Disgusted with myself. Terrified."

"Can I put my hands on your shoulders? I want you to take a step this way."

"I don't want you to see me."

"Humor me." Dale nodded slightly, so Ari gently guided her closer to the porch. She hooked a finger under Dale's chin and forced her head up. "Look at me."

Dale squeezed her eyes shut. "I can't."

"Look at me," Ari whispered.

Dale opened her eyes and looked at Ari, immediately flinching as if the sight caused her pain. "I'm so sorry. For whatever I say in the future or anything I do, I want you to know I'm so sorry."

Ari shushed her, brushed her hand over Dale's cheek. "Last time you called me a mutt after reading the essays. You just called me puppy. You said Mom, not Gwen."

"It didn't happen immediately last time," Dale said.

"Okay," Ari said. "But I'm looking at you right now, and all I see is fear and shame. I don't see any hatred. I don't see disgust. I see a woman who thinks she did something horrible. How do you actually *feel?*"

"Sick to my stomach."

"Right. Any rage? Any urge to run away from me?"

Dale took a deep breath. "I don't want to hurt you."

"That's not what I asked."

"I want to hold you so badly," Dale sobbed. "But if something snaps in me..."

Ari stepped closer and wrapped her arms around Dale. "I know it won't. I have complete and utter faith in you."

"I wish I did." Dale's arms hesitantly slipped around Ari's waist and pulled her close. "I had to do it, Ari. He needed to think he could trust me, and if I hesitated... I had to get her home. I had to do it to get Mom home."

"I know," Ari said. "You did good, baby. You did amazing. I'm so proud of you."

Dale lifted her head and looked at the house. "Are they okay?"

"Go see for yourself."

"I can't go in there, Ari. I'm a time bomb."

"Would you stop? You're not."

Dale stepped away from Ari. "You can't know that."

"I do," Ari said. "My faith in you isn't blind, Dale. It comes from years of experience. It comes from watching you standing up to do what's right. Not just for me, not just for *canidae*, but for everyone. You're a good person. You beat this brainwashing once, and this time you saw it coming so I know you didn't let it get any hooks in you. Last time when it tried to make you a huntress, the only thing you even came close in succeeded at was running away." She cupped Dale's face in both her hands. "You are Dale Elizabeth Frye, and a book can make you say awful things, but it cannot change who you are inside. That gives me more hope than anything else in this whole mess. The essays might make more hunters if they get released, but I don't think we have to worry about it changing every single person who comes in contact with it."

Dale sniffled. "Dale Elizabeth Frye... Willow."

Ari bit back a gasp. "I, uh... I wasn't... sure. We hadn't talked about it."

Dale shrugged and said, "Well, if Gwen and Milo are going to be the Willows... I don't want to feel like the odd one out when we have dinner together." She wiped at her eyes. "Hyphenated. I think? Maybe just on paperwork... I don't know. We can talk about it later."

"Yeah." Ari tucked Dale's hair behind her ear. "Are you okay? If you want to be alone I can drive you home, sit with you~"

"I want to see Mom and Milo."

"Then let's go see them."

She took Dale's hand and squeezed it before leading her away from the car. She went in through the laundry room and stopped in the kitchen, which was now empty. The living room was also vacant, and Ari felt a twinge of concern.

"They were here just a second ago." She started forward, but Dale reached out with her free hand to grab Ari's elbow to pull her back. "What..."

"Uh, puppy."

Dale nodded at the floor, where the jacket Gwen had been wearing was lying in a crumpled ball. Ari frowned at it.

"Mom was wearing that."

"Puppy," Dale said again. "That's *all* she was wearing."

Ari looked at her. Dale looked at the ceiling. Ari looked up as well, and finally figured out what had happened.

"Oh, for crying out loud," Ari groaned.

Dale chuckled. "What do you expect? They were held prisoner, haven't seen each other in ages, they're *married* now. Technically, in all the ways that matter. And I'm surprised it took them this long to get upstairs. I still want to see Gwen, to apologize to her for how I acted in the car. But it would be weird to just sit down here and wait, right?"

"A little, yeah." Ari walked away, as if putting distance between herself and the jacket would erase what it meant. "I was going to go wander around by the viaduct to see if I could find any clues about where they've been hiding, but now that Mom's here, we can pick her brain. And seeing her again might make Milo remember something useful. So I feel like waiting is the best course of action. But... yeah. A little weird." Ari looked down at Dale's hand in hers, then glanced over her shoulder at the stairs. "Would it be... less weird or a lot more weird if we used the time constructively?"

Dale furrowed her brow.

"My old room is still fully furnished," Ari said.

Dale's eyebrows arched up. "Are you serious?"

Ari shrugged. "You're worried about being a time bomb. What better way to prove you're still a big wolf fan?"

"Your mother and Milo will be right down the hall." Dale was whispering as if they were in the same room. "Are you honestly... implying we..."

Ari raised an eyebrow.

Dale slowly, reluctantly, began to smile. She stroked her hand over Ari's bicep. "I have spent a few nights in your bedroom up there, and it never really felt right without you there with me. I guess it would be nice to make amends for that."

Ari started walking backward toward the stairs.

Dale groaned and let herself be led. "Okay, but seriously, how good is a wolf's hearing...?"

"Honestly?" Ari said, looking toward one bedroom as she guided Dale to the other. "After everything those two have been through, I'd be surprised if they remember the rest of the house exists."

Gwen pressed her lips to the inside of Milo's thigh and let the kiss linger before she moved up to her stomach. Milo shivered and gasped, and Gwen smiled as she kissed a spot just above the sharp line of her hip. The first time they had sex, Milo had been the aggressor. Gwen hadn't had sex in years at that point, had barely even thought about it, and the idea of being with a woman wasn't even something she'd considered. After a few hours of debauchery and some soul-searching, Gwen discovered she was bisexual, but the label was just a formality by that point. She may have been attracted to men and women, but she only had eyes for one woman in particular.

And now that woman was flushed and breathing heavily under her. Gwen brushed her hair over the sweaty curves as she stretched up, pressing a kiss to Milo's slack but quickly responsive lips. Milo cupped the back of Gwen's head, raked her fingers through her hair, and wrapped her legs around Gwen's waist to pull her closer. When the kiss ended, it was only so Gwen could explore the curve of Milo's throat. Milo continued threading Gwen's hair through her fingers, and Gwen was hypnotized by the repetitive petting.

"The long hair looks good on you," Milo whispered.

"It drove me crazy at first," Gwen said, and kissed Milo's collarbone. "It probably looks like a rat's nest. I haven't washed it in forever."

"I love it." Milo grabbed a handful and draped it over her face, inhaling deeply.

Gwen laughed and sat up to flip the hair away. "Already sick of looking at me, Millicent?"

"Never," Milo pulled Gwen to her for another kiss. "Thought I lost you."

"I thought so, too." Gwen closed her eyes and rested her forehead against Milo's. "I could hear you sometimes. When they... did things. The experiments. I wanted to knock down those walls. It kills me that I couldn't help you."

"That's why they did it," Milo said. "I heard you, too. They offered to go easier on you if I cooperated and did whatever they asked of me. I almost did. So many times."

"They made the same promise to me," Gwen said. "They would have made us do all kinds of awful things and then thrown the agreement out whenever it didn't suit them anymore."

"I know," Milo said. "Doesn't help."

Gwen repositioned herself, bracing one hand on the headboard as she put the other between them. "How about this?" she whispered. "Does this help?"

Milo groaned. Her eyes rolled back in her head, and she put her arms around Gwen as she lifted her hips to meet the touch. "It's starting to..."

"Well," Gwen kissed Milo's cheek, then her lips. "You just let me know how long I need to keep going..."

"I'll say when," Milo gasped, letting her hands roam over Gwen's back.

Gwen smiled and began moving, prepared to go as long as it took, even if she didn't hear the word until morning.

***

Ari kissed the dimples in the small of Dale's back. Dale hissed and arched her back, looking over her shoulder. Ari slowly kissed her way up Dale's spine, eventually straddling her, eyes up to appreciate the way Dale's hair fell across the side of her face. Dale twisted as Ari stretched and they kissed, and Ari's hands went around Dale's sides to cup her breasts. Dale moaned and brushed her lips over Ari's cheek, up toward her eye.

"Any urges to hurt me?" Ari whispered.

"Not unless we establish a safe word," Dale said.

Ari grinned and kissed the corner of Dale's mouth. "Seriously, though. Are you okay?"

Dale nodded and kept herself propped up with one arm, using the other to brush the hair out of her face. "I don't feel anything like what I felt the first time I read the book. Not even a whisper. I think I'm okay. But keep an eye on me, okay?"

"How could I not, when the view is so pretty?"

"Well," Dale said, "to immediately ruin a very sweet sentiment, I'm going to go take a shower while the other people in the house are still occupied."

Ari lifted herself off Dale and rolled to the side. Dale sat on the edge of the bed and bent down to gather the bare minimum amount of clothes required to get to the bathroom.

"Don't use up all the hot water."

"Oh, I definitely need cold after everything you just did to me." She fanned her face and looked back at Ari, who was stretched out on the mattress. "God, you're pretty."

Ari struck a pose, one arm behind her head and chest thrust out. "Private eye, werewolf, model."

Dale bent down and kissed Ari again. "See you in a bit."

"Okay."

Ari dropped onto her back and stared at the ceiling, sweat drying on her skin. After a few minutes she heard the water rushing through the pipes. She considered staying there until Dale got back, thought about getting up to join her in the shower, but instead decided to go to the kitchen for some water. She put her undershirt back on along with her underwear and slipped out of the room, padding barefoot down the same hall she'd snuck down as a child.

In the kitchen she saw that the laptop on the counter was still on. She and Milo had been watching the livestream of Marin's imprisonment when they were so gloriously interrupted. Ari turned the computer around and saw that Marin was curled on her side, the blankets by her feet, head bowed with her arms raised protectively over her head. As far as they could tell, the lights in the room were never turned off. She'd been held prisoner before. She'd been in cages. It wasn't something she'd wish on anybody.

She finally looked away from the screen when she heard a creak behind her. She turned to see her mother standing in the kitchen doorway in a plain cotton robe. Her hair was wild, which revealed much more silver-gray streaks than Ari had noticed when Gwen had arrived earlier. They smiled awkwardly at each other before Ari went to the sink.

"Water?"

"Yes, please."

Ari opened the cupboard and discovered that none of the dishes had been washed in months. She took out two glasses and rinsed off the dust before filling them.

"Everything okay with Dale?" Gwen asked, looking at the computer screen. Her lips were pressed tightly together, and Ari knew she was kicking herself for being free when their fellow prisoners had been left behind.

"Dale's perfect," Ari said. "She wanted to apologize for how she acted in the car with you. She was just concerned."

Gwen looked up. "About what?"

Ari could tell her what Dale had done to get Hayden's cooperation, but she couldn't think of a way to phrase it that wouldn't make Gwen feel guilty.

"It's not important." She brought the glass over to Gwen. "I managed to put her mind at ease."

"Good." Gwen looked past Ari at the back door. "Can we drink these outside? I... I need to be outdoors."

"Oh, god, I'm sure you do," Ari said.

They went out onto the back porch. Ari brushed a layer of leaves off the patio chairs and took one, gesturing for Gwen to take the other. Gwen paused and tilted her head back to take a deep, slow breath of the night air, a beatific smile playing on her face as the wind moved her hair.

"I haven't been outside for months," she whispered.

"Do you need to run?"

Gwen shook her head, then shrugged. "Actually, I most likely do. But I can't guarantee the wolf would stop before hitting Canada. I need a little while to acclimate to being free before I hand over control like that."

"Probably smart," Ari said.

Gwen finally sat down and crossed one leg over the other. Ari couldn't help but feel reduced to a teenager at moments like these. It was just the two of them, alone in the quiet, and all the years in between fell away until they were just mother and daughter. Ari drummed her fingers softly on the side of her glass and looked down at her bare feet. Gwen chuckled quietly and Ari looked up at her.

"What's funny?"

"I never really pictured this moment," Gwen said. "You and me, sitting out here in the middle of the night, with our wives in the house."

Ari smiled. "Milo told you?"

"She did. I'm so happy for you, Ariadne. You chose well."

Ari put one foot on top of the other, awkward and shy again. "At least you could have imagined me with a wife. What about *you?* With someone like Milo?"

Gwen laughed, loud and genuine, and looked up at the sky. "God. Millicent Duncan... She was so rough around the edges when I found her. I thought she was just some punk wolf who would do anything for a little money. Do you know what she did with the money I gave her for trying to break up you and Dale? She gave it away. To her pack. One of them was pregnant, the rest she just wanted to help. She barely kept any of it for herself. I didn't expect to be in love with her. I didn't think I even respected her. Surprise, surprise, she turned out to be a better person than I ever was. I'm lucky *she* chose *me.*"

"I think you both came out okay on that deal."

Gwen smiled and sipped her water.

"Are you really okay, Mom?"

"Mm." She considered the question. "Milo and I went through hell these past few months. I think it would be ridiculous to say we're fine now. Milo obviously has a very long road to being completely fine. But I saw the woman I fell in love with upstairs, and I know she's strong enough to find her way back. With the right people helping her. Helping us. I think we'll bounce back."

Ari nodded slowly as an odd feeling filled her chest. She barely had time to identify it before the balloon burst in the form of a shrill sob. She put one hand over her mouth and leaned forward, her closed eyes useless against the tears that came out of nowhere. She was trembling so hard she was afraid she'd fall out of the chair, but suddenly her mother's arms were around her.

"I gave up on you," Ari managed to say. "I told Dale you were dead. I told her to stop holding out hope. I'm so sorry, Mom."

Gwen shushed her. "It's okay, Ariadne. It's okay."

Ari held her mother until she felt the unexpected touch of a third hand on her shoulder. She looked up and saw Dale, worry written all over her face, and twisted to embrace her instead. Dale cupped the back of Ari's head, and Ari pressed her face into Dale's stomach. Dale still smelled of soap and water from the shower, her hair wet and hanging loose around her face. She was wearing Ari's overshirt, buttoned wrong and too tight in the chest, and Ari breathed deep to inhale their mingling scents.

"What happened?" Dale asked.

Gwen said, "She's overwhelmed. It's understandable. We're all waiting to hit the wall, I think."

Dale stroked Ari's hair. "About that wall. Earlier..."

"Hush," Gwen said. "I don't need to know. You were there when I needed you, and that's all that matters. Are you okay now?"

"Thanks to your daughter, yeah."

Gwen smiled.

Ari sniffled and looked up, scooting to the side so Dale could squeeze into the chair next to her. "Does someone want to go get Milo so we can have the whole family here?"

"Don't bother," Milo said from the kitchen. She poured a glass of water for herself and one for Dale, bringing both out onto the porch. "Don't even offer her a drink? Some wife you turned out to be."

"Hey, I'm new at this. Not all of us could have a secret European ceremony."

Milo bent down to kiss the top of Gwen's head as she passed, sitting on the brick half-wall at the edge of the porch.

"I guess since we're all here and we've all had a second to breathe, we might as well address the elephant in the room. Milo doesn't remember where you were being held..."

"I know exactly where we were," Gwen said.

Ari sat up straighter. "You do?"

"Of course I do. I'm sure Milo does, too, but with her memory issues..." She shrugged. "We were in an abandoned building on First Street, just before it becomes Dave Niehaus Way. Between the Seahawks and the Mariners."

"We weren't looking far enough south," Ari said. "I assumed since Milo said she heard demolition, it meant she was under the last pieces of the viaduct."

Gwen said, "Try being down there and hearing anything else. Trust me, I had very little to do other than listen and take note of the things I heard. Traffic, ferries, demolition. There was a football game, and a concert that I assume was held at the baseball field."

Milo said, "I remember some of that. I kept track of the ships coming in and out. And if the concert was taking place at the baseball field..." She closed her eyes and held one hand out in front of her. She slowly swept it to the left. "Then that would mean the demolition noises were coming from the north. Because obviously the ship traffic was..." She swept her arm again. "To the west."

Ari leaned forward. "Can you find the building again?"

Milo's eyes snapped open. She said, "Absolutely," at the same time Gwen said, "Not now."

Everyone looked at Gwen. Ari was the one who finally asked. "Why not? Marin and Val shouldn't be stuck in that godawful place any longer than necessary."

"Agreed," Gwen said, then held out her hands. "So what's your plan? There are at least a dozen hunters there right now. Are the four of us just going to knock down the door and demand they hand over their prisoners?"

"We can call the police," Dale said. "Regardless of their motives, they're holding two women prisoner. It doesn't matter what the story is, they can't explain that away."

"And you can guarantee the police are trustworthy? Like your friend, Detective Lorne?"

Ari tensed. "Diana is rock solid."

"One cop in a city full of them," Gwen said. "I'm sorry, Ariadne, but this is how the hunters have operated for so long without causing any waves. They have friends in high places. If we call the police, the call will either be lost or we'll walk right into a trap."

Dale got up and went into the kitchen. The other women watched her rummage through the groceries they'd gotten for Milo when they set her up in the house. When she came back, she had a box of cookies and drinks from the fridge for all of them. She set everything on the patio table and turned to face the group.

"I don't think any of us are planning to go back to sleep tonight. And like Ari said, time is of the essence. So we're going to sit here and we're not going to leave until we've figured out what we're going to do to save Marin Cardoso and Val Byrne. Sound like a plan?"

Milo exhaled sharply. She shook her head, and couldn't stop a smile from spreading across her face as she turned to Ari. "You married up, girl."

Ari smiled up at Dale. "Don't I know it." She leaned forward and took a drink off the table. "You heard the woman. We've got a lot of work to do."

CHAPTER SIXTEEN

THE MAIN room of the building was filled with hunters by the time Hayden returned. He paused on the threshold and every eye turned toward him, and he knew word had traveled about his jailbreak. He sighed and continued forward into the room, hands out to either side to show he was unarmed.

"I assume Mr. Roemer is waiting for me up in his office."

One of the hunters, a squat and sturdy mustachioed man named Norman Izett, stepped forward and crossed his arms over his chest.

"Along with a special visitor. And we're gonna be waiting until they give the okay before we let you walk out that door again." He looked at the ground, scanned back toward the door, and locked his steadily-widening eyes on Hayden. "Where the fuck is the dog?"

Hayden stared at him and said nothing.

Izett leaned closer. It couldn't have been called a threat, but the intention was clear. "Where is our *prisoner*, Isaac?"

"It's none of your concern. I'll discuss it with Roemer, but not one of his lackeys."

Another hunter joined Izett. "You've never been one of us, Hayden. You're a tourist. This is our lives. Our legacy. If you do anything to screw this up..."

"Oh, shut the fuck up about your legacy," Hayden said. "Until a few years ago, none of you had even thought about being hunters. You went out to the woods with your dads and shared scary stories around the campfire. You pretended you were the big bad protectors of the world, but none of you believe a word of it until people like Keighley and Roemer came along. You want to talk about legacy? This has been the sole purpose of my entire adult life. So maybe you can accept I know what the hell I'm doing and get the hell out of my way."

Izett held his ground for a moment longer, then stepped aside. "Real big man," he muttered as Hayden brushed past him, making a point to bump the smaller man's shoulder.

Upstairs, Roemer was standing behind his desk, hands on the blotter and head hung low. A woman Hayden had never seen before was sitting in one of the visitor chairs. When Hayden reached the top of the stairs, Roemer bared his teeth and straightened to aim a finger at him.

"Just what the hell do you think you're doing, Isaac?"

"Strategy." Hayden looked at the woman. She was older, and dressed like she had just stepped out of a dinner party despite the fact it was the middle of the night. He didn't know anything about clothes, but he knew high-end when he saw it. He picked up a whiff of unusual floral perfume that he recognized as his grandmother's favorite scent, Jean Naté. "Who is this?"

She looked at him as if he was barely worth the energy of turning her head. "I'm none of your concern. Where did you take Gwyneth Willow?"

"That's none of your concern," Hayden said back to her.

Roemer came around his desk. "I am going to have Valerie examine her, and if there is anything amiss, if there's even a scratch on her~"

"She's not here."

The woman finally seemed interested in him now. "What do you mean she's not here?"

Roemer's eyes flashed. "What have you done?"

"Like I told your minions downstairs, I let her go."

The woman shot to her feet. She was much shorter than either of the men, but her rage added two feet to her height. "You did *what?*"

Hayden remained unshaken. He directed his response to Roemer, whose face had turned bright pink with rage.

"Strategy. Gwyneth Willow was never going to cooperate with you, or any hunter. It was simply never going to happen, no matter what delusions you may have held about turning her. At best, it was a liability to keep her around. Eventually you would have had to put a bullet in her head, and that creates the hassle of disposing of a body. Why invite trouble like that when there's a better solution that actually benefits us? I arranged Gwen's freedom in exchange for enlisting the help of Dale Frye."

Roemer narrowed his eyes. "The daughter's girlfriend?"

"She's been living with wolves for a decade. She'll be an invaluable resource, and she's agreed to help us because I freed her girlfriend's mother as a show of goodwill."

The woman wrinkled her nose and turned away as if smelling a bad odor. "Wolf loving little ginger bitch..."

"How do you know you can trust her?" Roemer said.

"She almost came with me willingly the last time I was in Seattle. The detective convinced her to stay, but she wasn't truly convinced. She's been having doubts. Once she knew I was back in town, she jumped on the opportunity to escape."

Roemer and the women exchanged a look. She shook her head and walked away.

Hayden hooked his thumb at her. "Seriously, who is this? Your mother?"

"We now only have *one* wolf in custody," Roemer said, ignoring the question. "And Ariadne Willow, who is a proven shit-stirrer, has yet another ally in her corner."

"And she's going to lose her partner," Hayden said. "How are you not seeing this as an absolute win? Willow is going to self-destruct when she realizes Dale has come over to our side."

"You are an *imbecile*," the woman shouted. "You think taking away the woman she loves will cripple her? Threatening that redheaded traitor only takes her off the leash. Believe me, I know what I'm talking about."

Hayden shook his head. "That may be true if we were holding her prisoner. She will be here willingly. She can't be saved because she's not in danger. Once she sees that—"

"Gabriel, kill this useless piece of shit."

Hayden blinked at her. "What?"

He was so startled by the order that he didn't have time to defend himself from Roemer's attack. One hand closed around his throat while the other grabbed his shirt, shoving him backward.

Hayden tripped over his own feet and was half-dragged to the open elevator shaft at the far side of the room by the stairs. The wooden slats nailed over the opening were easily snapped when Roemer slammed him against him. Hayden's heart pounded as Roemer bent him backward into the shaft. He could hear the planks clatter far below him.

"Wait! Wait!" He clawed at Roemer's hands, shoving down with both legs as hard as he could to keep himself on solid ground.

"Drop him," the woman said.

"We can... use her both ways," Hayden grunted. "She's with... Willow right now. She can report back. Tell us what they're planning."

"The Willow girl is a detective. She'll know something is wrong."

"Then we threaten to kill Frye if she makes a move against us. She's an asset, and she's a bargaining chip. She's much more valuable than Gwyneth Willow or Milo Duncan combined. We can use her to control Ariadne."

Roemer looked back at the woman, who considered the new tactic. Finally she rolled her eyes and made a sideways gesture with her hand. Roemer grunted and pulled Hayden back into the room.

The woman folded her hands in front of her and walked back to the desk. "There's another way to keep Willow out of our hair. We can just kill the bitch."

"Killing the wolves is a pipe dream," Hayden sighed. "We have no idea the size or spread of their population..."

"Not every wolf," the woman said. "Just one. Well, and her friends. If we're so concerned about Ariadne Willow and her family, then we should just kill them. We have a roomful of men and women downstairs who have been itching for a hunt since this whole mess began. Mr. Roemer, you were adamant that Gwyneth and Millicent remain unharmed for the duration of your experimenting. I agreed, for the time being, but circumstances have changed. We have the Cardoso girl. The Willows are free and probably plotting to cause trouble as we speak. We know where they are, and we know they have a mole with them."

Roemer raised an eyebrow. He looked at Hayden. "I suppose you have a choice, Isaac. We can either kill you or get the Willow wolves out of our hair for good."

Hayden rubbed his throat. He had no idea who this woman was, but she was clearly the one in charge. And she was clearly on the same page with Roemer about exterminating as many wolves as possible. If he had any hope of an actual victory, he would have to play along until an opportunity presented itself. For now, that meant agreeing to whatever they wanted. Ariadne Willow's life was a small price to pay for ultimate success.

"Fine. Frye is the important one anyway. To hell with the rest of them."

The woman grinned.

"Mobilize the hunters. With any luck, they'll have some new trophies by dawn."

CHAPTER SEVENTEEN

IT WAS Milo's suggestion that they needed more people to brainstorm an actual plan of action. Ari made the call and, twenty minutes later, Diana Macallan came around the side of the house looking like she'd dressed in the dark. She wore a button-down pajama top, jeans, and a hoodie. Her wife, Lucy, was a few steps behind her in a similarly mismatched outfit and a pair of chunky eyeglasses. Ari stood up and went to escort them the rest of the way to the porch.

"Sorry for dragging you out here in the middle of the night," Ari said.

Diana shook her head. "I'm a cop. I'm always on-call, especially with a case like this. Lucy's the one you should apologize to. I'm not sure why you insisted she come along." She looked at her wife. "Not that I'm complaining about having you along, babe."

Lucy smiled tiredly. "Happy to lend a hand, if possible."

Gwen stood up to welcome them. "We decided that if we were going to make a plan of action against hunters, we should have a quorum. Three wolves to one human was a bit lopsided. You help round out the numbers a little bit. We all have a stake in what happens here. Wolves, humans, and the police will all be involved if the video proves *canidae* exist and the hunters are mobilized to war."

"No pressure," Lucy said as she took the seat Ari offered her. "Just a comic book creator helping decide how to fight a war."

Diana hugged Gwen and Milo, then took a seat. "Okay. Where are we at the moment?"

"Okay," Gwen said. "Obviously Milo and I have gotten away from the hunters who were holding us prisoner. They currently have two women held captive: Marin Cardoso and Valerie Byrne. Marin is *canidae*, Val is human. We know where they're being held. We have--"

"Wait, *we know* where they're being held?" Diana was out of her chair again, pulling out her phone. "Give me an address and--"

Gwen held up a hand. "And you'll send a strike team to surround the building, leading Roemer to kill the prisoners. He would have no reason to keep them alive at that point. The police have to be a last resort. As long as we keep this small, there's a chance of doing it with a minimal loss of life."

Diana didn't look happy, but she sat down again.

"We have a deadline," Gwen continued. "But it's still very early considering the fact Marin was in wolf form when she was captured. There's practically zero chance she'll transform in the next week or so unless she does it deliberately, and she has no reason to do that. So I think we're safe on that account."

Dale said, "The SPD press conference seems to have helped quash the video a little bit. It's not being shared as frequently on social media, and most people are already moving on. But it wouldn't take much for the fire to reignite."

"Like, say, if the livestream started showing a police raid," Ari said.

"Or if a bunch of actual wolves showed up and started attacking everyone in military formation," Diana said. "So what are our options? Negotiate?"

Milo said, "Like we have anything to offer them."

"We do, actually," Dale said. Everyone looked at her, and she shrugged. "The cure."

"What cure?" Lucy asked.

Dale looked at Ari, who understood what she meant. "When I was in prison, Val gave me medication that would stop my transformations for six months. The other *canidae* in there had been on it for years." She laughed incredulously. "Dale, we can't give that to the hunters."

"Seems like a really dangerous idea," Lucy agreed. Her voice was meek, as if she wasn't sure whether she could or should interject.

"No, listen," Dale said. "One of the main themes in the Magnusson book is that hunters are *terrified* of being bitten. What to do if you think you've been 'infected,' how fast it can spread, how to amputate if you're bitten on the arm or leg. There's an entire essay dedicated to wolf tooth removal so they physically can't bite you. They're scared because a bite is a death sentence. If they don't transform within four weeks, their bodies will change against their will, and it's a horrible, painful, gruesome death. If we give them a way to prevent that from happening, we could save lives."

Gwen said, "Dale, I appreciate where you're coming from, but we absolutely *cannot* hand this medicine over to them. They can't even be allowed to know it exists."

"Mom's right," Ari said. "These people manufactured wolfsbane and put it in the food supply. What do you think they'd do if they had a medication that could stop us from transforming? How long do you think it would be before they found a way to put it in the food, or the water? It would still be a genocide, just a much slower version of one."

Gwen said, "Negotiation is a good idea. None of you saw how many hunters they had in the building tonight. Who knows how many are elsewhere in the city waiting to be called up."

"Nowhere near as many wolves," Milo said.

"We can't guarantee that," Ari said. "And even if we did outnumber them, are we really going to start an all-out war against the hunters in the middle of Seattle? We might as well just let them announce that *canidae* are real and call it a day."

Diana said, "Well, if we can't use the police, we can't fight, and we can't negotiate, what the hell does that leave us? We have two women in danger, and sitting here debating isn't doing them any good. If all our options are bad, then we should go with the one that gives us the most boots on the ground. I can have the building surrounded by SWAT in twenty minutes."

Ari grimaced and leaned forward. "I don't see a way that ends with Marin and Val still alive. Even if Roemer doesn't give the order, at least one of those hunters is going to see the end is near and take the opportunity to kill a wolf while he still can."

The women all fell silent.

"What about the thing Ari did last time?" Dale said. "She walked in, talked some sense into them. They might be hunters, but they're still regular people. They may not have any interest in going to war. She got that-that... what were they called again?"

"Venatorial Club," Ari said.

Diana leaned to her left, craning her neck to look at the far side of the yard. Ari caught the move and frowned at her, but Diana waved her off and focused on the conversation again.

"Right," Dale said, unaware of the silent exchange. "They decided to just walk away and then we only had to deal with Keighley."

Milo and Gwen were already shaking their heads. Gwen said, "Last time we were dealing with weekend warriors. People who saw hunting as a hobby. The people who held us hostage, who tortured us, they're the true believers. You're not going to change their minds no matter how good your speech is."

"No, I wouldn't have thought so. The speech really didn't work, either, if you think about it. It didn't even give us a decade of peace before they came back swinging. Whatever we do this time, it has to be more decisive. I don't want to go through all this shit again in another five years."

Diana seemed to resign herself to not going the official route. She was watching the far side of the yard again. "Okay, what do we know for certain? Is there anything we can use to our advantage?"

Ari said, "There's a book. The Book of Simon."

Gwen sat up straighter. "That would be a hell of a reach, Ariadne."

"I'm not familiar," Diana said.

Gwen sighed. "Simon Lehner was a wolf who wanted to kill as many humans as possible to create a *canidae*-only country. This was two hundred years ago. He had a whole manifesto that he spread around to recruit wolves to his cause."

"So like the opposite of the Magnusson book," Lucy said.

Gwen nodded, then shrugged. "It won't turn anyone into a hunter the way the Magnusson book creates hunters, but basically. Wolves who read it get riled up. It's pretty effective rhetoric. It would be useful if a war *does* break out and our ranks are starting to thin out, but I don't think we can use it to start a war against them."

"The war has already started," Ari said. "Right now we're just looking for a way to minimize casualties."

"Maybe we shouldn't be." Milo's jaw was tight, and there was a fire in her eyes. "The hell with playing nice with these bastards. They want to see us as monsters? They're going to come at us anyway, kidnap us, torture us, maybe we shouldn't worry about playing into their hands. There's no moral high ground if they just slaughter us on sight. We go in, we take care of Roemer and whoever else he's got in that building, and we let that stand as an example to any other hunters who decide to stir things up again. If we're going to keep their damn book around, why not keep the counterpoint around as well?"

Gwen said, "It could be equally dangerous. Other wolves rose up to stop Simon because they understood how humans would react to a wolf like him. If one of us starts acting homicidal, they'll use it as an excuse to slaughter all of us. Then what are we left with? A whole world at war until no one is left to actually live here."

"Sorry," Diana said, holding up her hand. She was sitting up straight, almost hovering above her seat. This time Ari turned as well to see what had drawn her attention. "Sorry," Diana said again, "but is the traffic in this neighborhood usually safe?"

"Yes, why?" Gwen said. They were all following Diana's gaze now. She was looking toward a section of fence that partially blocked the street from view.

"Because I've heard three cars drive by very slowly without their headlights on. I'm pretty sure one of them just parked at the curb."

Ari, Milo, and Gwen all stood.

"How can you tell their headlights aren't on?" Dale asked. "The road is blocked by the fence."

"She still would have seen their headlights," Ari said. "What are you thinking, Diana?"

"I think someone needs to get Lucy somewhere safe, now."

Dale got to her feet and motioned for Lucy to come with her. She looked at Diana. "Where exactly is safe? If they're on the street, we can't get to the cars."

"The house is probably out of the question, too," Milo said. "Do you think they're surrounding us? There's a gap in the fence that Gwen and I use when we go running. They can get to the next street over through there."

Diana said, "Probably the best bet. Another car just parked." She reached under her hoodie and pulled a gun from the waistband of her pants. "Any weapons in the house?"

Gwen looked at Milo and Ari. "Just me and my girls."

Diana shrugged. "Works for me." To Dale, she said, "Get Lucy home safe. Lucy..."

"I love you, too. Be safe."

Dale squeezed Lucy's shoulder and guided her across the yard. Diana watched until they disappeared into the shadows before she faced the others.

"So... shirts and skins?"

Despite the circumstances, Ari laughed.

Dale held Lucy's hand as they hurried through the fence gap, hunched over to avoid wayward branches. They emerged in a small runoff ditch between two properties. Dale turned to make sure Lucy had made it through unscathed and urged her ahead.

"Are you sure they're going to be okay?"

"As okay as they ever are."

She moved closer to the house where she hoped they would be concealed by shadows and scanned the street. She wasn't sure what she was looking for beyond "something suspicious," but the street was quiet and empty. The property they'd emerged onto had an overly landscaped lawn, full of thick clover and the type of greenery that a real-estate agent would call "topiaries" to make them sound fancier. She whispered for Lucy to follow her.

"It's bad enough being married to a cop," Lucy said, "add in werewolves and it's a wonder I ever get a decent night's sleep. We should start a support group."

Dale chuckled. "I think you and I might be the only two members."

"So we should just have lunch?"

Dale looked back at her. "I'd really like that. We'll set something up. After..."

"Sure, yeah, of course after..." She gestured at the air to indicate everything. Dale led her to the sidewalk and then turned south. "Where are we going?"

"We're going to circle around behind the hunters," Dale said, "just to keep an eye on things. In case our girls need backup."

Lucy hesitated. "Right. Makes sense."

Dale looked back at her again. "Is something wrong? If you'd rather we just hightail it and call an Uber, we can do that. Diana would kill me if you got hurt..."

"No, it's not that." She cleared her throat. "Diana told me to keep an eye on you."

"Oh," Dale said. "That's fair. I *am* pretending to be a double agent turned triple agent. I'm not even sure how many people I'm supposedly betraying right now. I'll go ahead and swear to you that

I'm on Ariadne's side, now and forever, but I'll also give you permission to hit me on the head with a flower pot if I start acting squirrely. No hard feelings."

Lucy smiled. "I appreciate that."

They reached Gwen and Milo's street and discovered the Diana's fears were well-founded. Three SUVs which hadn't been there when she arrived were parked in front of the house. She had a momentary twinge of panic when she realized there was a chance they'd followed her from the park where she picked up Gwen, but she'd been too careful for that. She was absolutely positive that no one had followed her.

Unless the essays really had messed with her head, and she was acting as a double agent without realizing it. Blackouts, lost time, false memories, she could be doing things she didn't even realize.

No. She dismissed that thought and refused to throw away any more time second guessing herself. She had Lucy to watch her back, literally and figuratively, and that was enough insurance for her, for now.

She crouched down and watched a group of men congregate near the front vehicle. It was hard to tell in the dark, but she counted at least four of them. Possible movement in the backseat of one truck made her think there was a fifth. The Willow house was dark and completely still, the front yard overgrown and poorly-tended in the absence of its owners. The front windows were blocked by bushes which hadn't been trimmed down since before Gwen and Milo left for Europe.

The hunter who'd been sitting in the truck finally got out to join the others. Dale watched him tuck something, presumably a weapon, into his belt, and then shut the door quietly behind him. She noticed he'd tried so hard not to make any noise that the door was probably still open even if they'd locked it. At some unknown signal, they moved across the street toward the house. When they spread out, Dale finally got a headcount of five men. Her fingers itched for a way to warn them danger was coming.

As it turned out, a warning was unnecessary. As soon as the fifth man was on the grass, a wolf that had been hiding at the edge of the property broke cover. Dale couldn't identify who it was in the dark. Whoever it was, she crossed the lawn at a fast crawl, a pool of oil sliding across the grass, matching the speed of the hunters until she was right on top of them. She pounced at the same moment the porch light came on, blinding the lead man as the wolf tackled the hunter bringing up the rear.

"Stay here," Dale said, already running down the sidewalk.

"Wait!"

Dale didn't wait. She ran up the sidewalk to the SUV she'd seen the hunter exit and pulled open the door she'd seen him halfway close. It was, as she'd guessed, unlatched. She climbed in and crawled into the backseat, then continued on into the cargo area. She saw gun cases, boxes of ammunition, and several things she couldn't identify. She also saw a bulletproof vest, which she slipped over her head because anything would be better than her pajamas, and started rooting around for anything that might help.

"Dale!"

She jumped, even though she recognized Lucy's voice through the glass. She was on the sidewalk-side of the car, out of sight of the house.

"I told you to wait!"

"You must be out of your damn mind. Grab me one of those vests."

Dale did, and also picked up a few of the weapons just to have them. She tried the back hatch, discovered it was unlocked, and opened it just wide enough to tumble out onto the pavement. Lucy closed the hatch behind her before any of the hunters noticed, but a quick glance over her shoulder revealed they were much too distracted to pay attention to their cars. She handed Lucy a vest, then carried the rest of their loot back to safety.

She looked back toward the house. The porch light was bright enough for Dale to identify the wolves now, and she saw that it had been Milo who tackled the hunter.

The hunters had come well-prepared, dressed in thick jackets with gloves tucked into the sleeves, their throats and faces similarly covered. They wore masks with holes cut out for dark goggles. Every inch of skin was covered, which they thought meant protection. They were discovering that the opposite was true. As soon as Ari, Milo, and Gwen discovered there was no chance of infecting the hunters through a bite, they stopped pulling their punches.

Milo was standing on her fallen victim, his dominant arm trapped in her jaws. His free arm swung to punch her in the ribs, but she jumped and twisted enough to evade most of the blows.

Ari and Gwen had come around the side of the house when the lights came on, and they each had taken a hunter. Ari was on one man's back, and Gwen had bowled over another and dropped him hard on the grass. The front door was standing open and Diana had come outside wearing Milo's motorcycle helmet and leather jacket like it was a suit of armor. She had a tire iron hanging from one hand, and she swung it like she was Lou Gehrig. The first hunter she hit was by accident, a direct blow to the side of his head. He was wearing a helmet but it still knocked him to the ground. Diana angled her arm to use the rebound of the blow to strike the hip of the hunter next to him, and he collapsed with a shout of pain that even Dale could hear from down the street.

"Flashbangs," Lucy said.

"What?"

"You got flashbangs."

Dale raised an eyebrow. "How do you know that?"

"Research. I put them in my comic book. You draw something a couple dozen times, you learn to recognize it on sight." She looked toward the house. "The only downside is that there's no way to use them without also hurting the girls."

"We'll hold those back as a last resort if things start looking bad."

Two of the hunters were trying to fall back. Milo was still gnawing on one's arm, and the other was trying to pull her off. He had an arm around her neck and was leaning back with all his weight trying to pry her away. Judging by the screams of the man on the ground, it was only making her dig her teeth in harder. She'd stopped twisting and jerking, however, so some of the blows with his free hand were actually landing hard.

Ari had been thrown from her hunter. Dale watched her get back to her feet and launch herself between his legs to avoid the aim of his pistol. He fired and a clump of dirt flew up where Ari had just been standing. He twisted and took aim again but Ari was already blocked by one of the other hunters so he couldn't take the shot. Diana saw the gun and cracked the shooter's wrist with her tire iron. He howled, dropped his arm, and turned to face her fully. Diana headbutted him, the smooth front of the helmet cracking against the smooth material of his mask. He went down hard, and he didn't try to get back up.

Sirens were echoing through the neighborhood now. In this area, the houses were widely-spaced and surrounded by enough foliage that she doubted anyone had a clear view of what was happening in the Willow front yard, but the noise had definitely carried. The hunters were beating a hasty retreat back to their vehicles.

Dale looked down at the canister Lucy had identified as a flashbang. "What's the delay on these things?"

"Uh, not long. I would be dropping it as I pulled the trigger." She pointed and mimed the motion needed. "But if you throw it, you'd just be blinding our girls at the same time."

"No, I'm thinking of something much dumber than that."

The hunters got to their cars and got inside. Diana and the wolves gave chase, but remained wary of the weapons the men carried.

"Oh, I'm dumb, I'm dumb," Dale chanted.

"It's not too late to *not* be dumb," Lucy said behind her.

"Nope..."

Dale straightened and ran for the corner at the same time the lead car lurched forward. She was barefoot, she remembered, and she was in her damn pajamas. The bulletproof vest slapped against her chest and shoulders as she ran. It was heavy and seemed like more of a hindrance than any kind of real protection. She pumped her fists and picked up her knees, watching the cars, gauging their progress. They had no idea she was there. They assumed all their enemies were behind them. The lead car would have to slow down to take the corner. If she wasn't there in time, there was no point in even trying her stupid, stupid plan.

She reached the corner just before the truck did. She barely slowed down, grabbed the passenger door and yanked it open. Time slowed down so that each second seemed to drag by for a full minute.

The driver and passenger had taken off their goggles and turned wide, terrified eyes on her.

The men were too startled to raise their weapons. The driver hadn't even stopped moving.

The car kept rolling forward as Dale let go of the door with one hand, triggered the flashbang with the other, and lobbed it into the car.

The forward momentum of the vehicle caused the door to swing shut. Dale kept running, unable to stop her own tumbling run, throwing her weight to the left as she tripped over her feet so that she would land and roll in the grass. She saw the windows of the lead car light up with an impossibly bright flash, and then the windows were completely fogged. The driver finally stepped on the brakes, which caused the following car to slam into it from behind.

Dale pushed herself up onto her knees and looked back toward the house. The third SUV had gone the opposite direction and missed the accident entirely.

The driver and passenger from the lead car fell out and collapsed on the pavement at the same time a Seattle Police cruiser came around the corner with all lights flashing. The driver saw the men in the street and skidded to a stop, both officers leaping out with their guns drawn.

Diana ran down the middle of the road, badge held high like she was an Olympic torch runner. She'd lost the motorcycle helmet and looked only a little manic as she approached the other officers.

"Detective Diana Macallan, SPD!" she shouted. "These men are connected to the kidnapping of Marin Cardoso!"

Dale looked back at the house. All three wolves had vanished, presumably back into the house. She got back to her feet and brushed herself off, glancing up when she saw Lucy coming up beside her. One of the officers went to the men lying on the ground and knelt to check on them. A second cruiser had come up from behind, and those two officers were taking care of the hunters in the second car. People were starting to risk coming out on their lawns now to see what all the commotion was about.

One of the officers spotted Dale and Lucy. "Ladies, stay where you are."

"They're not related to this," Diana said.

"They're wearing bulletproof vests," the officer pointed out.

"They..." Diana looked at them, pure confusion crossing her face. "They, uh, they are. That's... the vests are mine. I'm... they... they're staying at the house these men just attacked, and I decided to let them wear the vests just as a precaution."

The officer didn't look convinced, but didn't pursue the questions any further. "Is anyone else in the house?"

"Three other women," Diana said. "They're instrumental to the case as well. We were combining what we knew in the hopes we could make a move. I guess these guys got wind of how close we were and decided to try tripping us up."

"Doesn't look like they were very successful."

Diana said, "There was a third truck that got away. I can give you a description for the APB."

"I can't wait to eavesdrop on this," the officer said. He lifted a hand, waved for Dale and Lucy to come with them. "Might as well keep everyone in one place until we get this all figured out."

Dale put an arm around Lucy and escorted her off the sidewalk. They joined Diana, who led the march back to the house with the other officers remaining at the wreck to sort out all their prisoners.

"Where the hell did you get bulletproof vests?" Diana asked. "And what exploded in the car back there?"

"Dale robbed a car, honey," Lucy said. "Arrest her. Arrest her right now."

"Traitor," Dale said.

"Is that where you got the bulletproof vest for my wife?"

Dale said, "It is."

"Then I think I'll let it slide, just this once." She looked back at the hunters. They were now all handcuffed, lying on their stomachs in the middle of the street. The officer who had done all the talking was now speaking into a radio mounted on his shoulder, most likely calling in for more units. "Four more hunters in custody," Diana said. "Guess that means the guy who got away was riding solo."

"Could've been worse."

"Could've been a whole lot worse," Diana said. "Come on. Let's get inside and get our stories straight for my colleagues here."

Dale looked back one more time. The police had opened the back of one SUV and was beginning to inventory the weapons there. Lots of weapons, lots of very deadly force, that these men had planned to use against Ari, Gwen, and Milo. She shivered and hugged herself as she went into the house. Any doubts she might have had about herself, any fear of lingering hunter seeds lying dormant in her brain, had just been effectively put to rest.

She would never be that kind of monster. And she was willing to do whatever it took, even if it put her in danger, to protect the people she loved.

Chapter Eighteen

Val's tension was so high that she twitched like an electric charge had passed through her when the door to her cell opened. Hayden came inside, glancing over his shoulder before he closed the door behind him. She'd been sitting on the bed and stood up, squaring herself for a fight.

"What the hell is going on, Hayden? Where's Gwen? If you hurt her..."

"Sh, shut up." He was holding his phone, which he turned around so she could see the screen.

At first she didn't understand what the picture meant, but she leaned closer and slowly realized it was Dale, crouching next to Gwen.

"This is tonight?"

"Just a few hours ago," he said. "Ms. Frye and I have an arrangement. I don't believe it's necessary to kill all the wolves. Roemer and I disagree about that. Hopefully we're making progress on a compromise that will keep Marin Cardoso safe when all of this is over. But for now, Gwyneth Willow is safe at home with her family."

Val said, "And Roemer knows?"

"Oh, yeah. Everyone knows. They just sent out a damn militia to the Willow house, so I don't know how long Gwen will stay free. But I did my part, Dale is going to do hers, and I hope I can count on you to do yours. Keep Marin safe and healthy until this whole mess is dealt with. If anything happens to her and we have to cut the feed, this whole thing will have been for nothing."

"Of course I'll keep her healthy. Not for this twisted game of yours, but because she's a person. She didn't ask for any of this. I'm not going to let her suffer out of spite."

Hayden nodded. "Good. Good, I just… I wanted to be sure."

Val clenched her jaw and crossed her arms. "So now the two of us are your only hostages?"

"I don't like the word hostages."

"How do you feel about kidnapper?"

He flinched. "I hate everything about this, but it's the only way. People will only believe the truth if they see it with their own eyes."

She laughed. "Really? How exactly is the livestream working for you? Are people out on the streets shouting about werewolves? Are there watch parties waiting for the moment the world changes? Or is it a joke? I imagine the late night comedians are having a field day with it." She tilted her head. "Actually, there's a woman being held prisoner in the video, so it's probably a touchy subject. Even if you do get a transformation on camera, what will it prove? That you have really good CGI? At best you're going to get some video essays on YouTube and a subreddit dedicated to *canidae* truthers. Honestly, those groups may already exist. So well done. You've stolen close to a year of my life to start a conspiracy theory."

"We're making strides. We're creating awareness. We're~"

"You're spinning your wheels. You want to let people know werewolves exist. To what end? Peace and cohabitation? Have you looked outside lately? Humans don't accept other humans for the tiniest, stupidest reasons. We're endlessly fighting wars because one person decides to believe one book over another one. How is this revelation going to be anything other than a bloodbath?"

"I have faith in humanity~"

"Me too," Val said. "I believe the majority of people are good. But I also believe there are those who will do awful things, and that a lot of people will suffer just because of what they are. My father would look at Ariadne Willow and consider her inferior. For a lot of reasons, actually. A woman, gay, a wolf. But she's a better person than him in every single way that matters. I'm not going to base my judgment of a person on how or where they're born. That's humanity 101."

Hayden worked his jaw, clearly fighting the urge to snap at her. Val didn't want to let him off the hook, so she stepped closer.

"What, Isaac? You want to scream at me? Or would it be easier to just hit me to shut me up? I've known enough people like you to make a guess which one it is."

She didn't know if he would have actually done it, because the moment was broken by the sound of someone shouting outside. Hayden snapped out of his rage and went to see what was happening. He neglected to secure the cell door behind him, so Val followed.

"Roemer! Get your damn ass down here!"

One of the hunters, a gym rat named Bruno Lutz, had stormed into the main room and was already halfway to the stairs. He looked like he was dressed for an assault but, going by the redness of his face, it hadn't gone to plan. Hayden moved to intercept the man before he got to the stairs.

"Bruno, what's going on? What happened? Where's the rest of your team?"

"I don't have a fucking clue," Bruno said. "The fucking wolves ran us off." He was breathing heavily, and he hadn't blinked since Val had been watching him. "They were waiting for us. It was three wolves, and some other bitch in a motorcycle helmet."

One of the other hunters said, "Probably their human bitch. The Frye woman."

"I don't think so," Bruno said. "Taller than her. But I wouldn't be surprised if she was the one who told them we were coming."

"Neither would I."

Hayden turned to see the mysterious woman had arrived at the bottom of the stairs. She advanced on the group.

"I've been monitoring the police band. There was a call to Gwyneth Willow's address a few minutes ago. Sounds of a brawl, possible gunfire, a car accident. Four men have been taken into custody and officers on the scene report their vehicles are full of unlicensed weaponry." She slowly turned her head until her eyes locked onto Hayden. "Dale Frye was, in fact, on the scene according to one of our men on the force."

Val could see the worry in Hayden's eyes. "Of course she was. We're using her as a double agent. The Willows have to believe she's on their side. Besides, Frye had no idea you were planning to assault the house. How could she have blown an attack she wasn't even aware of?"

The woman considered the defense. "Be that as it may, we've lost four good men to these damned wolves. I'm sick of it. I'm sick of letting them have the upper hand. They are *animals*. Beasts in skin suits. We will not be beaten back by them." She worked her jaw as she considered her next words carefully. Finally, she looked up, her decision made. "We still have a stockpile of weapons, correct?"

"Of course," one of the hunters said. "But if the cops are already at the Willow place–"

"We're not taking them to the Willows," the woman said. "There are more than enough other wolves in this city, and it's high time we start to show them how things will be from now on."

Hayden said, "You have any particular wolves in mind?"

The woman looked at him. "Marin Cardoso has a sister, doesn't she? And she's part of a pack?"

"Lot of eyes on them after that press conference stunt they pulled," one of the hunters warned.

"Good. I want every wolf in the city to see it and know who they're up against." She turned and walked back to the stairs, giving one last command over her shoulder as she left. "Willow, Cardoso, or any other wolf... I want pelts on my wall by breakfast time."

The hunters, all on the verge of insanity after playing babysitter for so long, jumped into action. Val watched them with dread, saw them open crates to remove weapons of every variety and size, while others disappear into other sections of the building to return with body armor. They'd been waiting for this ever since Milo and Gwen were taken prisoner, and now they had permission to run loose. She looked at Hayden, who seemed just as disturbed by this development.

He held his hands out, indicating helplessness. "This has always been a race against the clock, Dr. Byrne," he said. "I'm afraid the counter just hit zero."

Chapter Nineteen

After the police left with the arrested hunters, after Diana promised to get statements from everyone present for the official report, and after Ari got Dale some ice for the shoulder that was now starting to throb after her wildly ill-advised move with the grenade, the group gathered in the living room of the Willow house. The wolves had retaken human form and changed back into their clothes. Milo sat with Gwen on the couch, Dale took the armchair, and Diana and Lucy sat on the hearth. Ari was pacing, head down, worrying her bottom lip with her teeth.

"We can look at the bright side," Gwen said to break the silence. "Four more hunters have been taken into custody. It doesn't matter what our story is. They were caught red-handed outside a private residence with their cars loaded for war. Either they come up with some lie, and I can't imagine a plausible legal reason to have that kind of firepower, or they tell the truth and get locked up for ranting about werewolves."

Lucy said, "The video could actually help us in this case. We could say it caused some kind of mass hysteria. People on the verge of a mental break heard about werewolves and started seeing them everywhere. It's like that *Twilight Zone* episode where everyone was worried about aliens showing up so they turned on their neighbors."

"Mob mentality," Ari said. "It'll more than likely become a real issue soon enough, so it would be nice to use it to help us out while we still can."

She started to say something else but was interrupted by Diana's cell phone chirping. She checked it, answered. "This is Detective Macallan. Yes." As she listened, her expression became darker. She stood up and held out her hand for Ari to come closer. "Were you... good. Fantastic. How many?" She nodded. "Hold them on the scene until I get there."

Ari raised her eyebrows when Diana hung up. "Good or bad?"

"Little of both," Diana said with a sigh. "The officers I assigned to watch Eva Cardoso's house spotted a suspicious vehicle circling the block. They called in the license plate and found it was a rental. I told them to expect just what Lucy was talking about. Eva made herself a very public, very searchable face of any 'werewolves are real' conspiracy theorists who might want to take matters into their own hands. Looks like we caught a break."

Milo said, "But she's safe?"

"Oh, yeah. We moved her whole pack to a safe house after the press conference. It seemed like the best course of action. The officers let the hunters go ahead with the assault and caught them in the act. The condo will need a new door, but no one was actually injured."

"How many hunters were involved in the assault?" Gwen asked.

"Ten," Diana said. "I guess they decided to go whole-hog since they didn't know how many wolves would be there. All ten of them were taken into custody."

Ari stood up straighter, suddenly invigorated. She looked at Gwen. "How many hunters would you say were at the building?"

Gwen shook her head, uncertain. "Less than twenty, more than ten."

"And we just saw four of them get carted away by the police. That makes fourteen hunters in custody, including the one who was injured the other day when they were going after Eva's pack. There can't be that many left behind at the building where Marin and Val are being held."

Gwen and Milo both got to their feet. Gwen answered the question Ari hadn't asked. "I can get us there, no problem."

"Are you sure you're up for going back there?"

"Oh hell yes," Gwen said.

Milo nodded. "Same goes for me. I can't wait to even the score a little bit."

Dale stood. "You're going to need me, too."

"I always need you," Ari said, "but I'm not about to walk you into a potential war zone with an unknown number of hunters."

"Oh, cool," Dale said. "That's fine. So, uh, which one of you is good enough with computers to cut off the live stream? Milo? Mom?" She looked around as if she actually expected someone to raise their hand. "Anyone? Or is it just me?"

Ari grunted. "You're not smarter than me just because you can work the magic glowing box."

"No, no, I'm smarter than you for other reasons, too." She winked and folded her arms over her chest. "Besides, if I'm not there, Hayden may hold onto the idea that I'm really a double agent. I would like to personally dissuade him of that belief."

Ari shivered. "Okay. That gave me chills. You can come."

Dale winked at her.

Diana said, "I'll coordinate with the arresting officers. They should know that all our wolf hunters are part of the same organization."

Lucy said, "I'm not sure what I can contribute to the fight, but I'm willing to do what I can."

"You told me what the bangflasher was," Dale said. "That was a huge help."

"Flashbang," Lucy corrected, then shrugged. "Well, if you need any more esoteric useless information, I'm your gal."

"For now," Diana said, "you're needed safe at home. I think you've been at the heart of enough excitement for tonight."

"Since you're going to be more on the administrative side of things," Lucy said, "I'm willing to agree with you. I just wish I could be of more help." Her eyes widened. "Oh! The dazzler!"

"What's the dazzler?" Ari said.

"It's one more way my useless research information can come in handy. Do you have time to swing by our place to pick something up before you go after the prisoners?"

Ari said, "If it will help us succeed, absolutely."

Lucy grinned. "I think you'll be very happy with it."

Diana looked as confused as everyone else. "Well, if we've all got our assignments, I think we better get this show on the road. I'll keep you informed if anything changes with the hunters we have in custody." She rubbed her hands together and looked at Lucy. "Do you want to say it?"

"Say what?" Lucy asked.

Diana said, "Oh, come on. They're about to go off and..." She sighed and rolled her eyes, then raised her hand to give an exaggerated wave. She squinted one eye shut and spoke out of the corner of her mouth in an old person's voice. "Have fun stormin' da castle!"

Ari stared at her. "You're a dork."

"You're a heathen if you don't like that movie," Diana said.

"I love the movie," Ari said, "but whatever you just did was... sad."

Diana sighed and rolled her eyes. "Fine. Go put on your fur coats and kick some hunter ass."

Ari smiled. "Now *that's* a send-off."

The Macallans lived in North Seattle, but it was late enough that they didn't run into any traffic and made the trip in record time. They drove Lucy home and waited when she went inside and came back with a duffel bag full of riot gear: batons, elbow- and kneepads, safety goggles, helmets. Ari stared at the display with more than a little surprise.

"You just have this stuff lying around? You're a comic book creator."

"And I need reference material. One of Diana's colleagues loaned me all this stuff when I did a comic about a special-ops team. You can take all of it, it'll probably come in useful tonight, but the things I wanted to show you..." She put the bag down and dug around until she retrieved a small device that looked like a flashlight. "The dazzler. It's supposed to be mounted on the barrel of a rifle or shotgun or something, but you can also use it manually."

She aimed it at the wall and triggered it, creating a bright strobing flash. Even the reflected light was so bright that Ari and Milo both brought up their hands to cover their eyes.

"That's why I included the goggles. No sense blinding yourselves at the same time. It's perfect because even if you accidentally catch Dr. Byrne or Marin in the flash, they'll recover without any permanent effects." She returned the dazzler to the bag and handed it to Ari. "Never thought I would be a gunrunner for a guerilla army of werewolves, but I guess life surprises us all."

Ari leaned in and kissed Lucy's cheek. "You're a hero, Lucy

Macallan."

"I still feel like a coward for sitting safe at home while you're all out doing the dangerous stuff."

"You made it a little less dangerous," Ari said. "That's enough. Now get inside. We'll keep you in the loop as much as we can."

"Be safe, all of you."

Ari nodded and waited until she was inside before she picked up the bag and carried it back to the car. Milo followed her, glancing at the car where Gwen and Dale were waiting. She put her hand on Ari's shoulder to stop her on the sidewalk.

"Are we really going to let them help us out with this?"

"You're lucky I'm letting *you* help," Ari said. "You're still recovering from everything that happened. Mom hasn't even been free for an entire night. The idea of taking her back to that place is killing me. But we don't know how many hunters are there, and I don't want to risk being outnumbered. Mom can take care of herself. So can you and Dale. So if you're all willing, I'm not going to waste time trying to be the Lone Ranger."

"Works for me," Milo said. "Plus we got all these cool new weapons to use."

Ari said, "I was thinking I'd go in as the wolf."

"Me too," Milo said, "but it's nice to have options. And Dale should be nicely protected."

"My number one concern," Ari admitted. "Shall we...?"

Milo nodded and they continued on to the car. Gwen was in the back, Dale in the driver's seat. Milo joined Gwen in the backseat with the bag, while Ari got in the front next to Dale.

"Have a nice chat?" Dale said.

Ari said, "We decided to let you help us."

Dale wiped imaginary sweat from her forehead. "What a relief. Did Lucy explain what a dazzler is?"

"Yeah. Along with some other cool stuff. We'll fill you in on the way." She twisted in the seat to look at Gwen. "You ready?"

"Ready," Gwen said. "Drive south, Dale. Toward CenturyLink. Once we get there, it'll just be a matter of one or two turns."

Ari faced forward as Dale pulled out of the driveway. "Okay, then. Into the lion's den we go..."

New York got the credit as the city that never slept, but Ari wondered if any big city ever really went completely to bed. She looked out the window as Dale passed through downtown, the streetlights dimmed but still shining, traffic still flowing, container ships rolling through Puget Sound to deliver their cargo. She saw people out walking, shadows without detail, and wondered if they were out at this hour by choice or necessity.

"Have you thought about what you're going to say?" Dale asked.

Ari pulled her thoughts back to the car. "What? Say to who? About what?"

"The hero speech."

"I don't have any idea what you're talking about."

"You know," Dale said. "Last time the hunters showed up, you gave a big speech about how this whole thing was archaic. You got them to put down their weapons."

Ari scoffed. "Yeah, and look where that got us. They're already back, and they're worse than ever before. We're not going to talk."

Dale looked over at her, then glanced into the backseat. "You're... you're not talking about *killing* them, are you?"

"They planned to kill us, Dale," Gwen said calmly. "The raid on our home. The attempted attack on the Cardoso pack. Marin and Val are still in incredible danger. Ariadne is right. We can't afford to use kid gloves on them."

Dale looked at Ari. "I never thought I'd see you advocating deadly force."

Ari didn't answer immediately. She took a few deep breaths and watched the downtown lights for a few blocks before she spoke.

"We've tried to be peaceful. We've tried talking sense into them. It doesn't stick. There will always be people like Roemer who either want us dead or think they're doing the right thing by revealing us to the world. Either way, they're not going to stop unless we make them stop. Maybe that makes us the monsters Magnusson wrote about. I don't know if this is the right thing to do. The only thing I'm sure about is that if we don't do something drastic, a lot of wolves are going to die."

Dale pressed her lips together.

"You don't have to be there for it," Ari said.

"Do you still have my bracelet?" Dale asked.

Ari frowned. "Uh. Yeah. I think so." She reached into her pocket and retrieved the bracelet. She held it for a moment, then handed it over.

"Can you take the wheel for a second?"

Ari watched her carefully and put her hand on the wheel. Dale kept her eyes on the road as she unfastened the clasp, wrapped it around her wrist, and snapped it shut again. She took the wheel again and breathed out slowly.

"When I had this made, hair and fur, it meant that I was accepting both sides of you. If someone wanted you dead, if someone was actually sending SWAT teams to your house to kill you, nothing in Heaven or Earth would stop me from doing whatever it took to keep you safe. I'm all in, puppy."

Milo said, "Knew you were a true wolf, Dale."

Dale smiled, but it was weak. "Trust me, this isn't what I want to be doing. But if the option is between helping you and doing nothing, when I know that doing nothing means more *canidae* will die, then I don't see a choice."

The rest of the ride was spent in silence until the stadium loomed into view. Gwen directed Dale where to go, pointing her toward a nondescript concrete wedge of a building that could have been anything from a warehouse to a parking garage. There were only a handful of small windows, and those were blocked by thin sheets of mostly opaque plastic. Lights were on in most of the windows, but there was obviously no way of knowing how many people were actually inside. Ari heard a sharp intake of breath from the backseat. She didn't know which of the women had made it, but it didn't really matter.

"Neither of you have to be there either," Ari said. "You've both been through enough."

"I'm getting my closure," Milo said.

Ari nodded.

Dale parked at the end of the block and shut off the engine. "Battle plan?" she asked.

"I was going to say we go in as wolves, use the element of surprise, let the animal brain take over. But that was before Lucy gave us all these wonderful toys. So new plan. We take the bulletproof vests that Dale and Lucy so kindly appropriated from the hunters and we go in the front door. Hopefully we can catch them unawares and take them out before they have a chance to get their weapons." She twisted to look into the backseat. "What do you remember of the interior?"

Gwen said, "We didn't see much of it. Four floors. Multiple rooms on each floor. Milo and I were kept on the ground floor, I'm pretty sure Marin is on the second floor, and Roemer is at the top."

"Like a video game," Ari said. "Easy levels leading up to the big boss. I'll go in first. Then Milo. Dale, you and Mom bring up the rear."

Gwen said, "I'm~"

"Not arguing with me? Great. Because you understand that you and Milo have both been through something traumatic, and she's had more time to heal. Right? That's what you were going to say?"

Gwen curled her lip. "Smart ass."

"Well, you raised me," Ari said. "We ready?"

They geared up. Ari and Milo put on the bulletproof vests, protective eyewear, and slipped the dazzlers into their pockets. They also got batons, which Dale and Gwen were also armed with. They got out of the car and fell into the formation Ari had come up with. Ari kept them close to the building where they would blend in with the shadows. They passed three rusted-over loading doors with locks that looked like they hadn't been touched in decades, the metal defaced with indecipherable graffiti.

At the far end of the building they reached a gravel parking lot enclosed by a chain-link fence which had conveniently been left open by whichever hunter had last left. Only three cars remained, which supported Ari's belief that most of the hunters were currently in custody. She looked back to make sure she hadn't lost any members of the team, then motioned them to follow her across the lot.

Still hugging the building, Ari spotted a ramp that led up to a pair of double doors. She looked over her shoulder and pointed. Gwen understood the motion was meant for her and nodded. Ari returned the nod, then trotted closer. She closed her right hand around the knob and gave it a gentle turn. No resistance. She held up her left hand, all five fingers out, then counted down. Four, three, two...

On one, she yanked the door open and ran inside. Three men were seated around a card table in the center of a massive main room. Ari saw doors spaced around the exterior wall of the room, probably offices once upon a time, but all the doors were currently closed. The hunters were dressed all in black, all casually settled in folding chairs. One was looking at his phone, another looked to be asleep, and the third was playing solitaire.

The card-playing hunter was the first one to look up. Ari clocked the confusion on his face changing over to realization, then fury. They were obviously expecting their hit squad to be coming back. He shouted, words failing him as he fumbled for a weapon on his hip. Phone Man twisted around to see who had come inside. Ari fired the dazzler, shining a bright strobe light directly into his face. He howled, waking his sleepy companion. When he opened his eyes, the first thing he saw was the strobing flash. He threw both hands over his face and fell out of his chair with a confused cry.

Milo had stepped around Ari and launched herself across the room with impressive grace, rolling when she landed. The first hunter had managed to unholster his weapon. Milo cracked him in the knee with her baton and he folded, dropping into a crouch and opening himself up to another strike from the baton. This time she hit him in the chest, and he fell to the side. She took his gun and tucked it into her belt.

Lucy's care package had also contained zip ties, which Gwen used to secure the blinded and disabled men. Ari grabbed the shoulder of the man closest to her, Phone Man.

"How many people are upstairs?"

He spit at her, but missed her due to the angle. Ari let go of his shoulder and he dropped hard onto the floor. Milo was already running for the stairs, and Ari followed her.

"Slow down," Ari hissed.

Milo shook her head. Her whole body was tense, and her eyes were shining with a rage Ari had never seen in her before. When she spoke, her voice was flat and forced. "I recognize two of those bastards. If I stay down here with them, the wolf is going to take over and it's not going to be pretty. I have to keep moving."

"Fair enough," Ari said, clapping her hand on Milo's shoulder. "Lead the way."

They reached the second floor landing as a door opened and Isaac Hayden stepped out. He was walking briskly, clearly on his way to see what all the commotion downstairs was, but he almost tripped over his own feet when he recognized Ari and Milo.

"What was it you said last time we met, Hayden?" Ari asked. "Take this mutt down? Something about killing me?"

"Miss Willow..."

Milo howled and threw herself forward, the sort of leap that a wolf could do with ease but a human might have found difficult. She raised her baton and brought it down in a wide, beautiful arc that very nearly came down across Hayden's temple. She only missed because he threw himself forward and wrapped both arms around her waist. He pivoted and threw them both forward, slamming hard into the wall with Milo to cushion the fall. The air exploded out of her mouth with violent force and her arms twitched, went limp. She dropped her baton and dazzler as her head lolled disturbingly.

Ari was on Hayden's back before he could step away from Milo. She threaded her arm around his throat, grabbed a handful of hair, and pulled him off her. Hayden growled and scratched at her arms but Milo clearly had the upper hand. She held tight, wrenching his head back as he stumbled in a circle in a futile attempt to shake her off.

Gwen suddenly stepped in front of Hayden, appearing as if she was a ghost. She didn't waste time with a threat, she simply pulled one arm back and punched Hayden in the stomach with as much force as she could muster. He doubled over and Ari let go to keep from going down with him, stretching out one arm to brace herself against the wall to keep from falling over with him. Hayden, clutching his stomach with a wheezing cough, made a break for the stairs and ran up to the next floor.

Ari thought about giving chase, but wanted to make sure her team was intact first. Gwen was already at Milo's side, trying to rouse her.

"Where's Dale?" Ari asked.

"Dealing with the computers. They're downstairs. We had to take out another guy who was monitoring the livestream, but he wasn't much of a hassle."

"Ariadne...?"

Ari turned and saw Val. Her hair was much longer, her clothes were filthy, and it looked like she hadn't showered during her entire imprisonment, but still unmistakably herself. There was a caution in her posture, just in case she was hallucinating, but Ari could see the moment Val realized this was really happening. Her shoulders relaxed, her eyes widened and shined with tears, and she sagged as if she was about to pass out. Ari took off her protective glasses and went to the doctor, bracing her against the wall.

"Are you okay?" Ari asked.

"No. But I can definitely see progress in that direction." She gripped Ari's bicep and squeezed, then looked past her. She recognized Milo and Gwen, and her expression fell. "Oh, son of a bitch, we got you out!"

"We had unfinished business," Milo rasped.

"Milo, get Val out of here."

Val and Milo both protested, but for different reasons. Val's argument was the only one Ari heard: "I'm not leaving without Marin."

"Where is she?" Ari asked.

Val pointed. "Around the corner, in a dead-end hallway. Can't miss it. There are guards, though."

"How many hunters are still here?"

"Um." Val squeezed her eyes shut. "Um, four downstairs, two at Marin's room. Six. Just six."

Ari said, "And upstairs?"

"Roemer and the bitch who is running things," Val said. "Never got her name."

Ari patted Val's arm. "Okay. You did good. But now you need to go, get out of here. You've gone through enough. I'm here and I'm not going to leave her behind. Okay?"

Val's eyes filled with tears. "Promise me."

"I swear to you, I'm not leaving this building without Marin."

Val nodded and surrendered.

Ari turned to Milo. "As for you—"

"Yeah, yeah, yeah," Milo grunted. "Gwen talked some sense into me while you were getting your intel." She was standing up again, though clearly it was painful. She motioned for Val to come with her. "We'll get you somewhere safe, c'mon."

Gwen watched Milo head down the stairs, then looked at Ari. "Shall we?"

Ari nodded and led the way.

"They're going to know we're coming," Gwen said. "They must have heard the noise by now."

"Yeah," Ari said. "And Hayden is probably letting Mister and Missus Hunter upstairs know everything, too."

"So much for the element of surprise."

Ari shrugged. "I never much liked the element of surprise. I like people to know when I'm coming for them."

She saw the opening to the hallway ahead and stopped, shoulder against the wall. She breathed in deeply and smelled flop sweat mixed with cologne, and gun metal. They were armed, and they were nervous. They definitely wouldn't go down as easily as the guys downstairs. Ari was very aware of the fact she was mostly armed with a flashlight and a glorified stick. She looked at her mother, who was crouching against the opposite wall waiting for her to give a signal. Ari watched the corner carefully.

"Let's just get this out in the open," she said. "We know you're there. You know we're here. There's no point in pretending like either of us is being sneaky."

"Didn't hear a lot of gunfire," one of the guards called back. "Makes me think you're not very heavily armed."

"Makes me think none of your guys was quick enough to get a shot off."

Silence from around the corner.

"The fact we're even in the building is a really bad sign for you, too. Have you heard from the guys you sent after Eva Cardoso tonight? Were they supposed to check in, but they've been mysteriously silent? Yeah, you might want to stop checking your phone."

"There's a big difference between being arrested for kidnapping and an attempted murder charge," Gwen added.

"You don't want to be Butch and Sundance," Ari said. "You want to be Newman and Redford. Badass heartthrobs living live to the fullest into their eighties." She thought for a second and then whispered to Gwen, "Redford's still alive, right?"

"I haven't seen the news in six months. But he better be."

One of the guards said, "Redford's alive..."

"Cool," Ari said. "So come on out. You can move past this period in your lives, move on, have a solid second act. One of you can start your own salad dressing company. It'll be great. Just put your guns on the ground and kick them out."

She counted to fourteen before she heard the first clatter of metal. She resisted the urge to say 'holy shit, I can't believe that worked' when she saw the first gun slide across the carpet. A second followed it.

"Okay, come on out slowly."

The first man came around the corner, slumped in defeat. He looked at Gwen, then Ari, and she saw his expression slowly change.

"Oh for fuck's sake, there's only two of them!"

Ari ran forward, dazzler up and shining as he went for a second gun that was holstered at his side. The strobe blinded him before he could draw the weapon, and she cracked the baton across his jaw as she slammed into his chest. She wrapped her arm around him and spun him around to use him as a battering ram against the guard behind him. All three of them fell into a pile with Ari on top. Neither guard seemed to be wearing body armor, so Ari punched the one she had tackled in the stomach as hard as she could. He coughed and sputtered while the second guard shoved and wriggled in an attempt to get free.

The guard Ari was wrestling with had a bloody nose and a split lip. His lips were pulled back over disgusting red teeth, and she clapped a hand over his mouth before he got the idea to spit at her. He bucked up at her, twisted his waist, and threw her off of him. She hit the wall and dropped to the floor, instinctively bracing her fall instead of protecting herself. She tensed, expecting a gunshot, but instead she heard a solid thud followed by the man collapsing next to her. She looked up and saw Gwen drive the butt of one guard's gun into the remaining guard's face. He went limp and didn't look prepared to get back up any time soon.

"Damn," Ari said, using the wall to get back to her feet.

Gwen said, "You expected me to pull punches after everything they put me and Milo through?"

"No, ma'am." She bent down and patted the first guard's pockets, then tried the other's. She found keys and went to the door. The lock was pitiful, something she could have picked in a few seconds if she hadn't found the keys, and she eased the door opened and peeked inside.

Marin Cardoso was sitting up on the bed, straightening when she saw the unfamiliar face peeking in. Ari remembered the angle of the online video and looked toward where the camera had to be.

"There was a light," Marin said. "But that went out a few seconds ago."

"Good girl, Dale."

Ari came into the room and went to the shackle holding Marin to the bed. She crouched, grateful the keyring only had two keys on it. Marin twisted to watch her work.

"Who are you?"

"Just for tonight, we're the big bad wolves." She got the cuff open and helped Marin pull her hand free. "You okay?"

"Yeah. Mm-hmm..."

Marin was breathing quickly, on the verge of hyperventilating. Ari put her hands on Marin's shoulders and forced eye contact.

"Listen to me. My name is Ariadne Willow. I'm *canidae*. I'm a private detective. Your sister hired me to find you."

"Eva?" Marin's voice was small. "I've been trying not to worry about... sh-she's okay?"

Ari nodded. "She's safe. Your whole pack is safe. Let's get you back to them."

Marin gripped Ari's hand. Ari pulled her up off the bed and

put an arm around her waist. In the hallway, Gwen had just finished zip-tying the arms and legs of the unconscious guards.

"This is my mother. She's going to get you out of here."

Gwen said, "The hell I am. I'm seeing this through."

Ari glared at her. "Mom..."

"I'm not letting you go up there alone."

"She won't be alone."

Gwen turned to see Dale had joined them. She looked frantic, eyes a little too wide and hair wild, but she was breathing normally.

"You okay?" Ari said.

Dale nodded. "Lot of violence. But good violence, against the right people." She looked down at the bloodied guards lying between them and then pointedly looked away. She looked at Gwen. "You've done your part, okay? You need to get her out of here, go be with Milo."

Gwen still hesitated, but one look at Marin changed her mind. "Come on, sweetheart, let's get you somewhere safe."

Marin looked at Ari for confirmation before she accepted the swap. Gwen looked at Ari, monologues of warnings and promises passing between them as she led Marin away to safety. Dale stepped over the guards and cupped Ari's face.

"You're bruising."

"It's fine."

Dale pressed her lips into a disappointed line, eyes hard. Ari brushed her thumb over Dale's cheek. "Massages and long baths after this."

"Promise?"

"Swear." Ari looked past Dale toward the stairs. "Hayden retreated up. Roemer and some mystery person were up there this whole time. We could be walking into a trap."

"We're definitely walking into a trap." Dale took Ari's hand. "Nothing is stopping us from just going downstairs and getting the hell out of here."

Ari squeezed Dale's fingers. "Wanna run?"

"What kind of wolf would that make me? Besides, I think it's time we finally shut Hayden up once and for all."

"Sounds good to me."

Dale looked at the discarded weapons from the guards. "No hero speeches. Right?"

Ari looked at the guns. After a moment of hesitation, she stooped to pick them up. She handed one to Dale, kept the other for herself, and took a second to get used to its weight.

"Ready?"

Dale nodded. "Always. As long as you're at my side."

Ari leaned in and kissed her. Dale cupped the back of Ari's head, then dropped her hand down to brush her fingers over the leather of Ari's collar.

"Whatever happens," Ari said.

"No matter what." She rested her forehead against Ari's and then stepped back. "Shall we?"

Ari nodded, then led the way to the stairs and started up.

CHAPTER TWENTY

THE TOP of the stairs had no landing, leading directly into an open space. Ari stopped low enough that she couldn't be seen, but that meant she couldn't get a look at the layout for herself. She listened and heard whispered voices.

"Yo, Hayden. I can't see, are you waving a white flag? I'd really like to accept your surrender here, save us both a lot of time."

"Why don't you come on up, Ms. Willow?" a male voice Ari didn't recognize called out. "I assume Miss Frye is with you? She can come, too."

Ari and Dale glanced at each other. Ari went first, gun raised as the room came into view. It was almost entirely empty except for what looked like an office set for a very cheap community theater play. Hayden was standing in front of the desk, and Roemer stood behind it. Neither of them were armed, and Ari thought Hayden looked extremely smug for someone whose entire little army had just been neutralized. She looked for hunters lying in wait, but the only other person in the room was an older woman seated in one of the chairs in front of the desk.

"Hi, Hayden," Dale said from behind Ari. "Just in case it's not clear, consider this my resignation from your little hunting club."

"Of course," Hayden said. He didn't look particularly annoyed, or even surprised. In fact, to Ari's discomfort, he looked amused.

Ari eyed the woman in the chair. "Care to introduce us to your friend?"

"Oh, Ariadne, I'm hurt you don't remember."

The voice was familiar. When the woman unfolded herself from the seat and turned to face them fully, Ariadne couldn't even feign indifference. The woman was older, her face carrying more lines and her hair whiter, but there was no mistaking her. Ari's hands went cold and she backed up a step. Dale put a hand on Ari's shoulder.

"Ari, I thought she died."

"She did," Ari said, her voice barely above a whisper. "She died in prison. Cancer."

Katherine Gavin smiled. "Oh, that wasn't a prison. That was a hospital with a few extra guards posted outside. And I was a rich woman with cancer and a bullet wound." She looked at Dale. "I owe you for that last one, Ms. Frye, and I always pay my debts."

Ari stepped in front of Dale. Katherine Gavin, once one of the richest women in Seattle, a recluse who hired Ari to follow her daughter, then tried to frame her for her murder. Dale had shot her when she was fighting Ari, and all her crimes had been revealed. Ari distinctly remembered seeing online that she'd died while she was in prison, weakened from cancer treatments and her fragile state shattered by the gunshot wound.

But this was definitely her, unmistakably alive and well, smiling like she'd just won a very long game of chess.

"With the kind of money I have," Katherine said, "it was easy to make my guards look the other way. And money is also very persuasive to doctors with student loan debts. A few thousand dollars here and there, I was officially dead. I hadn't shown my face in public for years before I hired you, so it was easy to slip back into the shadows. I found a little island off the coast, settled in, and spent the next few years trying to figure out what the fuck you were. Miss Frye helped with that as well. Right before she shot me, she gave me a word. *Canidae.* Werewolves."

Ari swallowed hard. "You've been funding Hayden's work."

"He'd already done so much of the research. Saved me a lot of time, and he was a useful tool. The same with Mr. Roemer. It's always nice to have professionals on the payroll. I just sat back and waited for their updates to come rolling in. It wasn't long until we were ready to put our plan into action: the complete extinction of the *canidae* breed."

"I don't know if you noticed, but you're short an army," Ari said. "All the people you sent out tonight have been taken into custody. The ones who were downstairs are dealt with."

"Maybe not exactly as we planned it," Hayden said, "but I can't say we're disappointed with the results. This whole thing was building to you, Ariadne Willow, standing alone. The troublemaker, the wolf who made the hunters give up wolf manoth. Alone and surrounded."

Dale said, "Uh, not alone..."

"Oh right," Hayden said. "Miss Frye. I apologize." He faced her fully and put his hands behind his back, rocked on the balls of his feet, and in the most smug, self-assured voice, said a single word.

"Feather."

Ari stared at him, then looked at Dale. Dale looked at Ari and shrugged.

"Was he talking to you?" Ari whispered.

"I don't think so. Why would he say 'feather' to me?"

"And why'd he say it in that weird way?" Ari deepened her voice and mocked him. "Feather." She faced Hayden. "What's that, intimidation?"

Hayden finally looked concerned. "No, I... I was..." He cleared his throat, snapped his fingers at Dale, and said it again. "Feather."

Dale snapped her fingers back at him. "Okay, dude, feather to you, too."

Roemer's face was red. "Mr. Hayden..."

"No, wait. It's..." He rubbed his temple.

Katherine also looked enraged, but only glared at Ariadne.

"Feather!" Hayden snapped.

Ari said, "Why do you keep saying that?"

"Because she's supposed to turn on you!" Hayden growled. "The essays! The essays have a, a failsafe. A trigger word. If a hunter becomes confused or addled, the word 'feather' brings them back to their senses. It's the entire reason I had her read the essays in front of me!"

"She was supposed to be the nuke," Roemer said. "She's supposed to be putting a bullet in the bitch's head right now."

Ari leaned closer to Dale. "You're not going to do that, are you?"

"Nah."

"Cool." Ari leveled the gun at Hayden. "This has been real

swell, Isaac, but I think we're done with playing games with you. So we're going to give you the chance to do the right thing. Surrender, turn yourself in for kidnapping, torture, attempted murder, all that fun stuff, and I won't pull this trigger."

"You honestly expect me to believe you'll shoot me in cold blood?"

Ari shrugged. "Depends on what you call 'cold blood.' Gwen is my mother. Milo is her partner. Val is a woman I care for very much. And Marin... well, I don't know Marin, but she wants to work in an aquarium and I think that makes her a cool person. So I'm not too concerned about the morality of putting an end to all of this. But I feel like I should at least give you the option of going out on your own terms."

Katherine stepped closer. "And these are *your* terms, Ms. Willow? A *canidae* using a firearm? That hardly seems like a wolf tactic."

"Last time I went up against you, I used the wolf. But it was Mrs. Frye-Willow, in the foyer, with a fucking firearm that finally put you down. So I think I'll stick with this."

The hair on the back of Ari's neck stood up, aware before she knew what she was aware of, and a smile crept across her face.

"But if you want wolves, I'd hate for you to be disappointed."

She didn't have to turn around. She could smell them as they reached the top of the stairs. Gwen was out in front, the growl in her throat low but with enough bass to fill the empty room. Milo was behind her, then Marin, then Eva and members of the Cardoso pack. The wolves spread out in formation behind Ari, none of them poised to attack but clearly ready if the moment came.

Dale whispered, "Hey, Isaac. Try saying 'feather' again."

Ari smirked. She could smell the rage of every wolf in the room, felt the fire from each one of them. She could hear sirens in the distance, which meant Lucy had finally had enough and called in the reinforcements. Katherine Gavin, Isaac Hayden, and Gabriel Roemer stood in front of her, defenseless, and she remembered what she'd told Dale about her plans to end this night bloody. She could even envision the way Roemer's head would snap back when she put a bullet in it.

She lowered her weapon. "It wouldn't help," she said. "Talking you out of doing something else when the heat dies down, killing you all here, it doesn't matter. Other hunters are out there. I kill the three of you, I make martyrs for the next guy, and the next one, and the next one. I'm not going to do that. You're going to pay for what you did to my friends and family. But I'm not going to be your executioner."

Dale lightly brushed the back of Ari's hand with hers. "There's my puppy," she whispered.

Ari lowered the gun to her side, not daring to drop it and potentially arm the people she'd just spared. "This is over. You're going to be arrested, you may get to plead insanity for the whole werewolf claim, but the internet is going to forget this by the weekend. Everything you've done, all the mental torture you've put these women through, it was for nothing."

Dale said, "We should get all these wolves out of here before we have to explain them to the cops."

"Right," Ari said. "You can all have a seat. I'm sure the police will be with you shortly."

She turned and put her hand in the small of Dale's back to guide her to the stairs. The wolves reluctantly filed out, a few of them making disappointed chuffing sounds as they left.

Ari heard the footsteps pounding on the floor a second before she heard Katherine growl, "It won't be for nothing..."

Ari turned, pushing Dale out of the way as Katherine tackled her. They rolled, Ari more concerned with the other woman's age and fragility than she was about being actually hurt. She stopped the roll when she was on top, but Katherine punched her in the chest and knocked the wind out of her. Ari coughed and fell to one side. Katherine got onto her knees and tried to shove her back, but Ari wrapped both arms around Katherine's waist and tossed her. Katherine hit the ground, skidded, and then went over the edge of an open elevator shaft that Ari hadn't seen.

"Shit," Ari said.

Katherine had grabbed hold of a broken plank that had been blocking the opening, but the wood was already splintering. Her other hand was flat on the floor and sliding with alarming speed. Their eyes locked. Ari saw a look of pure hatred pass over Katherine's face as she let go and vanished into the darkness. A few seconds later, they heard a violent, final crash of a soft body on old wood and stone.

"Jesus," Hayden whispered.

A hand lowered into Ari's line of sight and she followed the arm up to Dale. She accepted the hand, got to her feet, and looked back at the men.

"We'll be watching at the bottom of the stairs until the cops get here," she said. "But feel free to try taking the express route like your benefactor. I won't kill you, but I'm sure as hell not going to save you, either. You can both take a flying leap off the roof for all I care."

She put an arm around Dale's shoulders and walked with her out of the room.

The gravel parking lot was full of police cars, lights shining brighter than the stadium lights down the street. Marin and Val had been taken somewhere safe to give their statements while a squadron of officers went through the building to gather up the hunters. Milo and Gwen had vanished after leaving the top floor office, and Ari didn't see any reason to tell anyone they'd ever been there in the first place. They'd been through enough.

The police wanted to speak to them separately, just to get a full idea of what had happened, so Dale had been taken away to be the first one questioned. Ari had been taken to a loading dock and told to "stay put," which gave her a front-row view of everyone being officially taken into custody. She let her eyes slip out of focus and mentally monitored the adrenaline seeping from her muscles. She'd gone from electrically wired to groggy in just a handful of minutes, and she feared a crash was coming.

Dale came out of the command center and crossed the gravel to Ari. She had a plastic-wrapped sandwich and a bottle of Gatorade, which she handed over before she hopped up to sit next to her.

"Figured you might be crashing."

Ari looked at the offering like it was gold. "Thanks, Dale."

"Mm-hmm. They're going to come get your statement soon, but I convinced them to let you eat something first. It's been a long night."

Dale let her feet swing, hands folded between her knees, watching the commotion as Ari devoured the sandwich. She shared the Gatorade.

"So. Feather?"

"There was something about a feather in one of the essays," Dale said, brow furrowed. "I think it means a hound has picked up a scent of its prey."

Ari watched Dale's profile. "Nothing? Not even a tickle?"

Dale turned and met Ari's gaze. "Not even a twinge. Not even for half a second, puppy." She smiled and leaned in, bumping her forehead against Ari's. "I think I'm actually free of it. God what a relief. I was so worried."

"I wasn't," Ari said.

"You walked into a room with me at your back, holding a gun," Dale said. "I got the feeling you were pretty confident in my loyalty."

Ari chuckled. "I was worried about how worried you were. So I'm glad you can let go of that anxiety." She kissed the corner of Dale's mouth. "I love you."

"I love you, too." She brushed a crumb away from Ari's bottom lip. "There was something else in the essays. Something that's come up before. Something that really is still bugging me."

"Something I can help you with?"

Dale shook her head. "I don't know. I don't think it's something that can be helped." She looked away. "*Canidae* live a lot longer than humans. A couple of the essays say that a hundred years is pretty much the baseline. I'll be lucky if I make it that long. It's just something I have to live with."

"Maybe," Ari said. "But you forget that I'm not a full-blooded *canidae*. Keighley was a hunter and, like it or not, I have his genes. He's the reason I wouldn't have been able to transform if Mom hadn't taken drastic measures. Maybe a shorter life span is another one of the deficiencies I got from him."

Dale hummed and shrugged. "Well, I'm never going to root for you to die young. So we can just play it by ear."

"Works for me. And if you ever need to talk about it, I'm open."

"Good to know."

An officer came out of the command center and spoke to an officer. Ari watched him, expecting him to motion her over, but he went back inside without even looking in their direction.

"The two of us sitting here like this kind of defeats the purpose of talking to us separately, doesn't it?" Ari asked.

Dale shrugged. "Let them try to pull me away." She looked around the lot. "Any sign of Mom and Milo?"

Ari shook her head. "They probably did the smart thing and headed home to lie low for a while. Smart of them. Wish I'd done the same. An anonymous call to the police and they show up to find all the bad guys tied up waiting for them."

"Like Batman."

"She-Wolf," Ari said. "I'll start designing a mask."

Dale put her head down on Ari's shoulder. "I'm glad you didn't go through with it. I absolutely would have supported you if you had. But I'm very glad you didn't."

"Me too. And I did kill Katherine Gavin."

"No, she committed suicide," Dale said. "Besides, she was living on borrowed time anyway. She's the one who came out of her hidey-hole after all this time. She should never have crawled out of it in the first place. But maybe now that she's actually dead, the hunters funding will dry up."

"Here's hoping," Ari said, even though that meant her mother's source of income was also in danger. "Roemer and Hayden are in custody. We'll probably still have the weekend warriors to worry about, and we don't know where the book of essays ended up. That's worrying. But for now, I think we've earned a day off."

"We can go in to work late tomorrow."

"Today, technically," Ari said.

"Right. Sleep in 'til noon."

Ari smiled. "You're too good to me, boss."

Dale found Ari's hand and held it in hers. Ari covered their linked fingers with her other hand. She didn't have any intention of moving until someone with a badge forced her to.

CHAPTER TWENTY-ONE

ARI SPENT the next few days rushing from one office to another, rarely knowing who she would be speaking to until she was sitting in front of their desk. She gave her statement multiple times, starting with Eva Cardoso hiring her, to the tip that led her to the abandoned building near the stadium. She left out any mention of Milo or Gwen's kidnapping, having decided it was easier to just erase them from the narrative all together instead of trying to explain why the kidnappers thought they were also werewolves.

To her surprise, Roemer and Hayden dropped the werewolf accusations once they were in custody. They were "confused" and "misled" by Katherine Gavin, who they now believed to be suffering from dementia. Her behavior from a decade ago, which resulted in the murder of her own daughter, helped sell the idea that the woman was on the verge of a mental collapse. The men were spared a mental evaluation but charged with kidnapping and attempted murder.

Gwen and Milo were both adjusting to their regained freedom. They went out as wolves every night, sometimes not returning for days. Milo said they'd been as far as Mount Baker, camping out under the stars and running with actual wolves. It was therapy for both sides of their psyches.

Before long, it seemed like the entire mess was in the past. Anyone who remembered the livestream thought of it as a vicious hoax, as Ari and Dale had both predicted. A few days before Halloween, Eva got in contact and asked Ari if they could meet at Union Square. Ari agreed and they set the meeting for the next day.

When she arrived, Eva and Marin were seated on the stone edge of the water feature next to the stairs. The sisters got to their feet when they saw her, and Eva greeted Ari with a hug.

"I never got a chance to thank you for getting my sister back," she said. "I don't know how I'll ever repay you."

"Consider any debt repaid." When Eva let go, Marin took her place. Ari laughed and returned the hug. "Oh, hey, lots of hugs today."

"Sorry," Marin said, stepping back and wiping at her eyes. "I dealt with a lot of what was going on by shutting down. I didn't let myself believe it was actually real. It's the only thing that kept me from going crazy. Once I was free, though, it's like my whole brain said, 'okay, let's process this.'" She tucked her hair behind her ears. "I know things would have gone much, much differently if it wasn't for you. I wanted to actually tell you that in person, face to face."

"I appreciate it."

"We were also wondering about the woman who was there with me," Marin said. "She said her name was Val. Is she...?"

"She's okay. She's dealing with the fact she was abducted and held prisoner for six months. Therapy. She's staying with my mother until she can get back on her feet."

Marin shook her head. "I keep thinking about her job, her apartment... I mean, she must have lost everything."

"Her apartment was long gone," Ari admitted, "but the building manager put most of her stuff in a storage locker in the basement. The electronics and a lot of her valuables had mysteriously gone missing, but a lot of sentimental stuff was recovered. And she has most of her clothes. That's not much comfort, but after living in a dirty T-shirt and sweats for months..."

Eva had a hand on Marin's back, a constant and supportive pressure. "I can't even imagine," she said, looking at her sister with an expression that, to Ari, meant she was at least doing her best to try. It was also clear that they were talking about Val because it was easier than talking about themselves, or Marin's recovery.

"My mother has pretty deep pockets," Ari said. "She's made it clear that Val doesn't have to worry about anything."

Marin said, "It shouldn't be too hard for her to find a new job, right? She has a great explanation for why she had to leave her last job."

"Sure," Ari said, "but she really did love that job and her patients. Part of her feels like she's abandoning them. I'm sure it's all going to work out in the end. It's just the process of getting there that's rough. The important part is that she has a strong support system."

Marin looked at her sister and smiled knowingly. "It's vital."

Ari smiled. "I think she's going to come out of it okay."

Marin wiped at her eyes. "I also wanted to ask for business cards. I know a bunch of people at school who might be able to use your services. And there are other *canidae* out there who should know about you."

"Oh." Ari panicked and patted her pockets. She was positive she didn't have any cards but, when she checked her wallet, she found a dozen slipped into one of the larger pockets. She smiled and said, "Thanks, Dale."

"Support system?" Eva guessed.

"The best in the world," Ari said as she handed over the cards. "The only rule to getting over this sort of thing is that there aren't any rules. There's no deadline, no right way to get back to normal. Normal isn't even promised."

"I'll keep that in mind," Marin said. "Thank you. For everything."

"You're welcome," Ari said. "Take care of each other."

She turned to watch them walk away, basking in the pride of a job well done.

"They'll be okay."

Ari almost jumped out of her skin, spinning as she took two giant steps to the right away from the voice. Conrad Rigas was lucky she'd recognized his voice or else she would've lashed out at him. He didn't look afraid; he was half-smiling, with both hands in his jacket pockets.

"Where the hell did you come from?"

"Didn't you catch my scent?" he asked, his voice far too casually.

Ari frowned. "No. I didn't. Why didn't I?"

"The same reason you didn't smell the hunters back when the Cardoso girl got abducted." He took his right hand out of his pocket and held out what looked like a thermos with a metal dome on the top. "This is an AOD," he explained as she took the object and turned it over in her hands. "They put it in the cupholder of their trucks when they're driving around and it disperses ozone. Hunters use it to mask their spray."

"I thought they used deer piss for that."

Rigas shrugged. "It's the future. There's a machine for everything now."

She handed it back to him. "So there's no way to stop people from buying this thing?"

"People protest products all the time, get them removed from the shelves. But there are a variety of things like this on the market, so it really doesn't seem worth the trouble."

"Great," she said. "So hunters have a way to make themselves invisible to *canidae* noses. That's really good news."

He shrugged. "It kind of is, to be honest. Firstly, I only found those things in the cars impounded after Roemer's sad little assaults. It seems like hunters in general haven't wised up to using this stuff."

"Let's hope their ignorance holds for a little while. I don't want to worry about ghosts every time I go out for a run. Thanks for the update, I guess."

He coughed softly and stepped closer. "Actually, there's something else."

"Yeah?"

"I told you about the Book of Simon. How it could be used to mobilize *canidae* all over the world to stand up and fight against the hunters if that video actually revealed we existed to the world."

She tensed. "Yeah..."

"You stopped that from happening. Things have quieted down. There's still a few odd YouTube videos, but they're blending in to all the other conspiracy stuff that no one ever pays attention to. So I think it's safe to say we're out of the woods. So..." He reached behind his back and pulled something from the waistband of his pants.

It was a book bound in red leather, gold lettering on the cover spelling out something in writing so flowery she couldn't even tell if it was in English. He held it out to her.

"The Book of Simon?" Ari asked.

"The only one still in existence. Trust me, I looked. It could be a weapon in the wrong hands, but I think you're the right person to keep an eye on it."

"Really?"

He nodded. "Gwyneth Willow is responsible for ninety percent of the victories we've had against hunters in the past thirty years. She funded action against them. She traveled the world, using money she skimmed from their own accounts, and tried to find ways to stop them from killing us all. She dropped out of sight recently, and a lot of us were worried, but now I think it's because she had a successor lined up."

Ari raised an eyebrow. "I'm not going to turn into some James Bond, Indiana Jones hero to the *canidae*. I'm staying right here in Seattle, I'm going to live my life."

Rigas shrugged. "Trouble has a way of coming to you, Ms. Willow. Whatever the future holds, I want you to be in charge of that book. Keep it safe."

"I'll do my best," she said.

"All I can ask." He looked up at the sky, framed by the tall buildings around Union Square. He breathed deeply and then lowered his gaze back to her. "The world is a little brighter today, a little safer for all of us. Because of you. There will always be dangers to those like us, but with the right defense, we can all survive to see another day."

Ari blinked. "Uh. Yeah."

He smiled and touched his brow in a salute. "Stay safe, Ms. Willow. I'll be around."

She nodded and watched him leave. She still wasn't entirely sure she liked him, but he seemed relatively harmless. He would be a decent asset to keep around if she really was going to follow in her mother's footsteps. And he was right, trouble had a way of finding her. It might even kick into higher gear if hunters found out she had Simon Lehner's book.

She looked down at it, drummed her fingers on the leather, and tucked the book tight against her side as she left the square.

***

Marin hesitated with her hand raised, considered leaving the card and going back to her car, but finally decided she'd come this far and knocked on the door. She told herself no one would be home. She would wait a minute and no one would answer and she could escape and no one would have to know how close she came to humiliating herself. Just a few more seconds before she could–

The door opened and Val looked out at her. "Marin." She sounded surprised, but pleasantly. "What are... how'd you find me?"

"Dale Frye, the woman who works with that private

investigator. I wanted to come by and see how you were doing. You look amazing."

Val chuckled and looked down at her T-shirt and baggy jeans. "Yeah. Amazing what a shower and clean clothes can do for a person."

"The hair, too," Marin said, reaching out to touch Val's much shorter hair.

"Oh yeah. Lopped it all off. And washed it. World of difference."

Marin smiled. "You look great."

"You too," Val said. "Are you, um... coping with everything okay?" She winced, knowing how terrible the question sounded.

"Honestly, yeah. School is being really understanding. The pack is there for anything I need. To an annoying degree, if I'm being totally honest. The biggest problem is that people expect me to have all this trauma, and it really wasn't that bad. I was abducted, which was terrifying, and I'm probably going to have a delayed reaction to that in due time, but the actual experience?" She shrugged. "I was pretty much just bored for most of the time. And that's thanks to you."

"I bored you?"

Marin laughed. "No. You made what could have been a really terrifying situation into something I know I can get over with time. You made sure they treated me well, they fed me. You kept me company. And when I think back to it, the feeling I get most is that I miss you. And I'd... I'd like to see you again. For dinner, or something."

Val raised an eyebrow. "For dinner?"

"Or lunch." Marin looked at her watch. "It's... it's around lunchtime right now, but we don't have to go right now. Unless, if you're hungry, we could..." She wet her lips and looked around for potential saviors. "I mean, it doesn't even have to be a meal."

"Are you asking me out on a date?"

"Basically."

Val took a breath, then let it go without saying anything. She leaned against the door. "You know what I am. Who my father is."

"I know who *you* are. As for what you are... you're a chance to turn a terrible experience into something positive. Yes, I was abducted and held hostage. But I met you. Maybe that will make it worthwhile."

Val ducked her head and smiled, looked back into the house,

and then examined her clothes. "I could run and change real quick..."

"Why?" Marin asked. "I think you look great."

"Well, you've only seen me in filthy rags after months of sponge baths."

"Yeah, so imagine how little effort it will take to impress me. You look red carpet ready right now."

Val laughed. She still looked hesitant but, after a few seconds, surrendered. "All right. I am hungry, and I've missed you, too. Let me get my shoes."

"Sure, take your time."

Val went back into the house, leaving the door ajar. Marin exhaled and let go of her tension and stress, shaking her shoulders with relief. It was just lunch. Just a meal between two people who went through a rough time together. It would be a normal thing, which is what Eva had been pushing her to do. And to be honest, it really felt great to be outside in the fresh air talking to someone. Even if that someone was a person who'd been in the hellhole with her. It was progress. And even if she and Val did just become friends after this, wouldn't that be just as great as anything else?

Val came back out. She'd put on a long-sleeved shirt but hadn't buttoned it. She smiled, the expression nervous but her eyes shining with excitement.

"Ready?" Val asked.

"We'll see," Marin said.

"What?"

Marin laughed and slipped her arm around Val's to walk her to the car. "Nothing, never mind. Let's go."

***

Ari came out of the bathroom after her shower to find Dale sitting up in bed, her legs tenting the blanket, Simon Lehner's book open in her lap. Ari raised an eyebrow as she traded her towel for a long T-shirt and went to her side of the bed.

"You can read German now?"

"Mm-hmm. It's very easy." She let Ari believe her for a second before she turned the book so Ari could see the pages. "Translations. German on the verso, English on the recto."

"Verso and recto?"

"Back and front of the page," Dale said. "I do know *some* things. Just not German." She put the book back down on her lap.

Ari sank back against her pillow, hands folded on her stomach.

"So? How is it?"

Dale shrugged. "How is any propaganda? Rah-rah, we're the best, let's go to war and kill those people who aren't like us. I was kind of expecting this to be the good book, versus the essays being the bad book. But it's not really that simple. They're both pretty awful. Like here." She flipped back a few pages. "Here. Simon is saying that humans are actually animals because we're stuck in one form. *Canidae* are superior because they were the best of both worlds. He thought eventually humans would die out, so why not help them along?"

"Sheesh," Ari said. "I can see why humans and wolves got together to stop him. That's Nazi talk."

"Mm-hmm," Dale said, then slapped the book. "I don't get these guys, you know? Magnusson and Simon Lehner, they were both just scared and decided the only way to get over it was to destroy the other side. They both wrote books for the sole purpose of indoctrinating people to go out and murder strangers. Can you imagine how many lives would've been saved if they just tried living together? Why does it always have to be hate? Humans and wolves *can* come together and live in peace."

"Humans and wolves can indeed come together," Ari said.

Dale glared at her and playfully kicked her under the blankets. "I'm being serious, puppy."

"I know, babe," She cuddled closer and put her head on Dale's shoulder. "I go for humor when I don't have the foggiest idea what else to say." She turned her head and kissed Dale through the T-shirt she was wearing. "I wish I had some big idea to fix things, Dale. I wish I had that hero speech you were hoping for the other night. I don't. There are always going to be hunters. There are always going to be *canidae*. We stopped them this time, but someone else is going to show up eventually. We just have to be there to stop them when the time comes."

"Yeah." She tilted her head away, exposing more of her neck. "You're too low, by the way."

Ari hmmed and moved her head. "Better?"

Dale sank down, pushing the book away with one hand as she pulled Ari to her with the other. "You're getting closer..."

Ari growled and climbed on top of Dale to get a better angle.

The next morning, Ari was woken by a series of very soft kisses on her cheek punctuated by a whispered chant of "Wake up, puppy." She uncurled her arm from beneath the pillow and reached out blindly to put Dale in a headlock, trying to pull her down to make a counterargument. Dale pushed back and Ari reluctantly opened one eye to see what she wanted. Dale looked excited, but there was a nervousness in her eyes. She brushed the hair back from Ari's forehead and bent down to kiss her again.

"Good morning, puppy. Get up, we have to go somewhere."

"It's the middle of the night."

"You can clearly see that it's light out," Dale said.

Ari grunted and burrowed her face into the pillow. "How important is it?"

"Life and death." She stood up and swatted Ari's ass through the blankets. "Get up, my wolf wife, we have a meeting with a lawyer."

Ari was intrigued enough to get out of bed for that.

Thirty minutes and one shower later, Ari was no less grumpy about being pulled out of bed. An egg sandwich from Skillet helped improve her mood a little, but any gains were immediately soured when Dale pulled up in front of Donald Keech's office.

"I thought you said we were going to a lawyer, not some ambulance chaser owned by hunters."

"Trust me, puppy," Dale said.

Ari followed Dale into the building. Keech was in his office and glanced up at the sound of the bell over the door. He flinched, his shoulders sagged, and he hauled himself up out of his chair to shuffle around the desk with one arm raised to fend them off.

"You get out of here. I have nothing to say to either of you." He looked at Ari. "I assume you're Willow, right?"

"You're smarter than you look." Ari slipped an arm around Dale's elbow. "C'mon, babe, we're not wanted here. Let's go home."

Dale shook her head. "No, we need to be here. Mr. Keech, you're probably very busy dealing with all the men who were arrested in connection with Marin Cardoso's abduction."

"And women," Keech said, aiming a finger at her. "See? See, it's easy to be accidentally sexist, you assumed they were all men."

Ari rolled her eyes and wondered if she needed to be present for whatever Dale was planning.

Keech continued. "And no. I'm not as busy as you might think, because apparently free counsel isn't as appealing to them when the stakes are this high. A lot of them have taken their business elsewhere. And good riddance, honestly. These cases are all losers, and I don't need the marks on my record. So let them throw their cash away on some flashy suit who can't do a damn thing for them anyway. No skin off my nose."

Dale said, "But you're still in contact with them? The hunters?"

He sighed and flailed his hands in a lazy shrug. "I guess. I'm not going to give you their information so you can go off on some witch hunt."

"We don't want you to give us anything," Dale said. "We want you to tell them something. Arrange a meeting."

"What?" Ari and Keech said at the same time.

Dale didn't take her eyes off Keech. "Columbia Center. Tonight, six o'clock."

Ari said, "Wait, who are we meeting?"

"Whoever is in charge now," Dale said. "Someone who can make decisions. Tell them they can bring a couple of bodyguards for security if they want, but they should know that we won't be alone, either. So it's going to be a nice, civil meeting. Can you do that?"

Keech looked at Ari, confused, but she only shrugged.

"I think I can arrange that. They're going to want to know why, though."

"They'll find out at the meeting," Dale said, backing toward the door. "Six o'clock. Columbia Center, the Sky View Observatory. We'll be waiting."

She left and Ari followed her. "Do you want to fill me in on the plan, Dale?"

Dale stopped in front of the car. "I could. I don't quite have it all figured out yet. I mean," she gestured at her temple. "I know what I want to say up here. But it's not quite all put together in words. I can give you the general~"

"No," Ari said. "I trust you. Whatever is going on, I trust you."

"Enough to bring Mom and Milo into a room full of hunters just because I said so?"

Ari didn't hesitate. "Yep."

Dale smiled. "You trusting me makes me trust myself."

"That's how this marriage thing is supposed to work, I think." She nodded at the car. "Come on. We have a lot of time until six o'clock and you need to figure out how to say what you need to say. Let's go to the office. You can bounce some ideas off me."

"Just like normal," Dale said. "Just in reverse."

Ari smiled and got in the car. Whatever Dale was planning, whatever unspoken idea was in her head, Ari had no doubt or hesitation about following where she led.

CHAPTER TWENTY-TWO

THE SPACE Needle attracted all the tourists, but Columbia Center was home to the truly unbeatable view of the city. The observation deck was high enough that the neighboring buildings didn't get in the way, granting unbroken views of the entire city from north to south. Ari walked up to one of the walls of glass and looked out over the water, hands in her pockets as she drifted north. She could see downtown, all the way to Queen Anne and beyond. The sun was just beginning to set, and Elliott Bay glistened with the same brilliance of every downtown building.

Milo came up to stand next to her. "Never thought I'd call somewhere besides London home," she said, "but this place kind of gets under your skin."

Ari smiled. "Are you sure my mother doesn't have anything to do with that feeling?"

"It's either her or the fish market," Milo said. "Neck and neck."

Ari laughed. "I'm still not calling you 'mom'."

"That's it, go to your room."

Ari bumped her shoulder against Milo's and turned to face the room. Diana and Lucy were standing by the bar, which was currently unstaffed. Gwen and Dale were close to the elevators, speaking quietly. Ari had a better idea of what Dale's plan was now, but she still wasn't convinced it could work. But she had faith. That, along with trust, was enough to get her in the room and to support the big swing they were about to make.

Diana moved closer. "I'm still not sure why Lucy and I are here."

"Dale will explain everything," Ari said.

"If she expects me to represent the police in some official manner, I can't—"

"It's—"

They were interrupted by the arrival of the elevator. Dale ushered Gwen deeper into the room as the doors opened. Ari motioned for Diana and Lucy to get behind her and Milo. Diana's cop instinct caused her to hesitate before she accepted she didn't have the authority in this situation, and she did as she was instructed.

The new arrivals were mostly men, mostly dressed in dark suits, like someone had a casting call for Secret Agent Douches. They remained by the elevator while the only woman in the group continued forward. She was also dressed in a suit, open at the collar. Her hair was either very light brown or very dark blonde, slicked back against her skull. She stopped a few feet in front of Ari and Dale, put her hands behind her back, and smiled.

"Ariadne Willow and Dale Frye. It's an honor to meet you both."

"You represent the hunters?" Dale asked.

The woman inclined her head. "Captain Grace Lang. Air Force. Here unofficially, of course, just like your law enforcement representatives are here as civilians. I was chosen because we understood you would respond better to a female counterpart in... whatever this may be. I've been given the authority to hear you out and, if need be, make decisions for the group. We're all very excited to hear what you have to say."

Dale stepped forward. "The last time we were this close to war between humans and *canidae*, it was stopped by a union between a woman and a wolf. They represented hope that the two species could live in harmony. These are very different times. Something so relatively small would never hold the same weight now. Ariadne and I are married, but we don't honestly believe that will sway any hunters in this day and age. We needed something bigger.

"We needed a pack."

Ari stepped forward. "My mother was raped by a hunter. I was born a hunter, but made into a wolf. I've spent the majority of my life as both. Transforming hurt me, it was agony, because of the genetics I was born into. I've been healed of that, but the fact remains that I have a foot in both worlds. Hunter and *canidae*."

Dale said, "I'm a human, but reading Magnusson's essays changed me. Even though I clawed my way back to the surface and found myself again, I know that I'm not the same person I was before those essays. I also have a foot in both worlds. Human and hunter." She stepped back and held her hand out to indicate Gwen and Milo. "A union between two *canidae*." She moved her arm to Diana and Lucy. "A union between two humans."

Ari said, "Three wolves. Three humans. Representing both sides equally. Dale and I aren't hunters, but we've been irrevocably influenced by them."

Grace raised an eyebrow. "Not enough to appropriately speak for us."

"Of course not," Dale said. "For this to work, we need cooperation. Someone to step in if there's ever a disagreement between the two sides."

Val stepped out of the snack bar's kitchen. "Is that supposed to be my cue? Sorry. It's surprisingly hard to hear back there."

Grace looked intrigued. "Valerie Byrne."

"Daughter of Gabriel Roemer, indoctrinated into the hunter lifestyle. She was raised on a steady diet of hunter logic. And when she grew up, she decided to take that knowledge and use it to help *canidae*. As a child, she was forced to fight a *canidae*. She was forced to make an awful decision to survive that day, and she was scarred by what she did. Val took that pain and she turned it into something good. She's saved countless *canidae* lives. She will always be a hunter, but she has the trust of every *canidae* that's ever met her. She's suffered at the hands of hunters and at the claws of wolves, and we have faith she'll be a bridge between the two sides."

Val looked at Grace. "I won't advocate for genocide of the wolves. But at the same time, I will never agree to a mass extinction of humanity."

"I'd call that fair," Ari said.

"We wouldn't be a single union," Dale said. "We'd be a pack. Human, *canidae*, hunter. The Willow Pack. Dedicated to protecting the peace between the three groups. We stopped Keighley. We stopped Hayden. We stopped Roemer and Gavin. We're already doing the work, we're just making it a little more official."

Grace pursed her lips and lowered her head like a robot processing information. The observation deck was silent until she raised her head again.

"You could have made your little pack without putting yourself at this risk. Why invite us? Why announce yourselves like this?"

"Because this is going to be official and agreed-upon by both sides." She pointed at the sunset-gilded city outside. "Look out those windows. That is our city. Seattle, all of Washington, and the Pacific Northwest, will be a peaceful zone for *canidae*. Hunters are allowed, naturally, it's a free country. But you will be here at the blessing of your wolf hosts and you will treat them with respect when you're within our borders."

Grace laughed. "My, my! That is quite a request. And what do you have to offer to make such a huge leap?"

"We won't build an army."

Grace's smile faded. "Pardon?"

"We have Simon Lehner's book. A book that was once used to raise an army of *canidae* to rise up against humanity. If you agree to this plan, we won't post the contents of the book online for any wolf who wants to read it."

Ari said, "We'll also release it if the Magnusson essays get posted anywhere."

"And we *will* be checking," Dale added. "Religiously."

All the humor had left Grace's expression, and she looked darker, meaner. The sun had also sunk lower and caused the room to dim as well.

"What... exactly... are you proposing?"

"The Pacific Northwest is a safe haven for *canidae*. Since that's kind of a vague term, we'll just say pretty much from Portland north, and everything to the west. Canada included."

"Cascadia for *canidae*," Ari said.

Dale looked at her and said through her teeth, "I thought we agreed to drop that."

"Oh come on, it's perfect."

Dale cleared her throat and looked at Grace again. "It's basically pretty simple. No hunting within the borders. *Canidae* will be safe here. Hunters will be safe from *canidae* if they come into the borders. We all learn how to coexist. And if any issues come up, the Willow Pack will be there to deal with it. Because we always have been in the past, and we're not going anywhere."

"How do we know you actually have the Book of Simon?"

Ari and Dale spoke in unison. "Simon is the one who will lead us out of the darkness and into the *light!*" They both punched the air. "He is *Alpha!*" Another punch. "The ends will justify! Repenting is for the weak. We do as we must. We do as they do. We do what is needed to survive!"

Grace remained stoic but her face paled behind her makeup.

"In addition," Ari added, "if any hunter is ever bitten by a *canidae* - either accidentally or with malice - we will help save their lives."

Grace hadn't expected that. "A bite is a death sentence."

"Not if you agree to our terms," Ari said. "If they get to us before the first transformation, we can save them. It requires an injection twice a year, but the bitten person will be alive to receive it."

A few of the bodyguards looked shaken. Ari assumed they all knew someone who had been bitten.

"Nothing has to change," Dale said. "Not on the surface. Any hunters who live here are welcome to stay here and go about their lives. But they cannot kill. They will not hunt. They will not recruit or attempt to indoctrinate their children into lives of hate and fear. No hunter will thrive within the Pacific Northwest. Because the simple truth is that *canidae* will never be completely wiped out. *Canidae* will never eliminate every hunter out there. All we want to do is prevent a whole lot of unnecessary pain and suffering for individuals on both sides."

Grace turned to look at the men who had arrived with her. They had grown less robotic the longer the speech went on, and now they looked positively stunned. They were watching Grace carefully, which implied she really was the person with the final say. She looked at the group in front of her again.

"Keighley is dead. Gavin is dead. Roemer and Hayden are in prison. And here you stand in front of me, not just unharmed but thriving. Ariadne Willow and Valerie Byrne, you should have been legacy hunters. Dale Frye, you should have been a valuable convert. Gwyneth Willow, you have been a thorn in the side of hunters for the past three decades, and we are quite convinced that you're responsible for a black hole in our finances that we've never been able to locate, let alone plug. And if what you say is true about a cure for a *canidae* bite..."

She took a deep breath and examined each woman's face in

turn.

One of the men said, "Captain..."

She held up a hand, which immediately silenced him. "As for the rest of the world?"

Dale said, "We're only negotiating for the P... for Cascadia." She looked at Ari, who smiled proudly back at her. "Word will spread, I'm sure. If we prove that it can work here, it can work other places. And our pack will prove to hunters and *canidae* alike that we can live together in peace."

Grace squared her shoulders and stepped forward. She held out her hand.

Dale turned and looked at Gwen. She'd been fighting longer than any of them, suffered more than any of them, and it was her actions that helped make the Willow Pack possible. She came forward slowly, looking at Ari and Dale in turn before she continued on. She stood in front of Grace Lang and met her eye. She held out her hand, gripping Grace's forearm. Grace smiled and gripped Gwen's arm in kind.

"Your terms are accepted," Grace said.

"We have an accord," Gwen confirmed.

Grace nodded. They held the gaze, their grips tight, and then released at the same time. Ari looked at Dale, who looked stunned. Ari went to her and put a hand on her shoulder to keep her upright. Dale looked at her like she wasn't sure what had just happened, and Ari smiled at her.

"Now that's a damn hero speech," Ari said and pulled Dale to her for a hug.

EPILOGUE

SHE WAS naked again. Of course.

Ari stood and slumped against a tree, arms crossed in front of herself as she caught her breath and looked around for clues about where she'd ended up. Thick forest all around, a muddy trail, the scent of water nearby and the sound of a cruise ship... she was north, west, and... Queen Anne Greenbelt. The wolf had taken her away from the drug-infested area and the homeless encampments. She managed to orient herself with the sun and headed off the trail.

It didn't take her long to find the stash Dale had buried. She remembered the view from the spot and found the tree with relative ease. Kneeling down in the dirt, wet from the overnight rain, she dug up the duffel bag and took out the first packet of clothes she saw: button-down shirt and overalls. She wondered if Dale had been mad at her when she packed this bag, but it was better than nothing. She dressed quickly, put on the shoes from the bag, and found the money for a payphone. She checked the bag to make sure there was no leakage or mold, then reburied it and headed back for the trail.

Ari stretched as she started walking back to civilization. She was sore, but it was a good sore. She'd been out as the wolf most nights this week, mostly checking for any hunters who might not have gotten the memo that Seattle was a safe zone. Dale understood, because Dale always understood, but Ari was determined to make it up to her. A nice dinner, maybe a movie, and then a full night in the same bed. It was the least she could do after everything her wife had done for her.

She smiled at the thought. Her wife. Her friend, her assistant, her godsend, the woman who saved her life and her business and was always ready to swoop in and save her at a moment's notice. What an honor to call such a person her wife, and to be her wife in return.

Her mother was also easily adjusting to married life. She had agreed to stop siphoning money from hunter accounts as a show of good faith, so her wealth was no longer a bottomless pit. She was still very, very wealthy, but she and Milo were considering a move to a smaller house just to make things a little easier. Ari had gotten them real estate listings for Portland, but only as a joke. Mostly as a joke.

Ari left the Greenbelt using a cozy if slightly ominous path that led her under the Magnolia Ramp. She saw a few tents set up and moved quietly to avoid disturbing anyone who might still be asleep within. She'd spent enough nights as a teenager in places like this, and she didn't want to disturb any of them if she didn't have to.

The trail ended at a cluster of buildings corralled by chain-link fences. Employees had parked their cars between the supports of the ramp, huddled there like woodland creatures hiding from the sun. The car parked at the far end of the street didn't belong, however, and Ari smiled when she saw who was leaning against the front bumper with a breakfast burrito.

"Detective Macallan."

Diana smiled and raised her coffee cup in greeting. "I've missed running into you after a run, and... dear *lord*, what are you wearing?"

"Dale's revenge," Ari said, plucking at the overall straps with both thumbs. "*Canidae* chic."

"I wonder why I ever thought you had a drug problem. Stumbling out of the Greenbelt at sunrise dressed like a refugee from the world's most disturbing kids' show."

Ari sat next to Diana and peered into the takeout bag. She smiled, retrieved the extra burrito, and began unwrapping it.

"Want to use my phone to call Dale?"

"Yes, please," Ari said. "How'd you know where I was?"

"I didn't," Diana said. "I saw you out running and followed you. I saw you disappear into the Greenbelt and, given the time, I assumed you'd be transforming soon. There were only a handful of places you were likely to come out where you wouldn't be seen."

"Nice detective work, detective."

"Thank you, detective."

Ari took Diana's cell phone and dialed Dale's number. It only rang once before she answered. "Diana?"

Only after she heard the note of concern in her voice did Ari realize she would have seen Diana's name on the ID and jumped to a bad conclusion. "It's me. I'm safe. Diana stalked me and I'm hanging out with her. She'd probably give me a ride home if I asked nicely~" Diana pointedly shook her head no. "~but I'd rather start the day with you, if you're up for it."

"Always. You're running late today, puppy. I'm already up, showered, and dressed."

"I guess the wolf got a little wild."

"Tell Diana thanks, and I shouldn't be long. I'm already getting the keys."

Ari gave her the address and returned the phone. "Thanks. And for the burrito."

"No problem. I'll wait with you until she gets here."

"I appreciate it."

"Pack's gotta stick together, right?" She winked and sipped her coffee.

Ari looked at the cup. "Could've gotten me a coffee, too..."

"I did. This is yours. I drank mine while I was waiting for you."

Ari snorted and shook her head.

A few minutes later, Dale pulled up behind Diana's car. She got out and frowned at Ari's overalls.

"Puppy! What the hell are you wearing?"

"You're the one who packed it."

Dale said, "I definitely did not pack that monstrosity." She looked at Diana. "Hey there, hon. Having a good day?"

"Right up until I had to babysit your wife. Get a longer leash."

"She keeps chewing through them."

Ari rolled her eyes and escaped the mockery by getting into the passenger side of their car.

Diana grinned and gathered her trash before she slid off the car hood. "Lucy would kill me if I didn't arrange dinner. Sometime this month? Friday or the next?"

"Friday's good," Dale said. "We'll cook."

Diana gave a thumbs up and got into her car.

Dale pulled out first, waving goodbye to Diana as she pulled out and headed back to the main road. "I was going to take you straight to the office since you have clothes there you can change into, but I'll take you home so you can shower."

"Bad?"

"Not the freshest, puppy. And your hair is a disaster." She reached over and tried to blindly tame some of it. She gave up after a few strokes and rubbed the back of Ari's neck. "Good night?"

"Pretty good. I must have made some pretty good mileage if I ended up that far into Queen Anne. A shower will feel great. Especially if I have someone to do my back..."

Dale made a quiet noise of mock contemplation. "You have a slow day today. Someone called for an appointment, but that's in the afternoon. You could try serving that summons to Ike Berry again. The schedule his ex-wife provided says he'll most likely be at the Capitol Hill offices this week."

"Might be worth a shot," Ari said. "It would be nice to get that one off the books."

"Mm-hmm. Other than that, the day is yours."

"I'm sure we'll figure something out."

Dale smiled at her, then focused on the road. "Oh hey..." She pointed ahead, to the south. "You can see Mount Rainier."

Ari leaned to one side until she spotted it. "Good omen."

"Yep," Dale said. "It's going to be a good day."

Ari settled back in her own seat. Beautiful skies, a shining sun, she was on her way to work with her wife, and the mountain was out. It wasn't going to be a good day.

As far as she was concerned, it was already great.